VIRAL

A NOVEL

M.A. BARRETT

kin(d)
press

Printed in the United States of America

First Printing, 2016

ISBN 978-0-9983602-5-6

Kind(d) Press
85 Main Street
Maynard, MA 01754

0 1 2 3 4 5 6 7 8 9 10

To My Belle.
Without you, there are no words.
And all the light hides in shadows.

Pop.
If you could see me now. I won.

Nan
Thanks for teaching me how to do the Charleston
in the kitchen. It made me love art and taught
me to be fearless.

BEFORE

Last night in sleep I clutched my GoPro like it might grow legs and run away to a person with a better plan. I startled myself awake then sprinted to catch the 90 bus to Assembly Row just in time to make the orange line out to Forest Hills. I pushed through the crowd, yanking my contraband-stuffed backpack in behind me through the closing doors of the train and managed to grab an end seat like I like, you know for quick escapes. I slumped into it, my bag held to my chest, and stared across the train at a man of Middle Eastern descent. I felt clammy instantly, palms sweaty, my polo stuck in all the wrong crevices. He held his backpack to his chest, his forehead beaded in sweat. We stared at each other, but looked away the exact moment before either of us gave up our secrets. When I looked back, his eyes were darting around the train, waiting for someone to challenge him. Then dirty grey cotton and fluorescent reflectors obscured my view. I blinked, refocused, and watched as a transit guard stood in front of the man, one hand on his left hip, the other on his gun.

"Sir, I'm gonna need you to open your bag," the transit guard's East Boston drawl salting his tongue. His masseter twitched and moved in time with his thumb near his holster. He didn't ask me to open my bag. Nor did he ask any of the other fifty passengers to open theirs.

"Why you want to open my bag?" the darker skinned man stood as he asked this in a Latin American, not Middle Eastern accent. My pulse quickened. Guilt reverberated in my head in time with my weak-ass heart. Several passengers stood and moved away from them. I sat and waited, accepting my fate. If there was a bomb in there, it would be my destiny or else a surefire way to know if I was making the right decision about rigging my camera in the restaurant. I couldn't get my phone out in time to record the interaction between the man with the bag and the guard, but it didn't matter because behind me, all around me, hell even shot in the reflection of the graffiti-scarred glass panes of the train, my fellow passengers already had it covered.

"We've had several reports from passengers of suspicious activity, so I'm only going to ask you one more time. Open your bag. Now." The transit guard fingered the snap on his holster again, rounding on the gold brad of the button roughly. The train started to slow. The dark man's eyes darted to me and then the windows of the train like he was looking for someone who might help him, but there was no such person around.

"My sister. Please. *Feliz cumpleanos.* My sister," he said, pleading with the officer. He couldn't be older than twenty, black splotchy stubble moving on the peak of his chin with every quavering word. Three more transit guards now ran along next to the train, willing it to stop so they could jump in, like hockey players charging the ice for a gloves-off fight.

The guard stepped closer and I, and I'm sure the guy with the bag, saw a montage of videos of men lying in the street, their backs riddled with bullet holes while cops surrounded them and planted weapons. He slowly lowered the bag to the floor with his right hand. His left was already in the air, surrendering. The train stopped and the doors opened. Several riders bolted. I was the only one still sitting in the general vicinity. I couldn't move. The dark man looked at me, stared right through me, his eyes swimming in embarrassment, fear, anger. The guard didn't bother with me, but he yanked the guy out of his seat by the collar.

Then the bag squirmed. It's the only way I can describe it. I was too afraid to go anywhere, do anything. The other guards came. Four of them in all. The bag moved again. They pushed the dark man to the floor; trained their guns on him. He held his hands out in front of him. I'm not sure I would have done the same, but he'd been trained. He stared up at them, begging them not to hurt him, tears running down his cheeks.

"What's in the bag, Mohammed?" a lady transit guard asked.

"Jose. I am Jose. Please. *Cumpleanos*. My sister." He held a driver's license out to them as he said this, but they didn't bother with it.

My eye sockets were dry, but I couldn't blink as they held him on the floor. His cheek took on the indentations of the lines in the train floor. The train didn't move. Passengers stared in at us. I felt the pulse of the crowd on the platform. One of the guards ran a handheld x-ray along the bag and said, "What the hell?" before slowly unzipping it. People ducked, like diving down for cover on the platform would help them survive a blast that would blow a sinkhole into the heart of Boston. The guards moved back. We all waited for the shattering of our world, an implosion that would wipe out our fear. But there was a sudden moment of calm and quiet. Everyone released a universally held breath, like air gushing from a sucking wound. Someone on the platform burped out a laugh. An empty slushie cup rolled toward Jose on the dirty floor. He couldn't see it through the heels of his palms pressed into his eyes. Blue juice spilled into the lines on the floor and raced to his white t-shirted shoulder.

From inside Jose's bag, tiny white fluff shook off the darkness and from under cotton candy fluff, I saw two black beady eyes. Then I heard it: a squeak, a little yelp. It poked its head out of the bag and lapped the guard's face. One of the other guards let out a burst of nervous laughter.

"Are you okay?" I asked Jose, the words—the only ones I could muster— dry on my tongue. Dirty looks came at me from every angle of transit guard. I tried to make myself smaller under their gaze. Jose just glared at me, hated right through me, and I closed my eyes and took it. When I opened them, Jose was running toward the escalator with the puppy in his arms, his blue stained shoulder like a bruise as he sprinted the entire length of the station. The officers stood outside of the train talking in a small group, a board meeting to get their stories straight. Martha, the Sullivan Square squatter, yelled out, "Douches! Pigs! Pick on someone your own size!" as she waddled by with her cart full of bottle bags, rags, and whatever she'd found in the bin she'd just dug through. In my mind, where most of the reality happens, I thanked her for doing something, anything to fight them. I certainly hadn't been able to. The lady guard pulled her billy club out and stared Martha down. Martha looked away hard as the doors closed around all of us and the conductor said, "Sorry for the delay, folks. Next stop: Community College Station."

I clutched my own bag to me, the bomb inside, twitching to be let loose. I watched their faces recede as the train pulled out of the station and careered down the dark tunnel before us. Everyone on the train had forgotten Jose already. I popped my earbuds in and found solace in the darkness until Haymarket, until I could get off and carry on with my plan.

Now here I am in the dark again. This morning on the train feels like a lifetime ago. I'm in this closet, in the bowels of the restaurant, I'm still clutching my bag to me like it holds a puppy inside. I'm using it this time though to hold me, to keep the tremors at bay. I'm using it to wipe the images of what I've just witnessed out of my brain, to try to find some semblance of reason for what I've done, but fear is a tricky animal; an abusive, cursing clown of a monster that pulls my strings. Fear's the reason. Isn't it always?

I'm holding this bag the way a kid might hold her teddy bear at night every time she hears the closet door creak open another inch, the monster inside breathing death into the air of her bedroom. I'm using it as a place to rest my head, to pillow my thoughts, to sleep forever. But the only thing I know for sure is that I've failed. Again. Big time. Which wasn't the plan.

DURING

I am the black muck on the floor, eye level with his boots. Fried chicken turds are encrusted in the leather where the shoes are starting to wear near the toe. I have a horrible tingling sensation in my gut, like maybe I want him to catch me here, crouched on the floor with my skirt around my waist, my GoPro exposed in my hands. Maybe he'd understand what I'm doing back here or maybe he'd turn around and walk away. Maybe he'd grab me and throw me against the dry goods cabinet and suck my lips off, then scoop me up and carry me home, King Kong style. I could record that. I have a pretty good script of it in my head already. We could act it out. Right here behind the bread racks or in the closet behind me. It would be the only thing worth the wasted space on my SD card at this point. He takes another step closer, just a couple of feet from me. My breath catches. He thinks he sees something? I hold my exhalation, my heart thumping against my throat. Can he hear it? Can he smell me?

"Lucky, get off my clock!" Joe bellows from the bowels of the restaurant. Lucky steps back, teeters, finally turns and leaves me there alone. I wait twenty seconds before standing, making sure the coast is clear. There can't be many of them left. I'll have to wait here until the last one leaves, until I'm alone with myself and the nothingness of what I've done. I finger the crumpled stickie note that holds the alarm code in the front pocket of my apron.

Someone cuts the musak at the front of the house and I'm left with just the dull hum of the walk-in coolers all around me. I smell what was fresh bread this morning souring with bacteria. We'll serve it anyway. That's something I could have captured in the eight hours since I planted my GoPro—molding bread going out to unsuspecting guests. The Boston Globe would have jumped on that story. When this chick in Miami, Marni Reyes, stuck a camera in the prep kitchen at the Assisted Living Facility where she worked, she captured cooks dumping sleeping pills into the mash potatoes and serving them up to the kiddies to get them to stop banging their heads against the walls. She shot that. It went viral and the bastards were arrested.

But I will have to do this shit again tomorrow. I'll have to risk it again, sneak in early, rig the camera, maybe even manifest something; a little white lie, reality television style. Maybe drop the steak for table 27 on the floor on purpose and see how fast Joe snatches it out of the chemical jelly we walk through every day before sending it back out to the guests. That would do it. And it would only be a little set up on my part, not a lie really. A little produced reality never hurt anyone, until it does. But this is something Joe does every day, scraping fallen food off the floor and dumping it back on a plate. Except today. No one did anything revolting or that would violate health codes today.

If I could direct these bozos, I would, just like I used to, but I can't.

I duck down fast as a couple of cooks leave. I hear the front door slam. I check my camera and see that I've got about an hour left at 720p with 60 frames per second. When I stand again I feel a loose shard from one of the metal bread racks slowly dig into my flesh, tearing through the thick black tights I popped out of a plastic egg this morning. The new run dominoes up my thigh and gets lost under my regulation black skirt. I bite back a yelp as the blood drools down my leg, but as I move to adjust for pain, the sound my thighs make when I drag my no-slip shoes through the crap on the floor, is something like *pfft, pfft, pfft* and seems louder than my outburst of pain would have been. I wonder if the mic picked up my burning thighs or my insane heartbeat or the voices in my head screaming at me to get the hell out of here and stop trying to shoot for glory, stop trying to make something of myself. Just be here now and accept my fate. I am no longer a story producer. I am no longer anything, but a waitress. I am no longer a resident of New York or Los Angeles, but sometimes I go there in my head.

Margie leaves next and I dive for cover again. She pulls on her coat and comes right at me. I tuck my face into my knees as she looks back over her shoulder and says, "I'm out!" She waits for a response, but gets none. "Don't give the new girl a hard time, guys. She's never closed before," she says to no one in particular. I train my camera on her and find a moment of hesitation in her eyes, a *maybe I should stay* look that subsides quickly when she remembers that LaDasha's been with the babysitter for seven hours now. At this point, Margie just worked for free. There's no money left, not even for a pack of smokes, only one-way fare back to Watertown and cash in hand to the sitter.

She zips up her coat and walks by me. She hits the switch on the wall on the way, which casts the back of the house in an eerie blue haze from the security lights. My lowlight on the GoPro isn't great, but I can still see through it. The blue hue makes everything cold. I hear someone set the alarm. I reach into the left pocket of my apron and feel for the crumpled stickie note. Still there. I think of yesterday,

9

this morning—hell, half an hour ago. Time before now feels like another dimension, a dimension where the jerks I work with were perfect fucking saints all day. Not very interesting at all for my new YouTube Channel, which I haven't actually gotten around to creating yet. But I can do that part when I'm home. In five minutes or so I'll be in the clear, steady and on the last green line out of the Convention Center T station, headed back to Somerville, where the air smells like the sulfur of the Mystic River met up with townie beer breath. I can at least set up the YouTube so today won't be totally wasted.

"Don't worry. It's hard to get the hang of it." Joe's low, grumbling voice comes out of the shadows and it feels like someone opened one of the freezers just wide enough to chill my spine.

My breath catches in my throat. At first it looks like he's talking to himself, but then as he passes a ray of blue light, I see that he's with Quinn, the newbie who started floor training last week. Her bright pink polo contrasts with her dark, caramel skin and is stained with some conglomeration of ranch and ketchup like a birthmark in the middle of her shirt. The collar has been tucked under all night and no one told her. Her ponytail is at its wit's end, wispies gone haywire all around her head. She's all legs-for-days and hope on the verge of tears. I roll my eyes at Joe's lame attempts to play it cool with her.

"You don't owe us any money tonight, sweetheart. Everybody miscounts their bank in the beginning. We'll just call it even, okay?" Joe says and his voice sounds syrupy, teeming with bacteria.

"Thanks, Mr. Marino, but I can't keep doing this. I have rent to pay," she says and I can hear her words shake in her mouth. No one calls him by his Father's name. Joe has his hand on her shoulder. It's an awkward gesture tinged with possession. Without another thought I slowly pull my GoPro up and hope that it's trained on them. This might just be weird enough to capture. I start to pray that he'll make a move and ask her out. Workplace harassment. Bam. Fuck yes. Sure to make a splash on the old interweb. If I were still producing, I'd have two cameras on this, as well as a bird's eye view and I would bark orders from the safety of command central into Cam1's earpiece to get in close on Quinn's incredibly uncomfortable expression. I'd tell them to make sure they get the collar and the ketchup stains. Make sure you sell it that she's a mess and she's poor and he's an awkward dude with a whole lot of power over her and probably (definitely) a huge boner.

"I'll do whatever I can to help you out," he says, darkness creeping into the crevice of his words. This piques the interest of some tiny monster in my gut. At this I'd tell my camera guys to not make a sound. Let them forget that you're here. Let this moment play out, whatever happens. Don't stop shooting. Even if your hands go numb.

Through tears, Quinn says, "I just feel like I can't get the rhythm right." Joe smirks at this, an *I can show you a thing or two about rhythm* kind of smirk. I've never seen him act this way before. It's like he's parading around the house in a suit and hat that are four sizes too big for him, the heels of daddy's shoes banging on the marble as he walks. I notice then he's only half-paying attention to her, nodding and pouting like he understands what she's saying, but not listening to a damn thing. I see his eyes divert to the hot kitchen and he hesitates before leaning in to kiss her neck, only he misses her neck and his lips—and his teeth, I think—scrape along her jaw. She rears up suddenly.

"I...I don't think I should—" she starts, and I'm hoping my frame catches her fists pressing against his chest. She's being polite, as polite as she can be so she doesn't lose her job, but he's not taking her hints. As he leans in further she leans back and I imagine that yoga is a daily practice for young Quinn. The whole thing is cartoonish and I should want to laugh, but the immense fear rising in my gullet keeps the hysterics at bay.

When Joe finally lands one, he looks like he's trying to swallow her face. I can see his gummy teeth glinting in the light. She pushes him again and says, "Mr. Marino, I don't want to kiss yo—" and there is an awkward stillness between them for a few seconds while Joe pushes himself into her. She digs her knuckles into his chest and shoves him hard, her other hand sweeping his face, her nails raking into the mushy, rubbery, acnified flesh of his cheek. In the blue light I can see a sheen of wet on his face, but can't tell if it's blood or pimple ooze. He hits the coolers behind him hard. *Not yoga, CrossFit* I think, before a stack of fry baskets totters and almost comes down on Joe's head. He holds his cheek then pulls his hand away to look at his fingers. Now the scratches on his face look like black war paint and his palm is covered in what looks like a thin sheath of molasses.

I am panting. I can hear myself. Why can't they hear me? This would all be over if they realized someone else is here. My breath is running sprints around my ribcage.

"I'm sorry—" she starts to say when Joe grabs her wrist, draws it tight up her back, and spins her away from him. The move, another awkward one, almost doesn't land. But then the sound of her body smashing into the metal prep table and the subsequent crashing of pots and pans on the tile floor is astounding in the hollow space surrounding me. I know that she is trapped.

My phone is in my left hand and my camera in my right. I don't know when I pulled my phone out of my apron, but it doesn't matter. I swipe the lock screen and the sinking feeling in my gut plummets to the floor. I'm at 1% battery. I didn't have a chance to charge it this morning. Joe's voice again takes over the space around me.

"I know you're there," he says and my heart skips into my jaw.

He's seen me. This is over. Then he continues, "If you want in, you better grab her arms." His tone is calm and quiet, though his face is purple from holding Quinn's struggling body in place and he adds, "Quick." When I look up, I see two dark figures emerge from the kitchen. I feel a wave of relief that he's not talking to me, but the relief is quashed when I realize he's talking to Donnie, the kitchen manager, and his grill cook, Nate, who are staring at their boss with fevered anticipation. These two make a habit of tearing Joe apart over a joint next to the dumpsters out back every day.

"Dude, I bet his dick isn't even half the size of that schnoz," Nate said just this afternoon, passing a roach to Donnie.

"Motherfucker, his nose? How about the grease? I bet he doesn't even need lube to jerk," Donnie said and mimicked wiping his forehead before sliming up his cock with it.

"You're fucking disgusting, you know that?" I said. His face got stony before it cracked into gut-busting laughter.

"Yo, Scar, you wanna hit?" Donnie asked me. I took one before heading back in to the restaurant. Now I'm watching these two knuckleheads try to form thoughts, weighing out a list of pros and cons on whether they should get in on this. I feel sick.

"Grab her friggin' arms!" Joe yells, his voice catching as she tries to break his hold.

Quinn whispers, "No."

They don't hear her. Not that it would change what they're about to do. When she realizes this she starts making sounds like a wounded dog might, repetitive words that I can't understand, a different language that my skin can translate, but not my ears right now. Something like, "pleas—no—youca—please—no—no—no." This seems to make up Nate and Donnie's minds. They lunge at the prep table and grab Quinn's wrists. Something cracks under her and I know that it can't be her back, because she's still fighting against them, but the sound is deafening, like the sound a tree makes when it finally starts to fall after the first deep cut from an ax.

My phone. I swipe it on again, but get nothing but a black screen. I killed it with the last shutdown. The spinning wheel of the dead battery mocks me from the screen. My right hand has a mind of its own and is pointed right through the bread racks at the mess in front of me, the camera trembling in time with my whole body. I have about forty-five minutes of space left on the SD card, but I'm praying it doesn't last that long. Joe rips open his khakis once his cooks have the flailing creature in front of him secured. I hear the metal of his belt buckle smash against the metal of the table and then Quinn is screaming. I've never heard a scream like that, not even from my own mouth. It's animal in its nature. My mind draws a blank.

One of the guys, Donnie I think, clocks Quinn hard in the jaw with a balled fist and screams, "Shut it!" I'm pretty sure it's the hand on which he wears his high school ring. She screams as his fist comes for her and then her scream drowns in the choking saliva and blood in her throat. Joe's face is twisted so that he resembles a grinning animal. I stuff my phone in my bra and hold the camera steady with my other hand. Is this enough? If I can keep shooting, if I can keep from vomiting, or making a sound, I might have enough evidence. I just have to hold the camera up. I can't jump out. I can't make a noise. If I let them know I'm here, I will be next and I can't be next again. I can't go through this again.

Quinn screams, louder and with more moisture than before. She has her face turned to me, but she doesn't see me, otherwise she would yell. She would ask me for help. She is looking up at Nate, who is usually the sensible one, but tonight his senses were checked at the door as soon as he felt a tickle in his balls, as soon as he witnessed

Joe trying to contain the screaming, flailing woman in front of him on the table.

"Stop! Please. Stop! You can't do this!" she says quietly to him, her voice jutting with every tear of her clothes, but Joe smirks at his new friends, his cooks, and with dark, palpable triumph, he says, "Oh yeah? Who's gonna stop me?"

She kicks at him, but her foot only flies into the air at his side. At some point her shoe comes off and I can see her big toe poking through her nylons. *If I try anything, they'll get me too.* I'm going numb. The camera is shaking in my hands and whether I like it or not, I'm about to drop it and I can't make my feet move. I can't make myself do anything to stop this. I hear the same word over and over in my mind: *Coward. Coward. Coward.*

I see Joe stick his fat hand up her skirt and she screams louder. With every maneuver, every bad porn move he's ever studied, he's gaining confidence. He rips her cheap stockings down to the knee and his erection is bursting from his boxers. She kicks at him again using her knees this time. I have a quick moment of optimism, but then Donnie clocks her awkwardly in the stomach and the choking whoosh of air that leaves her crushes my hopes. Joe's movements become more precise. Sweat mixes with the grease in his hair, on his face. He looks like a rabid pre-pubescent warrior about to make his first kill. His stomach heaves and looks less flabby as he thrusts himself into her. My legs start to go numb with every hit she takes. I can feel this like a long lost memory. *If I make a move they'll do it to me too and I'll die. We'll both die. I'm going to die.* Tears well up in my throat, about to drown me.

I'm in a cage being forced to watch, up close and personal, a lion ripping apart a lamb. I close my eyes and immediately my skull pulses with a screaming siren. When I open my eyes, it is still there. I know this sound. The fire alarm. Not in my brain. Not my guilt. The fire alarm is going off. I heard it last week when the fire department made all of Newbury Street run drills. All of us worker bees stood out on the sidewalk, smoking our cheap cigarettes and complaining about the money we were losing, while tourists with foreign tongues and screaming children knocked into us, flailing their way through a zoo that let all the animals out of their cages. Even the animals at Burberry have to practice fire safety. The alarms banged off of the buildings last week creating a tunnel of blaring sirens. And here it is again, surrounding me. The fire alarm.

I open my eyes, scan the prep area, and find blues mixed with reds all around me. The restaurant is lit up like a front yard Christmas celebration. Joe and the cooks freeze, but Quinn takes this opportunity to struggle harder and then out of the shadows of the hallway leading to the dining room comes a ghostly white face. Lucky is flying at them, the handle of the fire alarm dangling in his hand. He must have ripped it off the wall when he pulled it. He's heading right for Joe.

I hear Quinn's scream pierce the blaring alarm and it mixes with Joe's guttural exhalation of breath as Lucky awkwardly, with an inward bent wrist, shoves him in the chest against the coolers, as if he can't make the choice between a shove and a punch. The brightest pink flies by me, turning to purple in the blue light, and Quinn is gone. Torn-stocking legs trail the indigo hue of her shirt and a moment of relief washes over me. Quinn moves so fast, she leaves her server book and apron behind in the air before they fall to the floor near the prep table. Donnie kicks them out of the way as both he and Nate rush in to yank Lucky off of Joe. Lucky stands a good half a foot below Joe's long forehead, but it doesn't stop Lucky from using all his might to strangle his boss.

I look at my hands. The camera is still trained on the mess in front of me, but my mouth is hanging open like I'm about to yell something out. My fear reminds me not to and I close it. Donnie gets a good hold on Lucky and yanks him away by the collar. Lucky's stunned body smashes into the coolers and his gut expels a pop of breath, the kind that happens to a kid who belly flops after a clumsy jump into the pool. He falls hard on the floor, struggling to catch his breath. Nate puts a murky boot to Lucky's chest to make sure he stays put while Donnie checks in with Joe, who hasn't moved from his spot by the coolers. From the look on his face, I can tell his eyes are still trying to tell his brain what just happened. In his right hand rests his semi-hard penis. He protects it with his other hand as if the scene in front of him is nothing his little dick would want to see. Finally he pulls his pants up. He buckles the belt without clasping the trousers.

In the distance the air is cracked by the high-pitched wail of first a police siren and then a fire truck. These two distant sounds mix with the whooping call that has turned the back of the house at the Topsail Bar & Grill into a rave. Nate kicks Lucky hard in the ribs and Donnie turns from Joe and pounces on him with his fists. I can see Nate's black boot print on Lucky's t-shirted chest. Lucky is no longer conscious. Joe snaps to when he hears the sirens all the while muttering, "Fuck. Fuck. Fuck." He actually sounds like he's about to cry. He shoves both of his cooks toward the door, though Donnie is trying to get in a few more kicks to Lucky's side for good measure.

"Get out of here!" Joe screams into Donnie's face. When the two cooks balk at him, dumbfounded, he yells, "The cops are coming, you morons! Get out of here. I will handle this." Nate and Donnie hesitate, hands still balled into fists, hopping around on their toes, like they're in a cage match.

"Go!" Joe screams at them, his desperation filling the space around me. Donnie and Nate turn tail and run out the back door. Joe stops, takes a breath, turns to stare at Lucky's body on the floor in front of him, smooths his hair back with a shaking hand, and finally drops to his knees next to Lucky. I can see him ball up his fist, but he waits, looking over his shoulder. Then, it's almost an afterthought, he puts Lucky's right hand to the cheek where Quinn scratched him and scrapes Lucky's finger nails over the scratches there, wincing but not making a sound. Seconds later police officers are running in the back door with guns drawn. Joe's fist comes down hard on the unconscious busboy's temple.

"Put your hands where I can see them!" A female cop runs to Joe with her gun pointed at his shoulder. Joe puts his hands up. He is sucking in breath and his knuckles are bloody.

"Stand up slowly," she says and he does.

"My name is Joseph Marino," he says between deep, stuttered exhalations.

I can't help but notice a couple of the officers who stand in front of my hiding place drop their guns slightly upon hearing his name. In fact, the female officer lowers her weapon completely.

"Marino?" she asks.

Joe nods. "I'm the general manager of this restaurant. The man on the floor is my bus boy and I just caught him trying to break into the safe in the office," he says and nods at the office door, slightly ajar, down the hallway. I take two defeated steps back.

Lady Law holsters her weapon, stares at the office door, glances at Lucky, and then does a once over of the room. She comes back to Lucky again and I am hoping she realizes the size eight boot print on Lucky's shirt does not match the size eleven loafers Joe is wearing. She gives Joe the once over, takes in his crumpled, half-tucked shirt, his unbuttoned pants sticking out over his belt. With clumsy hands, he tucks in his shirt and in the process quickly slips the clasp into its place.

"Will somebody shut that goddamn alarm off?" the lady cop says and another officer disappears down the hall. The alarm is cut seconds later. She walks past the sticky, sweaty outline of where Quinn's body was being held down on the prep table and approaches Joe, her eyebrows pulled together. I open my mouth to say something, but nothing comes out, just like in my nightmares.

"Mr. Marino, step slowly toward the other officers. Are you alone here?" she asks and I shrink back into the shadows slightly. If there's any moment when I should come forward, it's now. There are three police officers standing in front of me with their backs to me and fire and probably an ambulance on its way. I'm protected here. These people will protect me. Or will they?

My hands are still shaking as I take a step in the right direction, toward the officer's backs. I grew up in a country that protects its citizens and where the citizens should therefore trust in the police. I'm not black, or Hispanic, or a Muslim. What do I have to fear? And then I remember being a shaved-head, tattooed girl who wore ripped jeans, no bra, and combat boots in 1999, driving around with a "hate is not a family value" sticker stuck right next to a rainbow sticker on my car and how a redneck cop pulled me over for a taillight and the next thing I knew I was unconscious in the back seat of a cruiser heading to Marquette County. My friends scrounged everything they had to bail me out. I had been arrested for resisting arrest, but I only remember crying and telling the officer that I was driving to register for classes at UNMT.

I take a step back again, still feeling the bruises from the handcuffs on my wrists.

"Yes, ma'am," Joe says, his breathing regulated, his hands in the air. He moves to the other officers. One of them takes him by the arm and holds him as the female cop kneels down next to Lucky. She checks his pulse and then tugs her shoulder-mounted walkie-talkie to her mouth. From where I am hiding, I can see her lips touch the lined screen.

"Lopez 8976 to Dispatch. We'll need a bus to the Marino's place: The Topsail Bar & Grill. 2799A Newbury. One passenger, one on scene. Copy?" She speaks fast, the words running together.

One of the cops in front of the bread racks backs up a step and glances over his shoulder, almost sniffing the air. He starts to turn and I inch into a back corner, further out of eyesight. If I make myself known, they'll run my ID and find out that I have over $500 in parking tickets from before my car was repo'd. And then I'll go to jail. I can't sit in that cell. I have no one to call this time. I might sit there forever. Tears start to build up from my stomach. They begin as fear and turn to anger when they reach my throat. Joe glances in my general direction. His eyes look blank. He doesn't see me. At least I don't think he does.

"Copy that, 8976. Bus en route."

Lopez stands with her left hand on her utility belt and her right on the butt of the Glock holstered on her hip. I imagine she's practiced this stance every night in her mirror since police academy graduation. She turns to Joe.

"I should probably call my father…and our lawyer," Joe says, placing more weight on the word "father".

She nods, chewing on the side of her cheek, studying him. "You can put your hands down, Mr. Marino."

He does.

Lopez hasn't blinked. "You found him, huh?" she asks, nodding in Lucky's direction. Something isn't sitting right with her. She glances at the prep table, studying it. Joe nods but says nothing.

"What was he doing when you found him?"

"I think I should wait until my lawyer gets here," Joe says, smiling politely.

"Any security cameras in here?" she asks. My heart thunks to a stop in my chest. My eyes dart to corners of the room and I see one in the East corner of the room, staring at me like the eye of Mordor.

Joe can't help the corner of his mouth pull itself up into a quick smirk that dissipates with the shaking of his head, "They've been on the fritz back here," he says, and I start breathing again.

"Too bad," Lopez says before a darkly coiffed man in sky blue Armani walks right by my head, leaving behind a fog of Clive Christian No. 1. Followed closely behind him is a man recognizable to anyone who lives in the city of Boston: Jack Marino, the Governor-elect. But he's not smiling like he usually is in his campaign shots when he's shaking the hands of Little Leaguers in Southie or the old ladies ladling broth at the soup kitchens in Roxbury. This Jack is red-faced, bloated from restless sleep, and his stern jaw is lined with a Burberry Tweed popped collar. He moves past me and this time I smell power and leather and Lucky's demise. I inch slowly back toward the dry storage cabinet and move inside, like the rat I am. No one notices me. No one notices anything in the room besides Jack Marino as he moves to his son and places a hand on his shoulder, squeezing his affirmation that there's nothing to worry about. But I can see the doubt in Jack's face as he sizes Joe up. It's the same suspicious look Lopez has been giving him for the past five minutes, only Jack knows more than she does I'm sure.

Meanwhile Lucky is lying on the ground in his hero blood while six sets of feet stand around him like he is an empty Dunkin Donuts cup in the gutter. And me? I feel almost nothing as the tears of defeat light up my cheeks. I just need them to leave so I can get out of here.

CHAPTER 1

I'm good at running. The last time I hightailed it, it was from Manhattan to East Somerville, just a couple miles outside of Boston. I ran because I was evicted. I was evicted because my girlfriend, Taylor, threw me out on my ass with next to nothing to my name and I couldn't pay my rent. Taylor kicked me out on my ass because I had been fired from my job as a story producer on gTV's *The Real Real Life*. I was fired because, well…I'm not ready to talk about that. Everyone who asks why I left the industry gets the same answer: "It was the recession that did me in." Which is actually true, but not the whole story. So I keep the dark little monster of truth about what actually happened buried deep in the junk drawer in my mold-infested apartment. I'm not destitute anymore, but I used to be. The idea of being so again is making my skin crawl. If I lose this job, where do I go? I can't do it again. I can't live on Dollar Store produce or steal other people's quarters at the laundromat to be able to afford a train to an interview for a job I won't get. I can't pare down my belongings anymore. There's not much left.

I spent the one day I had to get my shit together before leaving Taylor's apartment, placing my life's possessions into two piles: live with or can't live without. The can't live without pile was small and consisted of old family photos, journals, my computer stuff, an Xbox with a Rock Band bundle that I would be selling on eBay by week's end, shoes, books, my Gramp's taxi driver license, my Little Orphan Annie coffee mug, and as I worked through our dresser, my clothes.

I was piling underwear on top of the dresser, separating mine from Taylor's, when I saw the Trader Joe's card. It was small, the kind that goes on your key ring. We'd won the grand prize of a loaded $50 gift card at the Hollywood Trader Joe's right after we'd landed in Los Angeles, three years before moving to New York to be closer to production on TRRL. We promised to save it for an "in case we're really broke" time and had obviously forgotten about it.

By the time I'd gotten my first real gig as a production assistant on a cat litter commercial, Tay and I had been eating butter sandwiches and living off of whatever the producers and advertising executives weren't eating at lunch. We could make Monday's Executive's lunch last us a whole week, but we were desperately skinny, which was amazing as far as Tay was concerned. She had been spending more and more time clocking hours on rexia.com, where she and thousands of sickly girls and boys traded war stories about starving themselves. *Don't eat that salad, gurl. That salad is the devil and the devil is fat. Don't be fat.* That kind of thing.

She thought looking like a crack whore would be best for her rock star image. At that point she was fronting a femme-punk-collective called *Slitter*, and was obsessed with Juliet Lewis' look circa Natural Born Killers. I remember accepting this as part of our life. I remember thinking this is what she thinks she needs to do to make it in this industry. I wasn't that extreme but there were three to four day stretches where I didn't sleep or leave set for fear of losing my job to the next hungry production assistant waiting in the wings.

24

While Taylor was studying starvation, I was growing hungrier. She stopped eating almost entirely, subsisting off of watered down hot sauce, which she called her calming soup. If only we'd remembered the Trader Joe's card. But there it was. I slipped it quickly off the dresser and into my pocket, my pulse racing. She'd take it just to spite me, if she saw it. She was that angry. But I got it into my pocket before she could see it. At least I wouldn't go completely hungry. I threw my clothes on the pile, stuffed it all into black lawn trash bags and three boxes, and piled it into my Sentra. I only lasted a few months after that before I ran home to Boston.

The card with its plastic protective sheath peeled back calms me. I never took it off my key ring. I run my fingers along the sharp edges when I'm feeling nervous like now, in here in the dark. I'd been cruising along at perfectly fine, a good flat line of even calm until tonight. I'd been able to pay my rent and keep my nose to the grindstone, but then I got this stupid idea to record my co-workers and now here I am, stuffed inside a dry goods closet, my heart in my throat as Lucky lies on the floor in a pool of his own blood and Quinn is probably running down Newbury Street, a trail of panty hose flying after her, heading straight for the police or the emergency room. I will check on Quinn when I leave. But I'm starting to realize that could be a long time from now.

The process in front of me takes hours. There's a big crowd now, which includes Jack's lawyers, and three sets of officers besides Lopez and her partner. A couple of obviously green officers take turns shooting selfies with Jack. At one point they all move to the front of the house so that Joe can walk them through what happened, or at least what he's quickly made up. When they leave the kitchen, I slip further into the darkness of a storage cabinet behind the bread racks and hide behind gigantic sacks of flour and corn meal. My breath is pasty in the dark. I talk myself down several times from sneezing in the dust and I close the door, finding solace in the darkness. I wait for complete silence and the flash of the red and blue lights to subside through the sliver at the bottom of the door, then wait another hour after it's completely quiet, just to be safe. Finally, I slip out into the semi-darkness of the now silent kitchen and head for the back door.

I pull the alarm code out of my apron and am about to hit the seven on the alarm screen, but my finger stops, hovering over the numbers. I step back, not trusting myself. *7391. Just type it and get out of here.* But I can't. I pull my hand all the way back, just in case I slip. If I enter the alarm code, they'll be able to see that the alarm was disarmed and they'll start trying to figure out who was here after everyone left. There's no way out of this. I've got to stay. I feel the hot sting of tears in my throat again.

I turn and walk past the small pool of blood left behind from Lucky's body, careful not to let any of it touch my shoes so I don't leave tracks. I should clean it up. To just leave this part of him pooling on the floor seems callous. But I can't. I can't change anything. Every move I make now puts me at the crime scene or it doesn't. There is no in-between. I have to be careful. I stare into the blood like a wishing well before finally moving on through the swinging server doors to the front of the house. I go to the bathroom and sit on the toilet in the dark, voiding my nervous bladder at long last. Something like relief washes over me, but it's gone as soon as it comes. I wish I had a joint or a shot of whiskey or a gun. I wait for the sound of someone searching for me, but there is nothing except the hum of the coolers behind the bar. I finish and grab paper towels, squirt them with the bubblegum pink, plastic smelling soap in the wall dispenser, and wipe down the toilet seat before leaving.

I stand in the dining room for a long time. I've never been here by myself. The air smells like old fry oil, nicotine soaked vinyl, and cheap beer. I slip under the bar and with my hoodie sleeve covering my hand, reach for the bottle of Jameson. I pour a shot and throw it back. The liquid mixes with the tears caught in my throat and I take one more shot to wash it all down. Finally my hand stops shaking and I can close my eyes. I glance at my phone out of rote for the time. It's still dead, the screen smeared with my nervous fingerprints. I wipe it against my polo and shove it in my apron. I look up at the Budweiser clock on the wall to find it is 4:17 in the morning. I'll have to be on the clock in about four hours. I look down at my uniform shirt and see that it's pretty encrusted from my shift. I grab a rag, soak it with water, and begin the process of de-ranching myself. When I look up, I see two dark pupils over dirty cheeks staring at me through the window and the rag falls from my fingers.

The only time I've ever felt someone distinctly watching me from afar, someone from behind, watching me, studying me, spying on me, was Sam. She was sort of like my shadow on set, even though she wasn't my production assistant. Clark, a Kennedy-esque New England college kid was my PA. She was Gary's, but from the day she came to us on TRRL, she watched me. The time I talked Jaron into staying out of the hot tub, in order to do a confession booth, she was there. Jaron was HIV+ and he didn't listen to me. Later I found him fucking some idiot from his philosophy class bareback, his lethal jizz floating in the bubbles all around them. Sam was there. In the middle of a fit that production and crew let it happen, I slipped on the steamed boards beneath the hot tub and bit it hard on my ass. Sam helped me up. We never spoke, but she was the first one to get to me because she'd been watching my every move. Three months later, as

27

I accompanied Chastity, the youngest and saddest member of the house cast to a rehab clinic for an extended stay with a skeleton crew, Sam was there. She'd volunteered to go with me, even though Christmas was in two days and she'd miss her flight back to North Carolina. So she, Clark, one camera operator, and I filmed a very honest episode about heroin addiction that turned into a Christmas special for us. I gave Sam a bonus out of my own check for her help, and she watched me in the rearview mirror as she drove our crew back to the cast house.

I get the same feeling now, that heavy gaze weighing on me. Someone is studying me. I see those dark eyes, glinting between palms held to the glass at the front of the restaurant. Cliff, our resident homeless guy, doing recon, on a mission in his brain. I wonder if he thinks I'm an insurgent, like he did last week. I hit the floor hard again and try to stabilize my breath. Inching my way to the bar entrance, I peer around the corner to the front of the restaurant where Cliff's dirty pant legs still stand, pushing against the glass, trying to get a better look inside. He's poking his finger at the glass and I am the goldfish in the bowl. *Bong. Bong. Bong.* My whole world vibrates as Cliff yells, "Hey you! Hey you! Hey you! I know you!"

If I crawl, I might be able to get back to the kitchen without him seeing me, but it's a big risk. I glance back. He's still there.

"Fuck you, Cliff," I whisper into the darkness and kick the small mini fridge that houses the mixers and Bloody Mary vegetables. The tears come again and now they're starting to piss me off. I'm trapped. Jameson is making my head swim and I can't seem to do the right thing, to save myself. Glancing around the corner of the bar, I see Cliff pissing on the window and laughing maniacally, holding his dick like he's riding a wooden horse. His feet dance a sort of jig and the marigold stream of his piss Pollocks the window. This is the only chance I'm going to have. I know this. I know that I have to make a run for it while the deranged homeless dude is making piss art all over the window and I have to hope that he's just addled enough not to see me or remember that he saw me if anyone asks. I crawl fast and hard out of the bar and head for the kitchen. I'm going to have to deactivate the alarm. I don't have a choice. They won't know it was me. I won't leave my fingerprints.

I crawl through the swinging doors to the kitchen. I don't look back even though I can hear Cliff's palm banging on the glass and his yells of, "I know you! Come back." When I get through the doors, I grab my bag next to the bread racks and head for the alarm touch screen. I pull the crumpled sticky note out of my pocket and start to punch in the numbers written on it, but the lights on the alarm pad light up in front of me. I haven't touched it. I pull back from it just to make sure. The alarm starts to bleep through the unarm sequence, but I haven't laid a finger on it. Another step back. I hear the keys in the lock on the outside and then the door is opening to fast voices. I have just enough time to dive behind the racks and pull my bag into the storage closet behind me.

Through the crack, I see three, four, five people walk in, three women and two men, yawning and speaking in rapid fire Spanish. They drag in a vacuum cleaner and a cart of cleaning supplies with a to-go container of steaming *chilaquiles* resting on top of clean rags. They stop dead in their tracks at the state of the kitchen.

"*Ay dios mio*," an older woman says through squinted eyes. "Mierda. Es que la sangre?" she asks, staring at the almost black pool of Lucky's blood. One the men moves to the pool, sticks his finger in it without hesitation, and sniffs it. He nods, looks back at the crew and says, "Si. It's blood," with a slight accent. The old mujer crosses herself, shakes her head, and starts picking up the fallen pans.

Head in my hands, I inhale deeply to calm the shuddering breaths raging war in my lungs. They are meticulous in their cleaning rituals. I watch in a rage as the head cleaner, Maria they call her, wipes down the prep table in three strokes, buffing away the minute spatter of Quinn's DNA and any evidence that she was splayed there a few hours ago. All around me Chicano music blares, climbing into the dark corners where I hide. I want to sleep, to forget this night, to start over, but I can't. I haven't really slept in 48 hours.

CHAPTER 2

At 8am I am still hiding in my cubbyhole. My own stink is starting to overwhelm the cornmeal and flour smell. I wait for the kitchen staff to enter and the cleaning crew to leave. I make myself purposefully seventeen minutes late for my shift and emerge when no one is in the kitchen.

Donnie is in the hot kitchen, pre-grilling burgers for the lunch rush. He mashes the spatula into the raw meat so hard, oil sparks and pops all around his hand. He holds his hand there, unflinching, like he's testing his own pain threshold. His backs hulks at me. I want to scream at him. I want to grab one of the knives off the rack and drive it through his shoulder blades, the big dumb fucker. He glances over his shoulder at me then, his eyes more bloodshot, than blue.

"The fuck you looking at, Scar?" But words don't even form in the saliva in my mouth as Margie backs into the server doors and pulls a tray of salt and pepper-shakers in with her. The glass shakers clink and the sound hurts my head. She turns to drop the tray in the prep area and stops in her tracks when she sees me. She makes a show of giving me the once over, so I can take that moment to notice how clean and pressed her uniform is and how she appreciates her job way more than I do, even though I usually get the better shifts.

"Did you even go home last night?" she asks, a knowing smirk lighting the corners of her mouth. But the reality of my dress and state hit her full on, and the smirk drags itself into a natural frown that grows until it takes up her whole face. Daily I make a mental note to quit smoking when I look at Margie's cracked and creviced leather skin. I shake my head and start to speak, but instead the Jameson I slammed the night before rises up in the back of my throat. I clamp my hand over my mouth and push past her.

"Oh shit," she says as I head for the swinging server doors, then, "That's either the plague, a hangover, or even worse, morning sickness. Looks like I'm opening on my own again. Story of my friggin' life." She talks to no one in particular, but I hear the tray of salt and pepper shakers slam down on the metal prep table. The sound knocks around in my brain, mixing with the noise of last night. I rush to the bathroom, bumping into Cookie on the way.

"What the hell, Scarlet?" he says while reaching out to right me. I shrink away from him, like he might do to me what they did to Quinn last night. He drops my arm, as if he'd just yanked on a kid's arm too hard and didn't want anyone to see. He watches me back into the bathroom door. I barely make it to the toilet before I vomit up the fear and Jameson and nothingness in my stomach. Cookie is waiting outside the door when I emerge a few minutes later, after splashing cold water on my face. I can feel my hair matted to my forehead and I try to smooth it away when I see him standing there, but I just end up smooshing it into my face even more.

"I've already called Patty in to cover for you," he says. Above him, the news is reporting the robbery at the Topsail Bar & Grill and I look past him to see Cliff with his forehead pressed to the glass again and just beyond his shoulder, a dozen or so reporters and news vans. I turn away from Cliff, as he starts jumping up and down and pointing, his finger *bonging* on the glass again.

"We obviously need everyone in top shape today," Cookie says as he glances at the reporters over his shoulder. "I need you back here for a staff meeting before dinner tonight. We're having family meal at 5:00. Scarlet?" He snaps his fingers in front of my face. I've only caught some of what he said. I stare at the reporters. I can't help imagining running out there and showing them the footage. I take a step, but Cookie grabs me by the shoulders and stares into my eyes.

"What the—Did something happen here?" I say purposefully, and probably badly, stumbling over my words. He crinkles his brow.

"Man, you really are effed up. You honestly don't know?"

I slowly shake my head and force my swollen eyes to open wide.

"Lucky tried to rob the safe last night. Joe beat the shit out of him," he says, but has a hard time acting like it's no big deal that Joe could beat the shit out of anyone.

"Joe?" I ask, my voice going up an octave. Cookie nods, smiles, and leans in to share a secret.

"Good thing it wasn't somebody other than Lucky. I think we'd be a little light in the cash department this morning." He snort-laughs into my ear. I laugh too, but I know it's too awkward, too loud. He straightens up, studies me, trying to figure out if I'm making fun of him or lying.

"Anyway, get out of here. Sleep it off and come back tonight at five. Joe and the family," he draws this last word out for emphasis, as if his comically raised caterpillar eyebrows weren't enough to slam the point home, "want to talk to everybody, so it would be helpful if you washed your clothes before you come back." I look into Cookie's eyes, really look. Is he capable of doing what they did? If he had been here last night, would he have reached under that belly and unbuckled his belt too? I nod and he joins me until we're both silently agreeing. *Oh yeah. You too. You could do it too, couldn't you, Cook?* I shrug out of his hands and move away from him, tears filling my eyes for no good reason.

Thirty seconds later I'm walking past everyone in the kitchen and out the door. I light up a smoke when I get outside and realize it's the first one I've had since clocking out at 10:30 last night. The first drag makes me feel dizzy. I put my palm against the brick wall to steady myself, close my eyes and count to ten. The air smells of trash and what I imagine war smells like; old blood and fire.

When I open my eyes, Cliff is standing in front of me, studying me with a toothless grin. He holds his hand out, palm up. I dig in my pocket for a dollar and press it into his palm as I walk past him, hopefully confirming our contract of silence. He doesn't say anything, which is a good thing, but when I pass him and head out of the alley, I hear him say, "Next time share the whiskey, bitch." I don't look back. It could be that I'm just hearing things.

Sometimes when I play scenes of what just happened or what could happen out in my brain, I give the characters dialogue. Sometimes this dialogue feels so real that I don't know if it is or not. I do this a lot when I fantasize about Sam. I imagine a scene where I beat the shit out of her. It's choreographed like a fight scene, a Kill Bill-esque assassination and I'm the ninja in charge. I think of myself as *Battle Scar*, the anti-heroine. I imagine my thighs are weapons. I say things like, "You shouldn't have come here, Sam. Now I have to kill you." Then I deliver her a serious ass whooping. She fights back, but in the end we are wrapped up on the floor, ripped leather pants, limbs bloody and bruised, and she dives for my lips and I let her. The fantasy always ends with sex and I hate myself for it. Sometimes I imagine that she apologizes and that we get a real opportunity to get to know one another. She says things like, "I was a shit. I'm sorry I ruined your life. What can I do to make it up to you? Can we start over?" It sounds so real in my head. I like this fantasy better, even if it doesn't include the sex.

When I round the corner and travel up the shit-stained, trash-encrusted cobble stone alley next to the restaurant, I start to breathe again. I'm on Newbury, where the commuter traffic is hissing by and steam forces misty air into my face from the T grates in the sidewalk. I go to the Starbucks next door and am happy to be wearing my hoodie again as it covers my uniform and most of the fry oil stench of me. Without thinking I order a quad espresso macchiato with extra foam, but dry, and the rolling eyes of the barista pull me out of zombie mode. I distinctly remember barking my coffee order to Clark, my old production assistant, at some point in my shitty existence. I shake my head at the memory.

"I'm sorry. I meant a dark roast. Drip," I say.

"What size?" The barista asks me and just to piss her off, I say, "Medium."

Outside the big Starbucks window, a few people run by in the direction of the Topsail. I pay in cash and take my cup to the service station, touch it with half & half and a splash of raw sugar, and watch the small crowd of people gathering outside the restaurant. I step outside, walk back to the Topsail, and stand at the back of the crowd of passersby and reporters as we all stare into the window Cliff pissed on. Some of the reporters are pressing their hands and faces against the glass to get a better look and I decide not to tell them about the urine sheen on the glass.

Margie is setting out clean salt and pepper shakers, but she turns to the cameras and waves, smiling, before flipping us off. She doesn't see me, or at least she doesn't register that I'm here. This gives me hope that Cliff really couldn't see me last night. I study a blonde bobble head in impractically high heels. Her heels keep slipping into the divots of cobblestone, turning her ankles sharply every time she moves, to the point that she now looks glued to the spot, fear lining her face. She speaks into a camera resting on the shoulder of bulky camera dude.

"I'm standing in front of the Topsail Bar & Grill on Newbury Street, owned by Governor-elect Jack Marino, where a violent robbery took place last night. Our sources claim that a bus boy, one Lucas 'Lucky' Walker, of Dorchester, waited last night after his shift for the restaurant to shut down before attempting to break into the manager's office where the safe is kept in an attempt to rob the restaurant of its lucrative three-day cash profits. The General Manager and Jack Marino's oldest son, Joseph Marino, caught Mr. Walker in the act and the two tussled, resulting in minor injuries to Mr. Marino and a hospital stay before heading to county lock up for Mr. Walker. More information will become available within the hour and Channel 5 has been granted an exclusive interview by the Marinos, so stay tuned for FX News 5 at 11. I'm Callie Criss for FX News 5 reporting to you live from the Topsail Bar & Grill in Boston. John, back to you." She signs off with a serious nod and waits five seconds for the camera to cut from her. Then she's flipping her hair off her shoulders and using the cameraman's arm to steady herself as they walk to a waiting news van.

The pain in my chest is getting worse. I want to go check in on Lucky to see if he's okay, but I can't. He's in a lot of trouble. Besides, I have to check on Quinn first before I decide anything. I start to walk toward the T and find that no one notices me. Not that they would, but sometimes you think the whole world knows who you are and what you've done. I head into the underbelly of the city at the

Convention Center T, squishing through the crowd coming out, and load a green line train full of surly passengers staring at their tablets or sleeping off last night. I get off at Park, grab the red line to Central, and walk toward Inman Square. She lives there.

I walked her home last week and we talked about her recent graduation from Harvard and how tough it is to get the hang of serving people their food, how they're always so angry, how understanding the certain nuance of balancing food codes, drinks, and making change in our heads isn't a natural thing. It's a non-thing, that we get paid—sometimes—for. We shared a cigarette and laughter. She said someone at table 54, an old woman in a pink mock turtleneck with a gold cross hanging between not-there breasts, said the word *darkie* under their breath to her friend with the oxygen tank, as she walked away already forgetting their order. There was a long stretch of silence between us before I apologized for them, but it didn't make a damn bit of difference. I told her it was okay that she wiped the bun of the old hag's burger on the floor before she served it to them. I said, "Good for you. I would have clocked the bitch."

She said, "If I did that, I'd go to jail. You'd probably get to keep your job."

We didn't say much after that, after I nodded my agreement. But we hugged before I saw her off to her apartment on Concord. I told her if she needed anything that I'd help in any way I could. Then I broke my promise.

I stand in front of 27 Concord now, a row of knockoff brownstone fronts lining the street. Another brown building, just like the one I live in. There must have been a sale in 1975 on baby crap brown at the paint store, because so many row houses, and triple-deckers in Boston are painted this depressing color. Quinn's shitty apartment is third from the left. The basement apartment. Can it get any more depressing? The apartment is dark. She could be inside staring out at me. I hope she's not. I hope she's at the hospital getting a rape kit and heading to the police station to file a report against Joe, but then I see movement and there she is, emerging from what I thought was a huge pile of blankets on the bed. She limps to the counter in the kitchen, pours herself a big glass of water and throws back a couple aspirin. I move in closer so I don't look like a crazy person.

Quinn downs the water and uses the counter to hold herself up. She's wearing a big, fluffy, worn bathrobe that's covered in what looks like unicorns or horses and from the pocket, she pulls her cell phone. I can see the deep bruises and swelling staining her face even from the stoop. One eye is completely swollen shut and there's a deep gash in her cheek. She contemplates the phone, swipes the unlock, types something in, and holds the phone to her ear, but then she stops, chews on her fingernail, and hangs up on whoever she was calling. She chucks the phone at the bed. I look away and light a cigarette.

I drop my bag on the stoop and dig inside for my apron. On my double yesterday, I made $137. I pull five twenties off of the cash roll, stuff it in an old paycheck envelope, Jackson's face staring out through the cellophane peep hole, and I stick it in the mailbox labeled FRANKLIN Apt. A. I walk down the steps and don't look back. I light another cigarette off the first and head toward the nearest bus stop. I don't know why I didn't knock, why I can't knock on her door. I don't understand my own weakness. I light another cigarette, shut down the feelings of assholishness and head into the wind.

I take the bumpy 91, walk from Sullivan Square home, and when I enter my sad little apartment, where the dishes have been piling up for three days, I drop my bag, strip off my clothes, scrub the kitchen clean in my underwear, and do the same to myself in the shower. The bed looks empty and perfect and when I climb in, sleep doesn't wait for me. It takes me over. Maybe this will have been a horrific lucid dream. But my dreams are the same. I long for the day when I have an anxiety dream about waiting tables and not about being a production assistant. I dream that I walk so fast I'm running. And then I am the reality again; in the beginning when I Taylor and I were starving, when my $500 a week PA salary paid our rent. I'm back there and I'm learning that lunch is THE most important part of the day and no one studied reality shows in college. They landed there because the film world wouldn't take them. They landed there because scripted television thought they were a joke. They landed there because the money was good when you're selling people out.

In the *real* world, a good fight between cast members or live, drunken sex after hours, picked up by the night vision cameras, well that's just good television, a *Jerry Springer* wet dream, a *Cops Gone Wild*. Good television entices the executives to order another season of episodes and we all kept working, until that formula didn't work anymore or the show wore out its welcome.

The four camera crews and their production assistants worked around the clock in shifts on *The Real Real Life*. The producers and the accountant got to work out of their suites at the Four Seasons. When the camera crews were shooting at the house with the kids, the Directors and some of the Story Producers (me), holed themselves up in the control room, surrounded by fifty monitors, showing them every room in the house. They barked orders to their camera crews through walkies, directing the camera and the kids.

"Hey, Toby, why won't you talk to Rodney? He definitely has a hard on for you." One Story Producer smirked at an imposing jock, who looked like he was about to punch him.

"Man, fuck you! That fuckin' faggot comes near me and I'll rip his cock lips off!" Toby stormed off and the director whispered to his camera operator, "Did you get that?"

"Hells yeah, I got it, but what the frack are cock lips?"

Later he confronted Rodney and they beat the shit out of one another, a calculated and persuaded hate crime caught on video. The editors in Post Production put their spin on it, raucous music and smash cuts, bleeped curse words and chyrons of the dialogue in case the audience couldn't hear Toby scream in fear, "I told you to back the fuck off of me, homes. I'm not a faggot!" The ratings soared because what Toby didn't know is I saw him slipping down the hall with a guy at the club the night before. I got it on tape as they groped one another in the shadows. We broadcast it and outed Toby to his basketball team and his housemates, and he was ripped apart on Twitter, Reddit, and Gawker for being a coward and an actual faggot. The network loved it. They ate it up. I got promoted for my part in the ratings.

I heard Craig, another Story Producer, speak into his walkie through a yawn, "Camera three. Get Anthony brushing his teeth. He's gonna talk about what happened between him and Veronica last night." *Spin. Spin. Spin.*

The best part? Veronica has a boyfriend of three years, even though she slept with Anthony the night before, their eyes glowing green, like bats, on the night vision footage, while they try to fit all of their limbs into the twin bed provided by production. We threw out so many busted IKEA twin beds that everyone on Skid Row could have had a good night's sleep for a year. We all watched them hump the night away. We watched them take showers and shave and eat and drink and fuck. We took them to class in the mornings in the production vans. We picked them up. We sent them to cast bonding dinners and ropes courses. We took them to Coretta Scott King's funeral and to protest the war in Iraq. Some of them couldn't get out of bed, so they missed it, but our cameras kept rolling on them while they drooled on their pillows.

When the first docu-reality shows came out in the 90s, they broke my worldview open. When I saw Kevin and Julie screaming at one another about race and inequality on the streets of New York City I was glued to the screen. Now these run of the mill shows feature a bunch of drunk dude-bros destroying property or just a guy with a ponytail in Birkenstocks talking incessantly about coding. Irrelevant. A game show. More like *Survivor* than *Big Brother*. But Julia and Kevin, they were the megaphone for a generation of truth seekers. It was meant to be good, a controlled social experiment. It was meant to shed light on our differences and give us a stage to talk about our diversity, our weaknesses. We were supposed to change. We were supposed to connect with the real kids on the screen, offering us a platform to discuss our differences, our weaknesses, and our baggage. Instead we bypassed the reality and begged for the fucking and the drama and the drunken pool parties, numbing ourselves with an HDMI cable to the brain.

We started thinking that Pookie, the perpetually drunk, pint-sized party girl from *Castle's Rock,* was a real representation of an actual human being, instead of a Hollywood creation, like Frankenstein. The cast, became sycophantic little shitheads. They do it for celebrity now. It's like the perfect post grad plan. They tell themselves that they want to be a part of something real, but they really do it for after-show endorsements, book deals, red carpets, and for the $700-$1000 a day "per diem" that I certainly wasn't making when I first started, even though I practically lived in that cum-encrusted house too.

All that stays with me now are the dreams, frenetic moving dreams of people, real and not real, flying at the walls of my brain, making my skin twitch like a dog dreaming of chasing a rabbit. I see the world through a surveillance camera, through a button camera strapped to my chest. I see the world through this lens that is untrue, unjust. I don't trust anything. I don't know what's real, real anymore.

Today the dreams mesh. I find myself sitting in the hot tub with Joe Marino and he has a raft-sized boner and a diamond studded grill. His lips are stretched around it in a monster clown smile and I'm trying to get out of the hot tub, but the water is bloody quicksand. I turn around and see someone standing in the shadows behind me and I reach out for help. They take my hand.

"Help. Please," I say.

She says, "Sure thing, Scar. I'll run out and grab you another macchiato." That voice. I can hear it smiling in the shadows and I'm comforted by it, but then the grip loosens and she lets go and she's gone and I'm falling into the quicksand, slipping below the surface of Joe's giant pulsing dick, gasping for breath.

I fly out of the bed and hit the wall like I'm trying to run through it. My throat feels sandy and bloody. I touch the inside of my cheek with my forefinger and feel the rocky terrain of my flesh near my molars. I've nearly chewed a hole in my cheek. While I'm back there, I touch the tooth and feel the hole rotting away into my sore gums. The tooth is sharp around the edges and has been going bad for months now, but I can't afford the dentist. I contemplate ripping it out myself with pliers, but have read on Reddit that it can go horribly wrong if I mess it up. I go to the bathroom and rinse and gargle with peroxide, brush my teeth and climb back into my bed. My MacBook is lying next to me like a sleeping lover and I touch it softly, pull it into my lap, open her up, and start to scroll.

I wish I could do something normal when I feel guilty, something like grabbing a plastic bag and going out to the playground down the street and picking up trash, just because I want to make the world a better, safer, cleaner space for our children, but I don't. I don't. I know that prisoners from County and the volunteers of Keep Somerville Beautiful will do that. No, when I get guilty, when it really starts to fester like a hot boil under my skin, I scroll it away. I overwhelm-it-with-internet-away I remind myself that the media is lying to us, molding us into little Play-Doh dummies, all blue arms, pink bodies and yellow eyes, yanking us in the direction of whatever sells.

I fall down the worm hole of a search about corrupt government officials, which turns into an article about a DC Madame, and that leads to a search about transgender porn stars, and then body hair removal options, and finally I'm stalking Sam on Facebook. I'm blocked from her, of course, but Beth McLeod, the fake Facebook persona I've created, a rabid fan of TRRL, is not. So I strap on Beth McLeod now and stare at Sam on the red carpet at the Emmys. She and Big Momma Cass Edwards are drunk with laughter after their win, and I think maybe I should just go fucking pick up the trash at the playground and stop this.

But I don't. I just drift into a mind numbing scroll again.

CHAPTER 3

The blatting alarm on my phone lets me know I've hit the snooze one too many times. I'm going to be late. I contemplate not showing up, but can't shake the fact that it might come off as suspicious. I roll out of bed, my body creaking like an old door, and throw on the cleanest Topsail polo I can find. It's bright orange and was given to me the day I started. It makes my skin look like I've spent five too many years broiling myself with baby oil at the community pool, but it's the only clean one on the floor. And really, who cares at this point? I can't understand what's supposed to happen from here on out. I don't know what to expect tonight, but I've got to get there. I've got to stay informed, stay ahead of this thing.

I turn on the news while brushing my teeth and find that the story is everywhere. Lucky came to in the hospital and is being transferred to Suffolk County, where he'll await the judge. He keeps telling his public defender that there was a rape he broke up, but she, like everyone else he tries to tell, doesn't believe him. They just look at him like a poor sack of shit, some dirty busboy who would say anything he could think of to get out of the trouble he's in. No one would ever entertain that Jack Marino's son would rape anyone. In

45

fact, Jack's lawyer has started a defamation suit against Lucky, as far as News 9 tells me. No one would ever believe Lucky over Joe. I study a freeze frame of Lucky's face, a grainy dusty picture of him in fatigues, holding a camera in some far away desert. Another vet gone off his rocker, stealing to get the bills paid. That's Lucky's new story. I'm expecting the next segment to be about his PTSD after three tours in Iraq. He doesn't look anything like he used to. In the photo he's all teeth, big blue eyes, and blonde hair. The desert photo is juxtaposed next to his mug shot. His left eye is swollen almost completely shut, his lip is busted near the flume, and his hair looks black, but it's just the dried blood. It looks like with one more solid hit, his face would have split right down the middle. He is somehow, miraculously standing in front of a measurement board, but it probably doesn't accurately show his height, because a rubber-gloved fist reaching into the frame, holds a clump of his blood-slicked hair, and I assume the helpful soul with the glove is keeping his head upright. Someone else's gloved hand holds a letter board in front of him that reads: BOSTON POLICE DEPT and just below that, WALKER, LUCAS, but the words are cut in half by the frame.

I tune out the news and stare in the mirror. My hair has gotten darker since I stopped traveling to sunny places. It's almost black now. My eyes too. They used to be bright, grey and light, but now they're burnt like the smoke from a plastic fire. Everything around me smells of rotting oranges. I close my eyes, erasing images of bloody fruit from my brain. *It isn't real. It isn't fucking real.* My senses are reaching into a memory of a memory. When I open them again, I stare, really stare, and it's the first time I've been able to look myself in the eye since this whole thing began. I only last a few seconds and then I'm out the door and running to catch a bus.

The air inside the Topsail is thick with anticipation. The almost-governor is coming. Everyone wants to know what happened. But only a few of us really know and we're all cowards. I come in through the back door, like I always do, but the kitchen is empty, save a quiet Nate who is tossing a huge basket of fries with salt. He glances at me, grimacing and as I walk by him he shoves the big basket at me.

"Take these with you," he says and I take them, trying desperately and failing to make eye contact with him. "What are you waiting for?" he asks.

"You coming?" I ask, but he never responds, just goes back to the fry-a-lator. I can see scratch marks left from Quinn's nails snaking down his arms from under his t-shirt.

I leave him there and head out into the dining room. The swinging doors hold back the sound from the other room, but as soon as I break the barrier, I see everyone; every server, every manager, cook, bus boy, prepper, dishwasher, everyone. There are about forty people filling in the dining room, which the Marinos closed for the evening to deal with this situation. The blinds have been pulled on the front windows to keep the press from looking in. It's like a cave in here. My eyes go directly to Jack Marino, dressed down in a white button up, sleeves rolled up to the elbows, two top buttons open so he can breathe. This is his *let's get to work* look, the one I've seen him wear when he visits construction sites, topped off with a hard hat. To his right is a stunningly attractive man in a slim cut, charcoal suit. The suit is not shiny, but in certain light, it glimmers like the man's smile. The point of a black handkerchief pokes out of his breast pocket and matches his shirt as well as his skinny, pinned tie.

He glances at me while listening intently to Jack. His left eye twitches slightly and then he smiles at me. It's flirtatious, a *trust me* kind of smile. I don't. He is the cleaner. I know this. I've known so many men like him. I feel melty for a second, moist to the touch, and then I take a deep breath and remember myself and where I am.

Jack, meanwhile, listens with a gracious smile, to Margie, who is vigorously shaking his hand. Donnie sits at a bench surrounded by Cookie and two of the other cooks, while Joe stands behind the bar and taps a few beers. He's not watching what he's doing, he's watching the crowd, checking each of us out, scanning. For who? Quinn? He can't imagine she'll show her face here. He locks eyes with me and I quickly turn away, dropping the basket of fries on the family-style table with all the rest of the food, mostly fried, that we're supposed to eat. I take a seat at a high top by myself and watch Joe bring his dad and the lawyer a beer. It isn't long before I'm joined by a blushing, gushing Margie.

"Oh. My. God. I could like, eat his fuckin' butt chin for dinner," she says, climbing into the tall chair next to me, Watertown dripping off her tongue in hot, minty waves.

"Who?"

"The gov-enor. Who else?" she says and smiles at Jack, who nods in her direction. "He's a fucking dreamboat." I nod and stare at the man myself. He's chiseled, tan, dark, and by many accounts handsome, just like the man in the charcoal suit. Jack still runs five miles a day and eats only organic. He supports local farms and the composting program Boston started this year, and he's Harvard educated. I wonder what he would think of his son if he knew that Joe raped a fellow alumna, or maybe he does know. Maybe Joe is an old hat at this. They certainly coddle him, surrounding him with a thick man-barrier, all dressed in expensive shirts and pants. Maybe he got in trouble at boarding school in New Hampshire and they've covered it up for him before. Or maybe Joe was caught diddling the family dog, so they got him a prostitute and covered that up too. With this PR and legal Dream Team surrounding him, all I know is Quinn, Lucky, and even me, if I'm not careful, we're all fucked up the river without a paddle. I watch Jack move. His eyes sweep past me and then come back. He smiles. It seems genuine.

"Looks like everyone's here," Margie says and I finally notice that she's not dressed in her uniform. She is dressed in the uniform of every woman from Watertown who's trying to get on the local news: painted on skinnies with fake jewel-embellished back pockets, Uggs, a Sox t-shirt and a fleece vest. She slinks out of the vest and smells her hand, sucking in deeply, then she shoves her palm in my face. It smells like a mix of Newports and Estee Lauder. I swat her hand away.

"Did you smell him?" she asks and I shake my head. "I got the governor on my hand." She bark-laughs and I roll my eyes and take a deep breath. "Come on! What the fuck crawled up your twat and died?" she says.

"Nothing."

"Scar, it's Jack-fuckin'-Marino and Sons," she says and when this doesn't faze me, she adds, "And we got robbed. What the fuck? You'd think you'd be concerned. Like a little bit."

I shrug. "I've met celebrities before," I say and scan the room again. "Besides, not everyone is here."

"Yeah, that skunk who robbed us isn't here and…" She searches the room and says, "That new piece of ass. Where the fuck's Quinn?"

Margie twists in her seat and again, I shrug. "We don't know what really happened. Maybe Quinn didn't want to come back to this shit hole. I wouldn't. Not after the way she was treated."

She looks at me like I'm a moron. "Of course we know what happened. Your boy tried to burglarize the joint and he got his ass beat for it. And if that little ho can't fucking hack it, I say good rinse.

She couldn't even carry a tray with one hand." She digs in her faux leather, fringed handbag and pulls out a piece of gum. Immediately she's chomping it like cud.

I start to argue, but think better of wasting my breath. Joe is about to address us. The sheen of oily sweat on his forehead is giving him away.

"Hey guys," Joe says, his voice shaky. No one hears him but Margie and me. "Guys," he says again, a little louder, and I can see a light colored bruise shaping up on his right cheekbone. Then the air is cracked by a high pitched wolf whistle and I look to my right, where Margie is standing on the rung of her bar stool with her finger folded into her mouth.

"Shut the hell up and let the man speak, you monkeys!" she says when the room quiets to a murmur. She plops back down in her chair and crosses her legs, resumes smacking her gum.

"Thanks, Marg," Joe says. Margie winks at the governor in response. "Thank you for coming, some of you on your day off. As you know, we had an attempted robbery here last night after hours. I hadn't left for the evening and was able to stop it—"

A round of applause explodes, hands bang against tables and boots stomp floors like we're at the goddamned rodeo. Joe holds his hand up to quiet them, his cheeks flushing with color. For a moment, Joe doesn't look like the grease ball with the giant honker who every football player tried to stuff into a locker. He looks softer, happier—less molester, more maestro. He stops speaking for a few seconds and takes it in. Now he's the seasoned bench rider who finally gets called up by the coach and nails a three-pointer at the buzzer to win it. Behind him, his father stands and grabs Joe by the shoulder.

"We Marinos don't back down from a fight," Jack says to the crowd of Topsailers, and it winds them up even more. Joe stares at his dad as if he finally understands the foreign tongue Jack's been speaking all these years around him, but never to him. Gunmetal Grey raises an eyebrow, but claps along. Then Joe scans the crowd of his fans, his chest swelling. He grimaces at me and I realize it's because I'm not clapping. I start clapping immediately and nod at him, so he knows he has my support.

"Okay. Alright." Joe smirks at his dad and to the crowd of employees he says, "Simmer down, everyone. I only did what you'd all do."

"Fucking right I woulda," Pickles, a fry cook, yells out. "I'da kicked that punk's ass to Glosta and back if I'd caught him." Pickles wipes a spot of drool from the corner of his mouth, which is burned and knotted, his skin melted back to the ear all the way up to his hairline. I can't help smelling bubbling fry oil when I look at Pick. He looks like he wants to fight right now.

Joe says, "I know, Pick. I know. He's where he belongs now, but the reason we're all here is to let you know what comes next and to ask some questions."

The hair on my arms stands on end.

"Last night, Lucky tried to break into the safe in the office and almost made off with about eighty thousand dollars."

Someone in the room whistles low until it peters off. The room is so quiet; I can almost hear the brain calculators being punched by thick fingers as everyone realizes just how much money these guys make compared to how much we make. I brought home two hundred and fifty dollars in three days. The Marinos made eighty thousand and still needed to rape a girl to feel like men.

"That's a lot of money. It took some planning for sure. First things first, we've ramped up security here. The alarms have been changed and the CCTV replaced," Joe says, nodding to the ceiling near the bar.

I glance over my shoulder and see, for the first time, a camera pointed right at me, like a gun. All the moisture leaves my mouth. "The story's gotten a lot of press lately, as I'm sure you've noticed, so we have lots of reporters hanging around and people who just want to know what's happening and this is it: there's an ongoing investigation with the BPD and we don't know anything. You get me?" Some people nod. "We are not talking to the press. If a reporter asks you a question, you should not discuss the case with them. Clear?" More nods, some whispering.

Joe holds up a piece of paper, but none of us can really read what's on it. "Before you leave tonight, we'll need you to sign a non-disclosure agreement. It just states that you will not speak with the press or anyone else about the goings-on at this restaurant or the investigation into the attempted robbery. I'm sure you all understand why this is important." Joe hands a stack of papers to Holly, one of the hostesses, and she starts handing them out to everyone. Margie gets hers and signs it without reading it. I put my palm over mine and continue listening. Gunmetal Grey glances at my hand and then his eyes find mine, but I pretend to be completely absorbed in Joe's words.

"We don't want to hurt the BPD's investigation at all, so this is important, guys. Don't talk to anyone. We're going to be swamped here over the next few weeks until the story dies down. Irregardless—" The non-word grates at my nerves. I squish my cheek between clenching teeth and taste blood as Joe continues, "We need you on time for your shifts, ready to work hard, and hopefully making a butt load of money, without gossiping to the press."

Mr. Grey stands and touches Joe's shoulder.

"Anyone with questions about the NDA is welcome to discuss them with my legal assistants any time. My name's Rick. I'm Joey's younger brother and I handle all the paperwork for him." He smirks and slaps Joe on the back. Joe glares at him. It's obvious who got the brains and good looks in the family.

"I'd like him to handle my paperwork," Margie whispers and fans herself with her non-disclosure agreement.

"Yeah, my brother's team will address any of your concerns. Now onto the second matter at hand," Joe says, shuffling a bit and putting his hands on his hips, something I'm sure he's seen Ricky or daddy do when they need to get down to business and command attention. "We're pretty convinced that Lucky wasn't working alone. It looks like he knocked out all of the CCTV cameras, except that one." Joe points to a camera behind him, close to the front of the restaurant. The camera is pointing at the front picture window and I can feel all of the breath leave my body. Joe nods to someone at the back of the room and I turn to see Nate standing next the kitchen door. Nate hits the lights and for a moment, Joe is in full spotlight, black and white video of the Topsail's front window shining on his body. When he moves, I notice the projector attached to a laptop. The image is now projected on the white wall to the left of Jack. For several seconds, we only see cars flying by on Newbury Street outside and then Cliff wanders into frame. After a few seconds his attention is snapped to something inside. He cups his hands over the window and peers in, then jumps back and pounds on the window with his palm, yelling, "Hey you! Hey you! I know you!" pointing inside.

My heart thuds fast in my chest. It's hard to sit here and not run. He's talking to me. No one knows it, but Cliff's yelling to me. I see Rick Marino staring around the room, studying everyone's expressions and I quickly put on a look of concern as I stare at the video unblinking. His eyes fall on me, linger there for a moment and move to Margie, who is shaking her head, and saying, "Fucking Cliff."

As Cliff pisses on the window. Some people laugh around me. Holly says, "Ewww. That's friggin' gross." The video cuts and the lights come back. I'm surely losing all the blood in my body now.

"So as you can see, it looks like our pal Cliff noticed someone or something inside. He clearly says, 'I know you'. This is all we have right now and it's not much, but the time stamp says it happened at 3am, about an hour after the police, me, and my family cleared out and an hour before the cleaning crew punched the alarm out back."

"Has anyone talked to Cliff?" The words are coming out of my mouth before I can stop them. Joe squints to see me.

"Yeah. Thanks for the question, Scarlet," Rick Marino says. I tense. How does he know my name? "The police have talked to Cliff and he told them he saw the Green Monster sitting at the bar drinking a Schlitz." A few people laugh. "We think he saw something or someone, but he's a bit addled, so we can't be sure. We'll be—Do you mind, Joey?" Rick asks his brother before continuing. Joe clenches his jaw and nods. Rick touches his shoulder again in thanks and continues, "We'll be meeting with each of you over the course of the next week to ask you all a few questions about the night of the robbery. You understand that we need to get under every rock, so to speak."

Margie is nodding her agreement and I'm trying not to glare at the smooth operator, Rick Marino, smiling back at me.

"Sure," I say. "Of course."

"In the meantime, if anyone has any information at all, please let us know. It could be anything. You remember Lucky looking at the CCTV cameras funny one day or someone asking questions about the after-hours operating schedule, the alarm code, anything. Could be someone who was complaining a lot about their pay or you noticed someone nicking condiments or silverware. We won't share who told us what. We just need to know if there's something funny you've noticed." He smiles a wide white grin. Several of the women melt, but some of us besides me look nervous. Pickles makes the briefest of eye contact with me and I smile reassuringly at him. I've definitely seen Pickles swiping Nyquil bottles from the first aid kits in the office. I wink at him and he looks away.

"So get those forms on my desk by Friday. And don't talk to the press in the meantime, guys. Help us out here," Joe says and steps back in, only to be met by his father, who stands between his two sons with a hand on each of their shoulders.

"We all work for one another here, am I right?" Jack asks and gets an enthusiastic response. We might as well be baa-ing at him like sheep. "We're a team and we're going to work this out. You help us and the Marinos will help you, starting with dinner and a beer on us!" Jack puts his hands in the air and everyone claps like they've just won a new car. I glance over my shoulder at dinner and my stomach turns. The table of fried food is cold and gummy behind us. The beer, though... *I'll take your candy, Mr. Govna.* I throw a Stella back, a trickle of foam seeps down my chin and onto my shirt. I order a second. I wipe the foam off of my chest and realize I'm wearing a work shirt even though I'm not working. Everything is ridiculous. I leave before anyone else can talk to me. I see Cliff out back by the dumpsters again. Again I stand in front of him and give him cash, willing him to show me recognition. He looks right in my eye and smiles a rotted grin at me. After I get nothing from him, I pat his arm and walk past. Just as I'm rounding the corner I hear him say, "I know you."

CHAPTER 4

I call in sick the day after the meeting. I just can't imagine going back there again, but rent will be due soon and if I don't have this place, I have nothing. I call in just for the day, just to get my head straight, but by the end of the day, it's even more twisted. I spend the whole day binge-watching the news. Joe is being hailed an unlikely hero and it turns my stomach. I stalk Quinn again, but this time online, scouring Facebook for a status that isn't there. Finally, unable to hide behind my computer, I sneak out and hop the bus to Inman Square. I stand in the shadows of the parking garage opposite her apartment, hoping to catch a glimpse of her in the windows, but I can only make out a slow moving shadow passing by the pane every once in a while. Knocking on her door seems out of the question, but this leads me to stare at my phone for a good three minutes, composing a text.

Hey Q. It's Scar. Wanna grab a coffee?

Too casual. I erase it.

Hi Quinn! Missed you at the meeting. Just wanted to check in and make sure you're still slaving away with us. I erase the word "slaving" and then erase the whole fucking glib thing.

Hey Quinn. It's Scar. You missed the meeting. I just wanted to check in and—

And what? Make sure she's okay? Make sure she's alive? Make sure she gets to the police department to file a report before the bruises go away? Fuck. Delete delete delete.

Hey Q. It's Scarlet. Are you okay?

I hit send, bite my cuticle, rip the skin away from the nail, and taste blood. And then I walk away and hop on the bus home. When we hit Broadway, my phone buzzes in my pocket. I look at the screen and see a text from Quinn: *Fine. Under the weather. Thanks for checking.*

I stare out the window and a sudden inspiration hits me and I tap the bell strip next to me. The stop request dings and the bus pulls over right in front of Masala, a tiny Indian joint in Teele Square. I hop out and find myself standing in front of the neighborhood police station. There I stand for the next five minutes until a burly, blonde townie officer smiles at me and says, "Can I help you, ma'am?"

"How do I report a crime?" I say, but the words are mush and come out something like, *Howiportacrim.* He squints at me and his hand hooks into his belt.

"Say it again?" he says, but I don't. I just stand there staring at him. "Did something happen to you?" he asks.

I shake my head. The SD card is in my bag. I don't have to say another word. I just have to hand him the card, but what if he doesn't know what it is? What if he can't figure it out? What if he thinks I'm a lunatic and tosses it? Behind me, I can hear the squeal of air brakes as another bus stops on the other side of Curtis, just one block behind me.

"Do you happen to have the time?" I ask, as if this isn't the lamest cover ever. He glances at his watch.

"Quarter of."

"One?" I ask.

"Three."

"Ah," I say and nod. "Thanks, officer."

He nods slowly and behind me the bus pulls into the stop. I turn and get on it.

I go home. I'm a danger to myself. I read PsychologyForToday.com and discover a new mindfuck called Fiction Depersonalization Syndrome, wherein the afflicted acts like she's on a reality show, cameras trained on her at every second of the day. We act in our real lives for cameras that we've created in our heads. We don't know reality anymore. We don't know truth, only our own spin. The article makes my guts feel heavy. I think, *I did that. Me. I did that to us.* I chain-smoke and stalk Sam on Facebook. In her profile picture, she's holding up a giant Swordfish, standing on the deck of some ghostly fishing vessel, a reality camera crew behind her, all holding their own swordfish. Her pea coat collar is popped and her lips are lush. I want to rip them off with my teeth and taste the salt of the ocean in her blood. When I piggyback my third cigarette, I realize I've been here too long.

I was having three different conversations like a crazy person the first time I met Sam, on season five of TRRL. As a Story Producer, I was responsible for orchestrating the Fiction Depersonalization you're addicted to and for *gently nudging* cast members down the rabbit hole of the drama I made up. I was your dealer. I was the production company's trap queen. Every night I needed two showers before bed, I was that dirty. When I met Sam, I was on the phone. My phone had become affixed to my right ear and on the other side I held a landline. Sometimes I said the wrong thing to the wrong person. Sometimes I also carried a walkie and spoke to the crews.

My crew PA, Clark, was making his coffee and tape drop-offs throughout the office and I was anxiously awaiting my dry quad espresso macchiato with extra foam. I was a long way from

Production Assistant myself and I had the designer jeans, Ray-bans, and Frye boots to prove it. I was a cunt, not in the weak misogynist sense of a slur slung at a footballer who missed a punt, no I was a business cunt, a get-shit-done-by-any-means-necessary-cunt, the feminist kind of cunt. It was in my job description. It was a part of my DNA. I wore permanent resting bitch face like it was my job and only came down from being a restless asshole long enough to catch a few hours of sleep each night. And I was paid well for my endeavors.

On the home front, there was no home front. I'd been on the road for three years more than I'd been home. I'd already cheated on Taylor twice, once with her bassist Gretchen, who had moved into our apartment in Park Slope with Tay, and once with Craig, my camera operator, who was now working on another in-house show, *Antarctica: The Wilds*. I wasn't proud of myself. I just hated my life. That's the only excuse I have. So I kept depositing the checks and Taylor kept spending the money and played at being happy.

I'd wanted to write books, not produce reality television. I'd also wanted to be an American Gladiator when I was a kid. That was the dream. Well it was my Gramp's dream. That reality show was his favorite and he always talked about how I could beat the pants off of everyone on it and take home the big bucks. Then with my cash winnings, I could buy a cabin on a lake where I would write the great American novel or stories about him, my Gramp, my hero. Instead there was no Gramp anymore. There was diabetes and heart disease and too much television. Instead, I was living in the cesspool that is Los Angeles for six months out of the year, selling laundry detergent and advertisements for W-Mart through a group of half-braindead coeds on *The Real Real Life*, while my fiancé, home in New York, headed up a garage band called *Gloricrux* when she wasn't working shifts at Café Orlin on St. Marks. My life was abysmal. I was on the wrong side of the country most of the time and when I wasn't there, I was crashing in my own apartment in Brooklyn a few days at a time, trying not to fuck my girlfriend's best friend before heading back out on the road, sometimes stuck in podunk southern campus towns where the Klan still hangs black baby dolls from the trees.

"Sergeant Carroll, my name is Scarlet Battell," I said into the landline. "I'm a production manager with *The Real Real Life*, a reality show shooting in town, and I'm wondering who I would speak with—"

Then into the cell: "Tell him we'll send over the releases ASAP," Stevie "Skull and Bones" McManus, my Supervising Producer, was breathing in my ear, trying to listen to the conversation.

"Bruce! Tell him I need the light packs here no later than seven!" I barked into a walkie. I glanced down to the entrance of the office and saw Clark handing off my macchiato. I started to foam at the mouth.

"No. Excuse me. Not you, sir. We're trying to get permission to shoot our cast members on one of your bases—ha, ha. That's shoot with cameras, not guns, sir. We'd like to have access to the tanks and set up a challenge between our cast members and your cadets—"

"Don't fucking take no for an answer like you did last time," Stevie said.

"Fuck. That's not good enough!" I yelled and squeezed my eyes shut, listening to the other line. "No, sir. No. I wasn't speaking to you, Sergeant. I'm so sorry."

Down the row of cubicles, I saw a tall, lithe, blonde girl, a woman actually; maybe twenty-five years old. She was coming at Clark with another tray of coffees. She handed a cup to Clark, rescued my macchiato away from Greg, the gaffer, and sprinted toward me. She handed off a stack of SD cards to a camera PA, dropped a few bags of snacks on the craft services table, swung a Whole Foods bag off her shoulder and handed it to Stevie, then started to hand me my macchiato. I, in an immense moment of stupidity, tried to hold on to the coffee with no hands. I didn't manage the task and the coffee and both phones went flying. Stevie grabbed my landline in frustration and I mumbled something to Bruce about getting the light packs here or I would eat his firstborn child.

Poor Sam tried to help me clean up the mess all over my desk that was turning invoices and petty cash envelopes a dark brown by the second. And me? I was covered. We ended up standing just under Stevie's nose, smirking at one another, paper towels littered at our feet and stuffed into her hand, which had made its way onto my tit. It was the first time I'd smiled in months. I noticed a tiny infinity symbol tattooed on the inside of her forefinger and made a mental note to ask her about it. She scrubbed away the coffee making me look like the winner of a very dirty wet t-shirt contest.

"I'm sorry, Scarlet. I'll run out and grab you another coffee," Sam said. She quickly swept up the mess, color rushing to her cheeks, and left me staring after her as Stevie continued to deal-or-no-deal behind me.

I remember that day, meeting Sam. I remember that it was innocent and funny and then it wasn't. I've never spoken about it because I signed a non-disclosure agreement. If I talk, they might have to kill me. Kidding. They'd sue me, which is sometimes worse. I wasn't shocked when Rick Marino handed me an NDA yesterday. I haven't signed it yet. I don't want to be screwed into silence about the goings-on at the restaurant.

Next up on my internet binge, I look up the laws governing recording images of people without their permission on MAPressLaws.com and find this:

In the Commonwealth of Massachusetts, it is a crime to secretly record a conversation. Whether the conversation is in-person or taking place by telephone or another medium. This law extends to video recorded with sound, subjecting the recorder to criminal prosecution. As well, violating the Commonwealth's wiretapping law may also open the recorder up to civil lawsuits for damages to the victim.

Damages to the victim. Who is that besides Quinn, besides poor Lucky, probably getting his ass handed to him in a jail cell right now? The sinking, burning hole in my gut feels like a fearsome, angry tumor growing to the size of a watermelon. Still I only want to capture all of this. Imagine the show I could create. Imagine the ratings. Victims. Abusers. Corporate greed or something. It's all there.

The thing that's actually eating away at me the most, besides the fact that Lucky is in jail and unless I can talk to Quinn, I can't get him out, is that Quinn hasn't gone to the cops, at least not that I know of. This is that thing everyone talks about. This victim's silence phenomenon, women not reporting being raped. I wish I could be mad at her, but I can't because I've done it myself and by the time you want to tell the right people, by the time you're past being ashamed of this thing, this horrible thing that happened to you between your legs and all over your body, coursing through the gray matter in your brain, tearing apart your insides with guilt; by the time you're ready, the bruises have faded and the skin cells and semen have been washed away. In this case there's video proof, but I don't think I can do it. I am the black muck on the floor of the restaurant and I can't for the life of me bring myself to show her this video that I took, because everyone will know that I did nothing. I did nothing to help. I will say I was scared, but that will be weak.

I can't go to the cops either. I realized that today. I can't further violate her privacy, but I should go just to exonerate Lucky. I shake the thought away. Too many broken eggs in this fucked up basket. The best thing to do would be to show Quinn the footage. I can stop being a coward long enough to show her the footage and she will know there is evidence and we can be a team and do this together and get Lucky out and he can be a hero and I can slip back into the nothingness that is my existence and just pay the goddamned rent and keep my nose to the grindstone. Maybe in like five years, I can write a book. Maybe I can write poems or a short story about this, or life, or—

I see Jenny on the screen in front me. It pauses all thought of my own cowardice or literary endeavors. I press the mute button. A jingle with heavy horns blares at me and the chyron, *EXTRA! DAILY*, flashes on the bottom of an image of Jenny sitting in front of a group of teenage kids. On the blackboard behind her, the words, *HIV is not a death sentence*. Background singers harmonize, "Extra, Extra, Extra!" each word rising an octave until they're screaming at me and making my head spin. This cuts to Jenny walking and talking with Kent Snyder, the tall, coiffed Extra reporter, near a nice park with a water feature.

"I met up with Jenny Lang, star of TRRL, season five, to talk about her very public HIV diagnosis and how it's affecting her daily life."

Cut to a set: two chairs facing each other, soft lighting. It could be a hotel room. There's a crocus on a side table near Jenny's head. *Nice touch*, I think. Jenny looks great, fresh faced, crisp, clean. Coming out has done wonders for her skin. Kent Snyder is smiling at her with shockingly white teeth and doing some kind of mind meld with her, while he chooses his words carefully for the next question.

"It's been three years since you came out as HIV+," he says, choosing not a question at all. Jenny takes a deep breath, smiles, and nods. "What's life been like after exposing yourself like that?"

"Some days are better than others," she says, but doesn't mean it. They're all pretty good, except for the whole HIV thing. "I find that once you've been truthful, like really truthful, you have no choice but to live in every moment like that."

"That's profound," Kent says, but I'm not sure he knows what the word means. "So let's recap for the people who might have been living under a rock for the past few years: You appeared on season five of TRRL. Though you weren't a main cast member, you did have an intimate relationship with one." He gives her a raised eyebrow and she demurs, smooths out a wrinkle in her jeans and nods, with pursed lips.

"Jaron," she says.

"Jaron Thibideau. Star forward for the University of Duke, star mac daddy for the house of TRRL."

I can tell Jenny is holding in her laughter. I can't hold mine. It bursts out of me like a gas bubble.

"He was a player. For sure," Jenny says.

"So let's get serious for a moment here, Jenny. Take us through what happened if you're able."

She takes a deep breath, plucking up her courage to tell the truth and says, "I'd seen Jaron around. I tended bar most nights at the Crocus, a pub on campus, and Jaron would come in a few times a week. He was sweet, and flirty, and said all the right things you know? So one night he asked if he could wait for me after my shift, just like ya'll saw on the show and I said yes, but I had to check with my babysitter to make sure it was okay." She pauses, thinks on it, working to get the facts straight in her brain and continues, "So I came out at like two in morning and he's waiting for me next to his Charger, blasting some old school R. Kelly and my heart just dropped."

"And so did your pants," I say to the screen through a wall of cigarette smoke.

"We danced. It was so romantical, you know," she says, really selling the dream. Kent nods, but concern is creeping into his smile.

"But then…" he says.

"But then it went downhill. Everyone who watched the show knows we hooked up in his car. It was stupid. A quick fling that probably should never have happened, but it did and now we both gotta live with the consequences."

"Tell us what happened next."

"I just had this feeling you know. I told one of the story producers—"

Me. She's talking about me.

"—that I felt like I should get tested. This was a couple months later. They wanted to come with me. That's the first time I made a decision to live my life out loud, you know, truthful."

"Did you think you were positive when you went in?"

"I felt like something was off. I didn't feel like myself. So I went with a small crew because the show was just wrapping up production and we went in to the local clinic and got the mouth swab and it immediately came back positive."

Kent puts his knuckles to his chin, stares at her in his best *I can't imagine the pain you must have experienced* facial configuration. He shakes his head and says, "And then you went back to the house and confronted Jaron. You knew for sure it was him? I don't mean to be insensitive, I just—"

"I'm sure. I'd only had two partners before Jaron and my youngest, Kristal, doesn't have it, so I pretty much knew it was him."

"And Jaron agreed to get tested on camera. He was positive—"

"And that started a chain, you know. They tested his girlfriend and Lacey, the girl he'd hooked up with right before me, and like four other girls, who had no idea what they were getting into and sure enough, all of us. We have a support group now."

"Wow. I saw the show. I've seen it several times and it still blows me away. What a harrowing ordeal for you all and Emmy worthy docu-storytelling for TRRL. So let's talk now about what you've been doing since the positive result."

"We're busy," she says and inhales deep, sucking in the story, tucking it away until the next time she needs to unpack it. "It's been really good though. We started *Posi+ive*, a traveling support team for women of all races and sexual orientation who are HIV+ or who have AIDS. We work with their kids, their families; we have informed, honest discussions with high schools—"

I can't watch anymore. I mute Jenny and sit in the silence, allow it to envelope me and I talk to my own breath. *I'm glad she's okay. It could have gone so wrong.* Guilt plucks at my heartstrings for a millisecond, but I shake it away. *I did the right thing. I did the right thing.*

It amazes me how this current situation is just like story producing. I have to figure out the best way, the best angle to get this footage to the right people, who will do the right thing with it. I pound away on the keys of the laptop again, while Jenny wipes away tears in front of me. The past doesn't change the future very much sometimes.

I wash my brain with a Google solution and research Demarcus Shine, the guy who recorded Malcolm McConnell getting gunned down in an alley as he walked away from trigger-happy Carlos Zimmer, a Philadelphia patrolman. Shine brought his footage to McConnell's family a week after the shooting happened and his family gave Shine permission to release the footage to the New York Times. Shine was arrested three days after the Times released the footage on a possession of marijuana charge and two days after that, he was found hanging in his cell in county lock up. He hadn't eaten in two days and had bruises consistent with an ass kicking. So there's that too. That's a definite possibility. If I do the right thing, the Marinos might try to shut me up. I close the laptop.

I squeeze the flesh on my upper thigh hard enough to raise a deep red welt. I don't realize I'm doing it until I see the color. I never feel the pain anymore. I should have stopped this. I can still stop this. I pull the camera out of my bag. I haven't watched the footage since that night. I drop the camera back in my bag and throw my apron in next to it.

I'll stop by Quinn's on my way home from the restaurant tomorrow and drop the card. It's the only way. I hope she doesn't sue me. I'm not worth anything anymore.

CHAPTER 5

The Topsail is full of guests by the time I show up for my shift. It's packed, just like they told us it would be. Heroes like Joe are great for business. I feel sick every time I stuff a 20% tip into my pocket. The news runs continuously. Two hours in, I join Margie by the bar and we stare up at the screens. The front of the Topsail flashes on the flat screen behind the bar and the patrons and workers clap and start the wave. We're all heroes, except me. Except Joe, that fucking pig rapist. But what does the public know? I'm shaking my head next to Margie while I garnish the rainbow drink in front of me with a grenadine float.

"Scar, you should be celebrating with the rest of us. I've been banking all week," she says, clapping along with the regulars at the bar.

I nod as Lucky's face flashes on the screen and everyone around me boos like we're watching a Bruins game. I feel a catch in my throat as I read the chyron at the bottom of the screen under Lucky's busted mug shot: "Topsail bus boy says he's being framed and was actually stopping a rape in progress when he was attacked. #TopsailRobbery #Marino"

I glance at Joe, who is in the middle of a heated debate with Nate and Donnie near the service bar. Donnie motions to the tube and I watch Joe's face darken as he turns around and reads the screen.

"That pussy-ass'll learn a thing or two about rape up in Suffolk County, amIright, Joey?" Jerry, a grisly, toothless, tub of a guy decked out in Patriots gear, yells from the end of the bar. Joe allows a forced smile to hit his lips as he nods back.

"Fucking right, Jer," Margie agrees and leans into me and under her breath says, "What a crock of shit, huh? Joe doesn't have it in him. He probably asks his dick permission before he takes a piss."

Another round of cheers makes its way around the bar and when I don't respond, Margie says, "Ooooh, I get it. You still have a hard-on for that douchebag."

"No. I'm just over the locker room circle jerk." As the words come out of my mouth, Jerry reaches over and grabs the whole right cheek of my ass in the palm of his hand.

"Lighten up, Scarlet. We're celebrating here! We're famous!" Jerry says.

"Fuck off, Jerry!" I swat his hand away and he shrugs, laughs, and goes back to his beer. I hear him draw out the word "touchy" as I turn and head for the two tables that have just been sat in my section without another word to Margie.

At Table 47, a mom, dad, and two kids sit staring at me impatiently, their menus stacked in the middle of the table to let me know that they were ready to order three minutes ago.

"Okay, a PBR." I set the beer down in front of Dad. "A skinny margarita for you, ma'am." The toxic green drink is taken from my hands before I can set it down. "And for you, little man, a super cherry Shirley Temple." The dirty little kid to my left grabs the drink from me and it sloshes all over the table.

"Kirby! Watch what you're friggin' doin'!" Mom yells, slapping his hand. I hand the lidded chocolate milk to the little one in the high chair and out of the corner of my eye, I see Joe and Donnie standing near the kitchen doors. Joe hands Donnie a substantial wad of cash.

"Hell-o! Can you take our order?" the mom says.

"I'm sorry. What can I get you all tonight?" I force a smile and half-listen to the mom's order of fried chicken salad (hold the onion, tomato and cucumber, add extra cheese, ranch, croutons) as Joe slaps Donnie on the back and Donnie heads through the kitchen. I don't have time to contemplate what I've just seen though, because the two-year-old is yanking my apron down, nearly pantsing me where I stand. The Marinos pay people off all the time. This is nothing new. I've seen it before, the Restaurant Depot drivers, the Health Inspector, but Donnie—why is Joe paying Donnie off? Is Donnie threatening to talk?

Just a year ago, Pickles was working a busy Friday night shift when he got the call that the line needed more blood. He dashed back to the walk-in to haul out a 20-pound sack of red meat, blood, and gristle. He rounded the corner next to the fry-a-later and his worn down no-slips glided right over a puddle that had collected just the right amount of grease. The meat bag flew into the line, causing several full plates to smash to the floor. The bag split on a corner, blood and flesh flying everywhere. I got hit with the splatter where I stood next to the expo line. I was clearing the blood from my eyes and watching Cookie's face turn purple with anger as he turned to rip Pickles a new one, but then he stopped. We all stopped.

Silence hit the kitchen as we watched Pickles struggle to regain his balance. He reminded me of a person standing on the edge of a cliff, arms flapping to stay upright before a plunge. For one second, Pickles smiled at me as he found a flat surface to brace his fall, but then faltered, just like his smirk. The heel of his hand slipped on grease then he fell, hand- and arm-first, into the deep fat fryer. His screams caused the entire restaurant to go dead silent, save the thumping "I Wanna Dance With Somebody" being piped through the speakers.

Donnie and Nate struggled to pull him out, but the grease was so thick, they slipped too, dropping him back into the bubbling brown liquid twice more before pulling him out. Pickles didn't feel a thing after the first time, just his blood hardening and his skin cooking to light golden, chicken-fried perfection. The Marinos paid for everything: his rent, medical—hell, they even bought him cigarettes. They gave him his job back as soon as he was ready and they never filed a worker's comp or insurance report. Pickles had no idea he could have taken them for all they were worth, or that he could have ruined Jack's chances in the election, or that he could have shut the restaurant down. The building inspector told Joe to fix those tiles two months before Pick fell, but he never did it. Pickles didn't know any better and now Quinn's been raped and Lucky's been beaten and it all could have been prevented if Pickles hadn't been poor and Joe hadn't paid off the health inspector. I keep my eye on Joe for the rest of the night, but nothing happens.

I stop by Quinn's street on the way home to wad up the hundred sixty dollars in my pocket and leave it in her mailbox. I watch the darkness behind the curtains for a long time, but just can't ring the bell. I smoke five cigarettes in the twenty minutes I stand there, holding the SD card in my apron with my palm. I can't just leave it. That would be a cruel prank I need to hand it to her, face to face. I need to explain.

This sensation is familiar to me, too familiar, this need to explain, to wipe away my guilt with words. I used to be able to wash it away, pack it away in the back of my brain, muted from the job at hand, but

I've slipped before. I've let the guilt pervade my senses enough to tell the truth before.

Quinn's light never comes on. I never see movement. If she's gone, really gone, then there is no truth, unless I tell it. I hope she hasn't left. I need more chances. I hope she's with someone who is taking care of her. I hope that she is being comforted and loved. I finger the SD card in my bag, hold it like hot coal, let it burn me. I inhale one last cigarette, the smoke dragging its way through the wet phlegmy tears in the back of my throat, bringing to life an old monster in my gut. It's awaking from its violent sleep and it's about to take me down. I turn and head for the bus.

CHAPTER 6

Quinn's screams and the sound of fists meeting flesh are all around me. I can't escape it. It's inside my head, coating the walls of my skull. I am staring at myself in the mirror over the sink in my shitty, molding bathroom. The metal from the medicine cabinet is showing through the glass of the mirror and mixing with the rust that serves as its bed. My eyes are bloodshot from crying. Sitting before me on the equally rust-stained white porcelain sink are four things: a razor, a knife, a pile of seventeen Xanax and an orange. My hand hovers over the Xanax as Quinn screams "No" and Joe says, "Grab her arms!" I wonder if my neighbors can hear their voices.

I could leave the SD card on my coffee table. There would be no need for a note. I could take the Xanax and hope I don't wake up. I could make a copy of the SD card and drop it off in Quinn's mailbox with my tips tomorrow and step onto the train tracks at Park Street and wait for something inbound to smash me. My hand hovers over the knife: the hard way out. And then the orange. I touch its cool skin and can feel the pores of zest. My nose hairs are already pricking up at the sweet smell, my favorite perfume on an old lover. My fingers close on it and hold it tight.

I stare hard into my own eyes. My pupils dilate slightly as the fire alarm sounds out from the next room. I drop the orange into a pair of my Topsail stockings and then with all of might, with every force of my muscles, I swing and drive the orange into my cheek and feel the sensation of being punched. The force knocks my head back for a second. The rat in my brain slows on its wheel. Before I can talk myself into doing it again, I do, slamming the rind into my eye socket. Again and again. I punch myself so hard with the orange, it breaks in the stocking and the juice seeps into the split skin below my swollen eye. It stings like alcohol on a gaping wound. I dig the remains out of the stocking and throw it at the wall in the shower. The bloody orange mess seeps down the yellowing tiles in time with the pulp and blood from my cheek and then, with no fruit left to use, I smash my fist into the same side, breaking the cut open even deeper until my blood spatters my image in the mirror and I black out.

My head must have hit the sink on the way down because when I wake up, I am lying on the tile surrounded by my own blood. My hair is stuck to the floor and the gash on my forehead is competing with the one on my cheek. I can't move. It takes every bit of strength in my neck to turn over. I stare at the molding along the floor and see a splotch of blood. I imagine it's someone else's. Not mine. It can't be mine. But then my tears are rolling down my cheeks and splashing in the puddle of black/red plasma under my head. I crawl into the shower and wash away what I can away.

Tonight the bruises will be pulpy, tender throbbing red spots and tomorrow, black, blue, purple, swollen shut and split open. They will be a reminder of what Quinn and Lucky went through. We will share a tattoo. Tonight I will bring the SD card to Quinn, whether she is there or not. If she is there, I will confess and we will make a plan together. I hope she'll let me help her. I guess I have to be okay with it even if she doesn't. I have to be okay with it even if she punches me, calls me names, looks at me like I'm just another white person who has raped her. I don't want to be that person, but I can see how she might think it. I can see that. I hate it. I hate myself because of it, but it may—it probably exists.

I need to be numb before I go there.

I have to accept everything that she needs to throw at me.

I need to accept my role.

I slowly make my way to the ratty old couch I found on the sidewalk two months ago. I can still smell the hint of cat piss in the cushions even though I've sprayed and scrubbed it with an enzyme cleaner a thousand times. Right now though, the scent is somewhat comforting, as is the scratchy cigarette burn hole that digs into my naked thigh when I sit down and pull my laptop to me. I light a cigarette and find that inhaling hurts quite a bit, but the pain is making me feel alive. I pause. I only have a few options. I decide on Craigslist, go straight for Casual Encounters, and click the link to "w4w". I scroll until something catches my eye.

Femme Needs to Dominate Femme.

I click it. Inside I find: *I work in a male dominated field and need to be in control tonight. I need to pin you down and make you cum. Please be femme, not necessarily sub and willing to let it go after tonight. I'm in town for work. No strings.*

A lump of fear drops from my gullet to my belly button and passes hard into my core. I've seen this before. I've seen this—something like this—before. In Virginia? Jenny's slight VA twang pings around my brain. My last season? My head is pounding and blood is filling my mouth from the hole on the inside of my cheek. What had she said? *I need to be in control. I'm lowly. The bottom of the totem and I need to pin someone down and*…so familiar. Maybe there's a genre of Craigslist I've never seen before. Maybe I should cruise this subReddit, if it exists. Or should I? The last time I answered something like this, it was the beginning of a slippery slope that led to my destruction. The thought oddly comforts me, tickles me even. This may be what I need, a re-creation that I can make my own. Craigslist088365932 may want to dominate someone, and I'll let her, but this could just be the catharsis I need to find my strength and get the fuck on with it.

"Downtown. Four Seasons. Just you. NO MEN, DBAGS. Female bodied ONLY. Strictly hard femme for femme."

I hit the email reply and write: "I've been bad. I need to be pinned down. I need to release. Make me cum please." Send.

I light another cigarette. Before I make my first exhalation, my email dings. I open the new email from Craigslist088365932: "Room 1013," it reads.

I close my laptop and smoke my way into the nicest thing I have left from before, my black trench coat. I look like an imposter, a hooker, a girl at the end of her rope, but there's a strong knot to stand on at the end there. I don't care that my face is busted. It gives me something to hide behind. I walk out of my apartment and hail a cab to the Four Seasons. The images fly by me, but everything is a kaleidoscope of monotony. I am the broken, crusty leather back seat of this shitty Camry. I am the blurred images of this town. I am the violence seeping down, down, down into the sewers.

"Tough night?"

I realize the weathered and nearly toothless Somerville native who smells of Newports and Old Spice has turned down the Sox game on the radio and is speaking at me through the rearview mirror.

"Not the worst," I say and attempt a smile. Blood drools down my chin and I wipe it away with the back of my hand. I hope this gesture will make him turn on the game again. The soothing monotone and fast pitch of the announcers made me feel calm for a split second, but Father O'Malley here in the front seat isn't taking my hints.

"That's a nasty split lip ya got there," he says, unblinking.

"I beat the shit out of myself."

His brow furrows and he investigates my other bruises as we wait at the light on Massachusetts Avenue just before Cambridge becomes Boston.

"Never heard that one before," he says. "My sistah used to say she walked into her husband's fist on accident."

I stare at him, also unblinking, but don't respond.

"You walk into someone's fist?" he asks.

"My own. I told you," I say.

"You need a hospital?"

"No."

"You sure?" I look away from him and he slowly pulls out of the stop. "We're not far from MGH."

"I need the Four Seasons."

He shrugs and nods like he totally agrees with me and we sit in silence for a spell. I can see the Citgo sign in the distance. We're near Fenway. The lights are up on the field; people are littering the streets, screaming and celebrating a win. The traffic and potholes worsen as we near downtown.

My lips are so dry, I can taste the chalky, rusty spit in the corners of my mouth. I dig in my bag for my lip balm and hope that I can pull the rest of this night off with little talking or smiling. I realize I haven't emptied my bag since the night Quinn was raped. My GoPro is sitting there staring back at me like an evil eye and I can't find my lip balm. I take my keys out of the bag and hold them in my hand while I'm looking for the little tube of lip lube, and even they feel different to me, like they're lighter, like they're not even mine anymore. I throw the keys back in, hoping they'll break the camera. I don't want to be tempted to record anything else, though it's too late for that. The cabby makes eye contact again in the rearview. He doesn't say anything, just turns up the game this time and steals glances at me in the mirror.

"You mind if I smoke?" I ask.

He shakes his head. "You mind if I join you?"

He doesn't wait for me to answer. He pulls a soft pack of Newports from the visor and shakes one into his mouth. He pops the cigarette lighter in and it pops out twenty seconds later. He hands it to me before lighting his own cigarette and because my lighter has gone the way of my lip balm, I take it from him and touch the red coils to the end of my cigarette. I inhale and have the same recurring thought I have every time I take the first drag on a butt and the smoke burns the length of my lungs: *I'm dying. I need to quit this shit.*

"I need to quit these bastards," Sean O'Toole says. I've just noticed his name on his paper license displayed on the dash. "Can't buy 'em at CVS anymore and everywhere else they're like ten bucks a pack. Highway robbery."

I nod my agreement as we pass Newbury and head down Boylston. The Topsail will be quiet right now. It's 12:37am, but that doesn't stop me from peering down the busy street to see if I can catch a glimpse of it. I can't. Better that way. I'll be walking up to room 1013 in a matter of minutes and I need to prepare for what's on the other side. Maybe the emailer isn't a woman at all. Maybe it's a man waiting for me. A man waiting to kill me. That would be the easiest.

I take another drag off my cigarette and Sean O'Toole stares up at the night sky through his smoke out the window. I could just jump out of the cab when he picks up speed, but that's not a surefire plan and Sean O'Toole will have to live with the image of my shattered body falling from his car, smashing into the concrete or oncoming traffic for the rest of his life. I know that I don't want to burden another human with that feeling. Not Sean, anyway. He seems okay.

I stare down at my exposed knee and imagine what I must look like to everyone else. I'm bruised and naked save for my best underwear and bra set, left over from my days of shopping at Journelle, under this heavy trench coat. My boots are short black booties that are crap for my feet, but in style as far as I can tell from the trickle-down fashion at the big box stores. If someone's going to murder me or worse, rape me, I look the part—at least that's what they'll accuse my corpse of when they find me. I asked for it. Obviously.

I catch Sean staring at the bruise on my knee and start digging in my bag for cash. I come up with a twenty and hand it to him even though it's $6 more than what my fare will be. He shakes his head. I shove it through the plate glass and drop it on the front seat. I don't wait for the cab to stop completely in front of the Four Seasons before opening my door, but Sean grabs my wrist before I can hop out. He puts a small card in my hand and says, "I'm around until 8am on this shift. You call me if you need a way out of here later." He nods so I don't have to, then turns from me, his jaw clenching as he stares at the city in front of him. I get out and he slowly pulls away.

CHAPTER 7

1013 is at the end of a long paisley-carpeted, plastic-scented hallway.
The walk seems endless. I can taste the crappy carpet spray
housekeeping used this morning, which is supposed to be lemon
verbena but just smells like "yellow." All the scents mixing with the
blood in my nose are reminding me of the last time I did this, the last
time I spiraled, the last time I went looking for someone anonymous.
The ad was so clean. So desperate for power and there I was with so
much power and still with nothing. I wanted that low-on-the-totem-
pole person to get me. I wanted to be carried like something dead in
a stranger's arms. I wanted to be taken, to be put on the bottom, to
be anything other than what I was.

I remember seeing her sitting alone in a booth at a local chain restaurant
near the hotel, drunk, her nose just inches from the rim of her glass.
She said to find her in the booth under the boomerang. She said she'd
be eating cheese fries. And there she was, under the plastic boomerang.
No fries, just three empty beer mugs. She was light blonde from the
back, but as I got closer, I saw streaks of color in her hair. It reminded
me of someone I knew. Gretchen? My heart plunked in my chest. I

walked faster. She was tall, her messy bun tilted and sitting well above the back of the booth. She'd said to call her Cam.

"Cam?" I spoke slightly over the musak. She didn't turn. I stared at her long fingers wrapped around the frothy glass of dark beer, "Hey, Cam?"

She turned on me fast, like an enemy had snuck up on her and then stood suddenly, six inches over me, color rushing her gin blossomed cheeks and running a course down her neck to hide somewhere in the folds of her puffy vest. I stared from her chestnut colored eyes to the walkie-talkie on her hip. Her shirt had ridden up and the milky skin of her hip was exposed over too big skinny jeans.

"Scarlet, I—"

I closed my eyes and shook my head, tried to gather my thoughts, tried to make a rational decision and when I opened them, I walked away from her to the bar. I ordered a beer and a Jameson neat.

"Battle Scar!" a chorus from around the bar greeted me. So much for anonymity. Several of the day crew members were in stages of forgetting their shitty lives all around me. Gary nodded to me and Clark, my PA, looked abashed that I'd caught him having a good time. I smiled and raised my glass and this seemed to settle him. He glanced at Sam and then me and smiled. When I turned back to the booth, I found Sam sitting again, her head in her hands. She looked like she'd been crying or at least hadn't slept in a few days. The latter was probably closer to fact. I sat down with her. We never mentioned Craig or his fucking list. Instead, I ordered us steaks and starch and she devoured what she could. I couldn't eat mine. The three-second rule was still banging around in my head and I didn't trust the greying meat in front of me for one second.

"This is really awkward," she said and I nodded my agreement, but she didn't see it. She was staring at my steak like a long lost lover.

"We can just forget about it," I said.

"I don't know what I was thinking," she said.

"I'm guessing you weren't," I said, "at least not with your brain. Just like me."

She nodded and breathed in a deep meditative breath. "I got lonely."

"I know all about it."

She smiled at me, but either didn't totally get it or was too absorbed in my steak sitting there untouched to care.

"You hungry? Have at it," I said.

"You sure?" she asked, but didn't wait for my reply before she started cutting into the bloody thing. "It's good to see you take a break, Scarlet," Sam said around a mouthful of rare meat. "The only time I ever see you stop is to take a sip of coffee before you keep talking."

"Or screaming or having a nervous breakdown," I said. She nodded, guilty as charged. "I had to get out of that hotel room," I said and felt shitty immediately for complaining.

"Yeah. I hear ya." She smirked sarcastically into her beer. "You know Cass is calling me a 'local' even though my apartment's over 500 miles away?"

I nodded. "I do. It's a standard deal memo for production assistants. I had the same contract when I started, though if I remember correctly, Cass screwed me out of my per diem because I didn't know any better."

"I'm paying to be put up at this shit hole hotel just so I can get some TV experience and I'm coming home with about three dollars in my pocket after paying my double rent and living off crafty. You didn't hear that last part," she said, smiling.

I laughed. I laughed harder than I probably should have, but it felt good. I was two beers in and my head was swimming while my empty stomach was doing flip-flops. Sam's knee touched mine under the table and it felt warm.

"I won't rat you out." I took a gulp of whiskey and slurred, "It's just because the network needs to survive off the backs of people like you and me. The shitheads in our quaint little house get another day of celebrity for no-fucking-reason and America eats it up with a cherry on top, like the mindless zombies they are."

"Like a double decker fucking hot fudge sundae." Her smile was delicious. She stared long and hard into my eyes. I was hoping she couldn't see the conversation I'd just had with Jenny about Jaron and the test and the drugs in there. I was hoping I'd buried it so deep that my eyes were blank and dead.

"So how'd you get where you are, Scar?"

Was her leg moving softly against mine? The subtle rhythm was making my thighs hot. Her lips looked soft and her eyes were kind, in a deep-hazel-for-days kind of way. I wanted to swim in her—fuck! What was I doing? It was all wrong. I knew it.

I told her about how I Gorilla Glued all the lamps to antique tables in a historic mansion in Kentucky under direct orders from my production manager.

"Her name was Danika Ivers and she said, 'these animals will break all of this shit if we don't glue it down. Get it fucking done, Scarlet. So I glued all of these priceless antiques down to wood that had been in the family since the turn of the century. I ruined everything. But it wasn't my call. Danika was the moron in charge. Cass gave her the boot and they bumped me up."

Sam laughed until beer came out of her nose.

I wanted to tear her clothes off.

"Just the way this business works. You fuck over everyone until you claw your way to the top or get canned or caught. But if you get to the top, that's when you really have to be scared. The hunting pool doubles when you're an exec." I swallowed the rest of my whiskey and used my sleeve to wipe the sheen of liquid from my lips. I was like Hemingway right before Pauline dragged him off to her apartment, right before he fucked everything up.

"What's the worst you've done?" she asked, suddenly serious. It wasn't a question, as much as a challenge. I looked into her clear eyes and shook my head. The story was on the tip of my tongue and in the crevices of my smile. "You can tell me," she said and a softness had crept into the dark corners of her voice. Again, I shook my head. No one could know that. No one would ever know that. She smiled and asked, "What's your hotel like?" It sounded more like an offer than a question.

"Do you want to see it?" I asked.

If my teeth had hands, they would have reached out, grabbed the words, and thrown them in the trash. She slowly swallowed the hunk of steak in her mouth and I plunked down a wad of cash. We held each other up as we stumbled out of the booth and toward the door. I don't think anyone noticed us go.

I could smell the dank, sweet, moldy air of Sam's shit hole motel room in her hair as she kissed me in the elevator. I wished, for just a second, that we had gone to her room instead of mine, so I could pretend that I was having a dirty, illicit affair in some run down motel. Instead, we were in my two-room suite with controlled air, my mini-fridge stuffed with rotting takeout, the mini-bar already restocked to fullness, my sheets crisp. The television was still on; I glanced at the image of a sniper's viewpoint in Iraq as Sam ripped off my bra and threw me down on the bed. The lone mint on my pillow bounced and hit my nose before falling to rest under my shoulder. I reached for

Sam's belt, but her strong hands shoved me away. She laughed, her big white teeth caging her tongue, as she broke the button on my pants and bit into my hipbone, my side, my nipple, leaving indentations of her teeth all along my body. I wanted the pain.

I yanked her on top of me again and grabbed at the button on her jeans, but she shoved my hands away and they snapped back on the bed over my head. Sam smirked at me and shook her head, a gentle admonition. She leaned that muscled, swan neck toward me and bit hard just above my collarbone. Her hands wrapped around my back, just above my ass, like I was falling backward off a cliff. I wanted her to draw blood. I didn't want a sucking hickey of a mark, I wanted her to suck my blood out of me, to prove that I was alive even if just for a moment—*the* moment, the one when she touched the tip of her tongue to my clit.

"Bite it," I told her and she did. I grabbed fistfuls of her blonde hair tinged with black and I came so hard, tiny specks of light skewed my vision. Then I came again and again, my frail body a shimmering, glimmering piece of hope in sea of hotel clip art. My walls sucked at her fingers. My folds bruised her. She came too, in her dirty jeans, and wouldn't let me help her. She came because I came.

Then, only the dead slept harder than me.

I hesitate to knock as I stand before the door to 1013. Tonight has a hint of that night floating around the edges. I stand for a long time and consider walking away. The door latch is out and I try to glimpse the stranger inside between the crack. I hold my hand up and use my palm, not my knuckles to quietly knock.

"It's open," the voice on the other side of the door says. It is buttery, deep, and calm, but it doesn't stop every hair on my arm from standing on end nor the otherworldly feeling that I need to get the hell out of here. I push the door open and find a tall, slender, woman with her back to me. She is at the bar, pouring a drink. I hear the ice clink and close my eyes. *No.* I shake my head. *This is all wrong.* And then she turns and I'm staring at her exposed navel through the split in her unbuttoned black blouse. Her heeled boots make her seem much taller than I remember, but that smooth stomach, the depth of her clavicle, the breadth of her strong jaw is exactly as I know it to be and her eyes— how could I forget them—are staring through me. The rocks glass she holds falters a bit and her swollen, candy lips chance a smile, like she's seen the puppy who ran away from her. She takes a step toward me.

"Scarlet?" she questions me, her voice dropping an octave lower than I remember, dry around the edges. She licks her lips and my solar plexus starts to wake up. I take a step back and close my eyes. It is my only defense. My heart is incarcerated in my chest. I have two moves as I see it: run or attack. Or a third option: attack, then run.

"Sam, you fucker," I breathe the words out, opening my eyes and taking on a fourth option that I hadn't realized I could muster: relinquish all power, then run. I shake my head in defeat and turn from her.

"Scarlet, no. Please don't go," she says and her voice sounds humble, pleading even, but I don't turn back. "Let me help you," she yells after me. It is the last thing I will ever hear her say as I close the door behind me and start to run the trippy hallway back to the elevator. When the reflective doors slide closed the tears come, but my heart still rages. I have nowhere to go but down, out, into the city. The city will help me think. For a brief moment in time, I imagine Sam in her room, slowly setting down the glass and her smooth, long fingers slipping the buttons into the holes of her shirt before she turns and flies through the door to chase after that dumb, almost-lost dog. Then I shake the thought away and know that no one is coming for me, except me.

CHAPTER 8

The noise of the city below gets my hackles up, like it's stalking me down a dark alley. I loathe its vibrant rhythm. High school and college kids scream around me at passersby just so someone, anyone will pay attention to them. With every pulse of their shrill voices, I shudder and wish they'd go home and get brainless in front of their devices like everyone else.

Sam. Here. Sam. In my city. I thought I'd left her and all that behind. I've spent two years now becoming a responsible citizen. I've spent all of my downtime meditating my shame away. I've spent nearly every waking minute trying to talk myself down from a cliff of guilt so steep it makes my nose bleed. I have asked for forgiveness from the gods, from the Universe, from the recesses of my repressed mind, from any-fucking-one who would listen. I was starting to forgive myself. I was starting to feel like a real human again. I can't have this now, not when I need to be strong, not when I need to make decisions. I stop walking and a guy slams into me from behind. *It's not real.*

"We're walking here," he says as he cuts hard around me, knocking into my shoulder. *She's not real.* I take a deep breath of air. Move out of traffic. Grab a trash can for support. Stare up at the hotel. It swims in front of me. I taste the Jameson in my lungs. It is my breath. *It can't be real.* That's the only logical conclusion. *What are the odds?* The Law of Attraction says that what you think about, you bring about. I've been thinking of the opposite of this, so therefore, it—she—is a figment of my overactive imagination, but at the same time, that kid in the hoodie with what looked like a walkie in his ear, looks vaguely familiar, like one of my old PAs. *No. No!* I just thought that woman back there was Sam. I've made it up. The whole thing. Maybe I'm dreaming now. To test the theory, I step into the street and a car careers at me and slams on its breaks inches from my legs. It's a cab. Behind it, another cabs flies into position, nearly ramming its bumper. I walk to the back door of the first and get in.

"I almost fucking hit you," Sean O'Toole says from the front seat, his chin resting on his shoulder as he peers over his hulking bicep through the scratched plexiglass separating us. "I just had a feeling, I should circle back," he says. "You decide on MGH?"

I shake my head. "No. Let's go to Inman."

He nods and pulls into traffic, the lights of the cab behind him shining into his rearview as it follows with its own fare.

The city is a rave; cars honk at a driver in front of them who waited a millisecond too long after a green light, air brakes on a bus squeal like the prolonged sadness of a pig dying, and a thousand languages are screamed into cell phones and ear buds all around me. I used to thrive on this wave of noise, but now I just ride it to my destination: the shadows of a concrete parking structure directly across from Quinn's apartment, which is dark, save for the light over the sink. I sit on the ground against the concrete wall. I'll just sit here until I can get myself together, whatever that is.

Fucking Sam. My hands are purple from the adrenaline building up inside me. I open my pack of cigarettes and stop staring at the SD card in my hand. I just have to put it in her mailbox. I just have to leave it with a note saying I'm sorry. *I'm sorry and this is your story, Quinn, not mine. Do with this what you will. I'm sorry I didn't stop it while it was happening.*

I'm down to two cigarettes and no lighter. I stand and tuck the cigarettes back in my bag. I'll borrow Sean's in a few minutes. He's waiting just on Beacon for me and I'll be inhaling my second to last cigarette as soon as I do this. I start to walk toward the street, the bustling traffic sounds bounce off the concrete behind me, as if I've left a hollow space behind me.

My feet move forward, across the street, my chest heaving like I've just done sprints. Out of my good eye, I see someone turn the corner from Beacon and I duck my head into my collar and move faster toward Quinn's apartment. I take the steps fast and drop the SD card in the mailbox. From atop the steps, I have a good view above of Quinn's tiny patio and front door and a direct view into her apartment. I turn to go, to get out of there before someone sees me, but then I stop midway down the front steps, my breath caught. I shake my head and feel something hot and wet leave the crease in my swollen eye. I'm bleeding again, but I can't be bothered to wipe it away. What I've just seen has stopped any motion in me.

I am cold, frozen to the steps. The person coming from Beacon is walking slower, but they'll be here soon. Time is running away from me and I don't have the guts to prove my mind right. But I have to. I run down the steps and slink into the shadows of the concrete wall of stairs, hoping the slow-walking stranger will pass by. Waiting makes the lump in my throat grow like a tumor. The stranger doesn't come. They must have slipped into their own apartment. They must be home now, their door shut behind them. They are probably crawling into their lover's bed, breathing alcohol into the hollow between their head and shoulder and in minutes they will be asleep, unaware that Quinn's door is open. I thought it was, back there on the steps, but my brain has been lying to me for days, maybe even years. How can I be sure what is real anymore? I listen for other pedestrians, but only hear the distant hum of traffic. With an outstretched hand and closed eyes, I wrap my fingers around the edge of the door and don't open them until I hear the creaking jamb.

The smell of blood hits my nostrils first from the semi-darkness inside the studio apartment and for a second, I convince myself that it's just my own, but it's an unfamiliar taste of sweet copper that comes at my tongue from my nasal cavity and it's mixing with days-old Indian takeout and a full litter box. I can see her leg. Her toes are bent at an odd angle, like she was about to take off in a sprint. They're stuck under her and the pinky toe sticks out with a tiny gold ring on it. I inch closer knowing that I'll need to stamp the details into my brain. I have to look. I have to know how.

Quinn's eyes are open and they are shocked, one cocked to the side like it was keeping an eye on her back where the blow came from. There's a hole there, a heavy, deep, cave of her skull, where the hair is matted and lining the cavernous thing. A manmade lake of blood lives there now, though some of it has overflown the sides of her injury and run down her cheek, contouring her face into a clownish drag queen grimace. She is no longer here. The liquor in my gut comes up, but I swallow it back. I have my wits enough about me to not throw up here for obvious reasons; I can't desecrate her blood or leave evidence behind.

I stare at the ornate lamp near her head and see that it was yanked out of the wall so hard that the cord broke off at the socket, as if she'd clung to it after falling off the side of a cliff. The dead wires, snagged on the carpet, mimic Quinn's fingers sprawled and clutching the blue Berber fibers beneath her. I register the gun near her head, but can't look past the grey pile of her brains. Tiny, bloody paw prints make their way past Quinn's head and right out the door. They make a path past my boot, just two inches or so away, and out to the street where they are lost in the debris. I step back into the shadows as a group of people walk by. My chest wants to explode. I sneeze hard knowing that I'm blowing my DNA all over the place and someone yells, "Bless you!" over their shoulder and then, "Hey, kitty. Hey, sweet kitty." I peek around the edge of the steps and see a gaggle of clackers chirping over a scraggly black kitten. One of them has the thing over her shoulder and is petting the purr box, but she has no idea the cat's leaving bloody paw prints on her grey cable knit. The cat catapults off her shoulder and heads straight for me. I duck as they all turn around and squimper, "Come back, kitty! Come back!" before laughing and moving on. The cat heads for the door, but bangs its hips against my legs on its way. A siren rings out from Beacon Street.

The SD card. I have no further thought. Without even chancing a glance to see who might be coming next, I turn to the wall of steps and run back up to the mailbox. I dig around in the old metal box and feel the metal latch on the mailbox scrape against the inside of my forearm. It's not deep enough to bleed, but still, my DNA will be there. I start to wrack my brain for excuses as to why my DNA would be at this—what? Murder scene? Suicide?—and I know that I can be eliminated because I work with Quinn, so, you know, maybe I came over and hung out occasionally. We've texted. It's all there. It'll be fine. I'll be fine. My fingers wrap around the SD card and I yank my hand out of the box. I take the steps in twos and notice a person coming toward me, the same person as before, I think, or my mind, or shock, or terror is making me sees things. To be safe I walk quickly in the opposite direction and just plan to loop the building to get back to Sean.

I hear people coming and going behind me, but my vision is blurry. Every sound is in a tunnel. I get to Beacon Street and cabs fly by. I puke into the first trashcan I can find. I blink into the noise of lights and Sox fans celebrating their win. I walk past Sean's cab and back to Concord, peering down the street to Quinn's apartment. Quinn's front steps are hazy and far away, but the stranger is there, standing atop the steps, their back to me, staring down into the open doorway below. Head down, the stranger moves toward me, back up Concord. I recognize the gait, the body, the height—from where? The Topsail? But before I can figure out who it is, I am being scooped up like a child and the world goes dark around me.

CHAPTER 9

Menthol cigarettes and Old Spice scent the air inside Sean O'Toole's cab. He dumps me in the back and jumps in the front, throws the cab in gear and starts to pull into traffic.

"Stop!" I yell and Sean slams on the breaks and quickly pulls back to the curb. The lights from a car behind him shine into the rearview mirror and blind me momentarily. Horns scream at us as they pass. I have to think. I have to fucking think.

"Listen, lady, I'm taking you to MGH. You almost passed out back there in the friggin' street," Sean says and I can hear a slight tremor in his voice before the familiar sound of his lighter clicks into life.

"Just give me a second. Please," I say. The back of his seat sags near the bottom as he falls into it, answering me. My phone is in my hands. I swipe it on, hit the phone button, and stare at the numbers. How many times have I contemplated calling 911 in the past few days? This will be the last time. I have to do this. It's gone too far. Sean reaches for the dial on the radio and scans until he finds a local station. We both sit and listen through a *Johnny Jakes Cars for Goodnesssake* commercial. I dial the numbers and wait while the audio goes on.

"A grand jury declined on Monday to charge a Philadelphia patrolman, Carlos Zimmer, who fatally shot twenty-year-old, Malcolm McConnell during a routine traffic stop. McConnell was not armed and was handcuffed when the officer shot—"

"9-1-1. What's your emergency?"

Sean glances at me in the mirror and turns down the news when he sees the phone to my ear.

"9-1-1. What's your emergency?"

Even if I tell the truth, they win. They always win. The horns scream at me out the window. *How do I stop them burying the truth? How do I beat them? What do I have left? Can they trace this call?*

"Hello. Is there an emergency?"

No. It's a burner.

Sean nods at me, encouraging me to speak, to tell 9-1-1 that my boyfriend beat me. If only he knew the real me. I hang up and stare at him.

"Can you take me home?" I ask him and he nods, his disappointment visible through the smoke from his cigarette.

He lights a smoke and hands it to me. The menthol chills me from the inside out. My fingers are numb, but my brain is functioning at full speed. I have a plan. It's not the smartest. It may not be the best, but it's the least I can do to make sure that some sort of justice is served for Quinn and Lucky. I have a quick flash of Joe handing Donnie that fat stack of bills and find my fingers balled into a fist kneading into my thigh. I'm so stupid. Why didn't I see any of this coming?

Union Square lights up my windows and I am a ghost flying through the city in an Irish cab. Sean is swerving around other drivers, flinging us from lane to lane. My head is pounding and Sean's agitation is making me excited-nervous.

"Get the fuck off my ass, you Haitian motherfucker," Sean says, glaring into the rearview mirror. His gaze shifts to me. "This d-bag's been following my ass since Washington Street."

I nod. Clarity is coming. It's so simple. It was the vision of Sam, the illusion of Sam, that made me think of it. Maybe that's what my brain needed tonight, an image of Sam to help me see the light, help me understand what I need to do. *Reality. Sam. It all makes sense.*

"You believe this fucker on my ass?" Sean goes back to his road rage and I nod again, start to sit up straight. He slams on his brakes. "You like that dickweed?" he yells out the window and then smiles into the rearview as tires squeal behind us. I hold onto the oh-shit handle and smile.

"Get him, Sean. Don't let him ride you like that," I say.

"Fucking right, Rocky," he says and swerves into traffic, cutting the guy behind him off. I am forgotten. I inhale deeply like it's my first minty breath. My hands clutch the door. I'm itching to get out and get started.

CHAPTER 10

I woke up in a fog of cigarette smoke. That much I remember after fucking Sam all night. The call sheet for the day was lying on the bedside table and Sam was gone, but the stench of her inadequate hotel now clung to my hair too. I rolled over into the pillows and let the comfort envelop my sore body. I grabbed the call sheet and scanned it. Sam's call time was 6am. She was on transpo, picking up someone from the airport. I crumpled the call sheet. I couldn't understand why Stevie still insisted on hard copies when something like the internet existed. What a waste. Not to mention, some poor PA, probably my guy, Clark, got stuck every night walking the halls of the hotel and slipping them under every crew member's door. I'd hated that part of my PA responsibilities. I was always so worried I'd get some regular guest's room and they'd have every personal contact information for every crew member, including Cass, at their disposal. It was a fireable offense. I still had anxiety dreams about it.

I got up and made a cup of coffee in my one-cupper, then slumped in front of the news, chain-smoking, until the smoke wafted into my bloodshot eyes. The news was barely audible over the monster emotions broiling in my gut: guilt, fear, sadness, relief. I remember thinking this infidelity would be the end of Taylor and me and for a second I felt free. Then my phone rang. Stevie, sounding quiet and stern, said I needed to get into the office pronto. I hung up, dressed in my least wrinkly t-shirt and jeans, pulled my hair back, and set out. The house party the night before must have caused some major damage. Stevie didn't like cleaning shit up, so they called me in.

I went down to the garage, climbed into the production van in the parking lot, sat for a moment hoping my head would stop feeling like a monkey with cymbals was pounding around in there, and then texted Sam: *I'm in the garage at the hotel if you're back from the airport and need a ride. Haha.* I waited five more minutes, during which time I accidentally took a huge gulp of three-day old coffee from an old cup in the console. The tinny, cold acid coated my tongue and I wanted to puke, but knew that I didn't have time to get upstairs and change. Sam wasn't coming. I texted again: *I'm heading in. Don't forget the camera gear in the van. It needs to be to the office in 10-15.* I figured falling back into boss mode would be best for both of us, until next time at least. Because I wanted there to be a next time, I added: *Your mouth is a thing of beauty. Thanks for last night.*

I started up the van and headed into the shit-show surely awaiting me down the street at the production house. They wanted me to fire someone or clean up someone else's mess. I was sure of it. I hoped it wasn't Greg. Greg and I had become pals. We smoked together and complained about the executive producers at gTV together. Greg was a great guy, but he was definitely stealing scoop lights from the show.

No one said a word to me when I walked in. The office wasn't buzzing like normal. I checked my phone. 9am on the dot. Someone should have been screaming at someone else by then, yet I could hear Len's teeth gnashing his corn chips from edit bay one. I dropped my bag next to my desk. There was no coffee waiting for me. Clark must be sleeping it off. There were no messages lighting up my phone. All my pens were missing from my desk organizer, even my favorite red Uniball. My sticky notes were gone, like some office supply rat had made off with everything in the middle of the night.

"Who the fuck took my pens?" I ask and glanced at Whitney, the production coordinator, but she didn't even swivel around in her chair to look at me.

"Scarlet. Get in here." Stevie's voice was like a gunshot piercing the wall between my desk and his office. No one else seemed bothered by it though, as they all quietly worked at their desks. I jumped to and grabbed a notebook. Before I left the room, I stole a pen off Whitney's desk. I never gave it back.

I didn't expect to see Cass sitting at Stevie's desk. Stevie was pacing near the window, looking annoyed that he was even in the room with us. It felt like someone had died. The back of my neck was sweating out the seven shitty beers I drank the night before. Cass didn't even look at me as I came in. She had her head buried in her phone, a laptop open in front of her, and she was listening to someone yammer on the other end of the Bluetooth device jammed in her ear.

Stevie made eye contact, but only for a second before he turned and continued to stare out the window. I looked out to see Sam exiting the passenger van. Jessie, a recent film school grad, and our newest PA met her and she handed him the keys. He opened the van and started pulling the equipment out. I couldn't help smile down at her. She was beautiful and light and even looked fresh this morning, her clothes clean and crisp, like she was heading to the first day of school. I wondered if she was dressing up for me. The thought twisted in my lower abdomen and radiated in my cunt.

"Sit," Cass said, drawing my attention back to her as she unplugged all three devices. She rarely disconnected all three. *Fuck. Maybe I'm getting a promotion.* My toes were starting to tingle. I settled into a chair, smiling. Cass sat back and studied me for an agonizing minute.

"You've done some really great work in the three seasons you've been with us," Cass said. I could feel bile rising in the back of my throat. If I moved up, they'd want more from me. More time, endless hours. Seventy-plus-hour weeks. No time to fuck Sam. I couldn't stop thinking about her. If I was really honest, I'd been thinking about her for months. The night before was a culmination. I think for both of us.

"Thank you, Cass," I said and smiled through the vivid thoughts of Sam's mouth. Cass stared at me hard, wide-eyed, and with what looked like a hint of disgust in the crease of her frowning mouth. I glanced at Stevie, but only saw his rigid back.

"That's why I'm having a hard time wrapping my head around why you would be so careless to have *coerced*," the word dripped with disdain, "a subordinate into a sexual act."

Blood rushed to my temples, just like the night before, when Sam had her tongue inside of me. My hand moved to my thigh where an exact replica of Sam's hand stood out black and blue against my skin under my jeans.

"I don't understand—" I said. Cass smirked. "If this is about Sam—"

She rolled her eyes. "I spent some time with Samantha this morning on our drive from the airport. She was in tears." I tried so hard not to roll my eyes back at her that my eyeballs must surely have been clicking in their sockets just to stay in place. Cass shook her head and now her mouth really curved with disgust. "Are you retarded, Scarlet?"

"No," I said, but it was weak. That wasn't the first time I'd been called retarded, stupid, a moron, or an idiot while working in Hollywood. I once had a line producer so hopped on coke and reeling from her most recent DUI on season six of *World's Grimiest Jobs* call me a fucking moronic piece of shit when I'd accidentally copied the wrong sunset time onto the call sheet for the day. The entire crew was there. Her boss, a bearded frat boy, sniggered into his fist, and stared at me, laughing with the rest of the production team.

"Stevie, I'm sure you'll back me up in saying that we are completely, utterly embarrassed that one of our story producers would stoop so low as to coerce a subordinate, a lowly production assistant, into a sexual situation," Cass said. My eyes started to swim. Stevie nodded his agreement but remained aloof, probably singing a song in his head or counting the birds outside—anything so he didn't have to participate in the conversation or remember his own misdeeds.

"She could sue you know."

"Cass, if I could just explain—"

"There's nothing to explain. Sam told us everything," she said and glanced at her phone. It was about to be over, before I'd had a chance to breathe or comprehend. "I agreed to give her a pay bump and accommodate her at the Four Seasons for the duration of the show. That should keep us out of litigation." Her words were mutating into incomprehensible tones. "As part of this new agreement, we have to let you go, Scarlet."

I sucked in the air around me and tasted copper. I shook my head, closed my eyes briefly, and mentally talked down the rat running its wheel into oblivion I my brain. I felt sticky with sweat and blood.

"You'll need to move out of the Four Seasons this afternoon and leave your laptop with Elle," Cass said. My eyes snapped open and I stared through her, while Stevie picked at his tooth in his reflection in the window.

"I had high hopes for you, Scarlet," Cass said and stuck her Bluetooth into her sagging ear, ending our meeting and our relationship with a finality that I had seen her use to dismiss so many others in the past. Stevie escorted me out of the office. I managed to grab my lucky Annie mug. "The sun'll come out tomorrow" it reassured me, before I was kicked out for good.

That was the last time I saw Sam until my brain used her to help me form a plan tonight.

CHAPTER 11

I ask Sean to stop at the bodega on the corner before he drops me home. I need to make a call. I can't make any more mistakes. I have to do this the right way. I hand Sean another twenty and squeeze his hand through the bill.

"You got my card. You call me if you need me," he says.

I nod. "I'm Scarlet."

His smile is touched by softness and he says, "Frankly, my dear, I don't give a damn."

Without another word, I get out of his cab and run up the front steps to my apartment.

When I watch the video again it doesn't even unsettle me. I don't see it anymore. I see a job. I almost don't hear the sounds of the metal pans banging on the tiled floor or Quinn's screams, the hollow whirring of the cooler motors or their panting, excited animal breaths mixing with my own terrified suckage of air. I have a task. I used to drown out the sound of Sarah Pearson's vocal fry as she went on and on about her obsession with Keith on Season 3 of *TRRL*, when I was logging tapes in post. I was deaf to the sounds of revenge porn when I was tasked with scouring the internet for the dirtiest snippets I could find for a five second insert into a montage for a ridiculous interstitial about problems plaguing the current millennial generation. I can ignore Quinn's screams now. I can do this.

When I plug my GoPro into my old MacBook, my hands are steady. I take a drag off of a cigarette from a new pack and tell myself this will be the last pack. This is a new beginning. I have no further thinking to do. Every time I shut my eyes, I see Quinn's lifeless pupils swimming on the insides of my own eyelids. I won't shut my eyes the same way anymore.

I open up YouTube, but know I can't use my own account. That's too easy to trace. I pull up Gmail and start a new account with the name Shewho Mustnotbenamed with the email "innominate@gmail.com." I verify and head back to YouTube, where I am welcomed as the brave, anonymous version of myself.

I hit "upload" and scan the pop-up list of my files. I move to the G Drive and hover my finger over the track pad before clicking "Topsail12022014". I adjust some of the settings while the fourteen minutes, forty-seven second video that I've pared down from almost eight hours of footage uploads. Fifteen minutes. Was that all it took?

When they find Quinn's body—which they will, because I called 9-1-1 from a pay phone on the corner of Indiana and Broadway, veiling my voice with my scarf because I've worked on a few too many true crime docu-reality shows to know that they always use voice recognition software, even if they have no way of knowing who I am—the world will know that Lucky is innocent. Maybe he'll be able to forgive me some day. Maybe we'll get that cup of coffee just like two normal humans who like to watch true crime shows on Netflix and eat dinner in the living room at the coffee table. Maybe we'll kiss each other goodnight and trade spoons while our dog fidgets between our legs all night long. Maybe we'll open our own restaurant and give it to our kids someday. Or maybe I'll never see him again. Maybe I only have this footage left to redeem myself and get the bad guys. Maybe that will be all that is left between Lucky and me.

I leave the comments open. I want the world to let Nate, Donnie, Joe, and even Jack know how they feel. I want their #PublicShame like I want oxygen. I want the world to know what a woman really goes through when she's raped. I want them to feel it, taste it, fear it. Maybe I want this more than anything else. They always say there's not enough evidence or that she brought it on herself because of what she was wearing or drinking or enjoying sexually. Well Quinn was working. She was doing nothing but trying to make a living. She was working while being black and pretty. This was her misstep. This is what made her into another statistic. This and the economy and the ugly man who was abusing his authority is what killed her. For this reason, I will not blur Quinn's face. Maybe this makes me a shitty human being. That's okay. Get it off your chest. You can't do any worse to me than I've already done to myself. The angle is just so that Quinn's face never fully comes into a spotlight and she is blocked a lot of the time by the animals holding her down, but we see her. The world should see her and they should mourn her.

I want everyone to see Lucky's face too. I want the public to be waiting for Lucky when he is released from Suffolk County. I want them to carry him over their heads and buy him breakfast and a cup of coffee. I want them to take selfies with him and explode social media with the image of this hero bus boy. I just want him to be free and ride on a wave of people celebrating his selflessness. He didn't stop and watch. He didn't join in. He is the antithesis of a human being in this day and age. He is perfect and he might be all I have left.

I type in every tag I can think of starting with rape, abuse, sexual assault, governor, Boston, Jack Marino, the Marinos, caught on video.

My fingers fly with words seeping out of them across the keyboard. I click on Advanced Settings and choose to syndicate everywhere. I tell YouTube that this video has never appeared on television anywhere and I click to allow embedding. I file it under the category News & Politics, though I consider clicking Education instead, then I click for an age restriction, and finally I type in the recording date, so the police will know for sure that this is the exact event that happened the night Lucky was arrested for attempted robbery.

I go back to Basic and see that the video is 95% processed. I set up a Twitter account while lighting another cigarette. I set up @TopsailShooter and link the YouTube to the Twitter so the video will automatically post to my feed. I stay away from Facebook. It's too difficult to jump their hoops of authentication. Twitter, YouTube and Reddit should be enough.

#TopsailMarino and #JackMarino have already been trending in the United States for the past few days. #TopsailRape will fit right in.

I check the video and see that it's still processing. This whole thing has taken twenty minutes. I choose a thumbnail for the video: Jack Marino and a seasoned old Irish cop taking a selfie; the cop's meaty hand squeezes the governor's shoulder, assuring him they'll take care of everything. Jack's concerned expression hides his contempt. Then my finger hovers over the "publish" button.

This is my last opportunity to stop. I'm at 98% processed. I hear sirens wail in the distance and hope they're on their way to Quinn's body. I hit "publish" and inhale finally, take a swig of whiskey and watch my screen like it's the Macy's Thanksgiving Day parade. More sirens. Fire this time. Suddenly I'm starving and I've just realized I'm still wearing my stupid trench coat. I take it off and let the cool air in my apartment chill my flesh. I am naked save a set of black lace underwear and bra and the bruises covering my flesh. I wrap myself in an old quilt, one of the pieces from my childhood that I've been able to preserve through my homeless travels. The cotton is worn, but it feels like cool butter on my skin. It's made of the t-shirts my grandfather wore when he was young. My grandmother pieced it together when I was in my teens because I was obsessed with the way my grandfather smelled of tobacco, aftershave and sweat. The smell of him is gone now, but the comfort remains.

I head to the kitchen, grab the rest of the oyster crackers and the two-day-old fish chowder from the Topsail to-go container in the refrigerator and eat it cold out of the cup on my way back to the couch. I glance between the curtains out the front window and see the cab still sitting out front. Sean is still watching me. His white cab with the green shamrock on the side sits idling, the exhaust fogging up the air and making the wet streets look ominous. He's a few spots down from my door and though I can't see him in it, I feel a little safer, knowing he's out there until he gets his next call. I sit down on the couch and hit refresh on the video. Though it's three in the morning, the video already has a couple hundred hits and a few comments. The comments are typical of middle-of-the-night YouTube trolls:

Classy0967: Poor girl. I hope that guys ass raped 4 eternity!!!!

NightJohn87: dafuck? Who the fuck shot this video and what kind of coward you gotta be to sit there and watch a woman get her ass raped while you do nothing but record and try to get famous. Pussy. I meet you in the streets homie I'ma kick your sorry ass.

CherylB00st7681380962: WANT MORE FOLLOWERS? Follow back and comment with code: I<3FOLLOWERS now. <3<3<3<3<3

Triggasays: Fucking limp dick fools imma come in there and rip #urnutsacks off. She a queen and yall aint nuthin but a buncha crackerass white boys. Least that one whiet dude did sumthin instead of standing there. Tho he was a little shit dont know what he was thinking going against them big dudes.

AmericanEaglez: I hope she's okay. Did she give permission to upload this?

CarterWashington: Ummmm JACK FUCKING MARINO- oh hey, MSNBC, HuffingtonPost, BostonNews. WTF???? Is this shit real?

TNbabey1488: WTFF? hahahaha balck b totally wantin that d fuck her up.

Women4Women: Fuck this shit. Reported. Douchebag.

Glstnbry92: You're ded, mate.

I look out the window as a car screeches by. 927 hits.

"How's that feel, Joe, you twisted motherfucker?" I mutter and stuff a few oyster crackers in my mouth. A knock sounds at my door, causing me to choke and blow cracker chunks all over the screen of my laptop. My brows furrow. I glance out the window and see the quiet wet street beyond. I shake my head and don't move a muscle. Maybe it's Sean. I search the street, but he's long gone. Maybe the person on the other side of the door is drunk. I wait.

A shock runs through my body. Another knock. Heavy. Insistent. Not drunk.

Another knock on the door sends me off the couch, backing away from my computer to choose between the lesser of two evils. I don't have a peephole, but next to the door is an Inuit walking stick given to me by a Tribesman from Alaska when I was working on *Earth's End*. I wrap the blanket tighter around me and maneuver an armhole to hold the stick in case I'm jumped as soon as I open the door. I take a huge deep breath, raise the stick over my head, and throw open the door.

CHAPTER 12

"Hi Scarlet. This is Meredith calling from Here & Now TV Networks. I looked over your resume. You have really good stuff here, especially your "stint" with Edwards…but yeah, we're just not sure it's the right match for "Maids in Manhattan". I'll call you if anything comes up."

"Hey, Scar. You have amaaaazing creds, but I'm afraid this Edwards thing ties our hands. Not the bitch to fuck with, youknowwhatI'msaying? Drinks someday soon. I'd love to hear what happened. Ciao."

Every time it was the same. I'd stop following up. Weeks would go by. I'd stay drunk. To stave off eviction, I'd gather up my boot straps and do a little script coverage, writing short breakdowns of a script that's being considered for production and give my opinion on whether the studio or producer can make money off of some poor schlep's blood, sweat and tears, so said Studio Exec or producer doesn't have to read the script themselves. I'd do this for $100 a script. Sometimes I'd even get a couple a week. I'd PA for a day or two on a commercial at $200 a pop for a 15-20 hour day. I'd come home to my shitty little hole, the only thing I could find after Taylor kicked me out, where I didn't have to share with anyone.

I'd gotten used to my hermitude and the sound of other people talking through the walls was enough company for me. Besides, the voices in my head were loud enough. I couldn't stop revisiting the past. I wasn't thinking about getting fired or how my career was in the toilet. I tried not to think about Sam. I tried not to imagine her fucking me again, every night before I fell into a Jameson coma.

To get my mind off of Sam, I'd dissect my actions, walking myself in and around them until I could pinpoint the line that I'd crossed and how no amount of suffering could make up for what I'd done. I'd drink and I'd blame the network or Cass. I'd tell myself I did what I had to. I'd soothe myself and lovingkindness myself into forgiveness, but the forgiveness never came. The suffering continued.

I couldn't tell myself I was sorry. It never came and it snowballed into a massive boulder of anxiety that wouldn't let me be. I'd shake when I was alone. I'd stare at the knife, the orange, the pills, until they talked to me, egging me on, tearing at my brain, fingers looping around the membranes and tugging and pulling my thoughts and my guilt into something they could work with, but I always chose the easy way out: the orange.

I'd lie to friends, the few I had left, when we'd meet for coffee or drinks, when I could pull myself out of my self-aggrandizing stupor and show my ugly face in public. I'd cover up what I could, but occasionally, they'd ask, "Scar, what happened?" and I'd twist my tongue and tell them, I'd fallen down the stairs at my walkup or I'd stepped in front of a dude who was about to hit his girlfriend on the corner in the Bronx. How very fucking gallant of me? They'd look at me with heavy faces burdened with even more pity and eventually they'd stop calling and stop asking me out for coffee.

Finally, the jobs started to dry up all together, like word got around that I was some night time clumsy vigilante who couldn't be trusted to leave people alone with their personal dramas and I found myself with only a few options left.

We're a very successful adult video production company specializing in real straight men testing their sexual boundaries and we're at the top of our game. That's why we need experienced "reality-style" producers to throw in the mix. Pay is commensurate with experience, but pay is good.

We were holed up a sticky, hot hotel room. This time, I was playing "production manager", but this really meant that I was wrangling cable for the only camera operator we had, since our second had called out for the day. Most of the time, though, I was getting yelled at for not moving because I would find myself just stopping to stare at the mess of greasy flesh before me on the stained sheets. I had never worked in porn before. This was all that was left for me.

Casey and Paul were no older than twenty-five, if that. They were so beautiful and I felt horrible for watching. They'd made a mediocre living off of fucking each other. During a break one day, I asked them if they enjoyed it or if they ever got scared. They each looked at me as if the question had aged them about fifteen years. They just smiled and worked on getting their junk hard for the next scene. An Assistant Director screamed for them to get their skinny white asses to set as a "makeup tech" slapped olive oil on their chests. They dug their fists into a canister of shortening and worked it up to the elbows.

I looked around at everyone, really looked at them. A grisly, dark director slamming his fluorescent green energy drink, sat tired and bored behind a monitor, aging and chunky tech crew lumbered about, new fresh "actors" sat in wait for their scenes. Casey and Paul walked slowly and painfully (they had been working for seven hours already) to set. I was standing in a graveyard.

They fucked each other senseless and unprotected because bareback pays more. They were so hopped up on coke that nothing mattered to them anymore, or anyone else in the room for that matter, except me. This was too low. This was the dregs of a forgotten and wasted life.

I dropped my clipboard with the scene scheduled and call sheet on it, took off my walkie and earpiece and slowly and quietly walked out. As I made my way down the hall, I could hear them calling my name - and then screaming for me to get to set. I took off running until I was home. I bathed for the rest of the day and had three glasses of two-buck chuck until my teeth stopped clattering. I smoked the dregs of my last bowl of weed and stared at the water-stained wall until it got dark and the dark made me sleepy.

Sam did this to me. I did this to me. We did this to me. Or maybe I split off somewhere. Maybe I chose the wrong side. Maybe Sam was my alternate and the real me, the true me, quit that fucking show and Sam got her bump anyway and I went home and I left Taylor of my own volition and I found this shitty little apartment on my own, without anyone's help. The apartment saved me and it gave me space and it let me heal and forgive myself and I wrote the great American novel and Jonathan Franzen congratulated me in a New York Times editorial about new voices and how he was impressed that I was one of the few, the proud who doesn't use the internet and I didn't correct him because he's Johnathan-fucking-Franzen and he doesn't need to know that I just couldn't afford the internet. When I woke with a headache the size of Brooklyn, a heavy, hairy hand was pounding on my door and I knew they'd found me and it was over. I was about to be homeless.

The knocking sounds similar tonight, but I know I am not being evicted this time. I pay my rent in cash now. This is not the landlord. This isn't even the police. The person standing in what is now pouring rain outside of my door ducks as I barely miss her head and when she stands again, shielding her face, the stick drops from my fingers, clattering to the floor at my feet. I am seeing ghosts.

Sam lunges forward, grabbing me by the shoulder and walking me across my own threshold.

CHAPTER 13

"How did you—" I start. I've heard the saying "struck dumb" before and here I am, a complete and utter moron. I squeeze the flesh of her shoulder and feel muscle and bone and then I shove her off. I lean over to pick up the walking stick and it immediately falls onto my right shoulder, my hands gripping it like a baseball bat. I feel my hips give a swivel, like I'm winding up. She doesn't say anything, just takes me in with her eyes. "Why. Are. You. Fucking here, Sam?" I scream the last part. She glances over her shoulder at a police cruiser stopped at Lincoln and Broadway and looks back at me, face pale and serious.

"I saw what you did—I saw that girl in Inman. I followed your cab." She gives me a slight push, moving me back. She is stronger than I remember. This is also the most unhinged I've ever seen her. Her breath is ragged, stuttering in and out of her mouth, her lips chapped from sucking air.

"I didn't do anything," I say, forgetting that the real conversation really should be about why the is fuck Sam Martin standing inside my apartment.

"Give me one good reason I shouldn't flag that cop down and tell him what you did to her. I saw her—I saw the body, Scarlet," she says and I have a hazy recollection of a figure cloaked in all black walking toward me down Concord Street. I remember the cab riding our ass all the way back here. Sam's hands are shaking. I move to stand in front of the door.

"I didn't—" I can't tell if I'm more offended that she would scamper to the cops or that she would think I killed Quinn. My brain starts to reel. It sloshes around in the Jameson and comes up with nothing smart. Not a goddamn thing. *Quinn. She saw Quinn's body. She thinks she knows—thinks I killed her.* Maybe I should just flag the cop down myself.

I close the door instead. This is the second solid choice I've made in the past hour. There are no words between us. I watch as Sam, this ghost, this person who is not here—cannot be here—wanders my shitty apartment, dirtying it up with her presence. I hold the walking stick as a precaution. I even contemplate using it, cracking it into her spine while she stares at my dirty clothes on the floor near the couch, but my crimes are stacking up and now it looks like the end game is in sight.

"Why did you follow me?" I say, breaking the din of silence that feels more like the seconds before a bomb explodes than just awkward stillness. The skin on the back of my neck pricks up as she runs her long fingers down the velvety seam of my couch cushions. She's staring at my MacBook. The video is open and paused, blurring the images on the screen; the blue light from the security lights casts a weird glow and strikes through the four people entangled on the prep table. I am also acutely aware of how cold I am and glance down to find that I am still only wearing my underwear. I grab the quilt from the floor and throw it over my shoulders. Sam turns to me, her dark eyes tracing the line of muscle and bone along my hip that leads to the black lace bow in the middle of my fancy pants. Her eyes move slowly to my navel, her hot gaze burning a trail up to my lips. I am cold and hot all at the same time.

"Don't move," I say, pointing my weapon at her. I walk into the bedroom, which is to say, I walk behind the bamboo room divider and throw on a heavy Emerson hoodie and pair of red boxers printed, unfortunately, with tiny white hearts. They are all that is left of the clean clothes here. When I emerge, she is sitting on the arm of my couch, staring at her clasped hands in her lap.

"You looked hurt. I just wanted to—" The words escape her. She shakes her head as if her inner child is telling her she fucked up again. "I'm in town on a job," she says finally.

"Congrats. Who'd you fuck over to get this one?" I ask. She shakes her head and bites her lip as if she's stopping herself from retorting.

"Listen, I wanted to make sure you were okay, but then the girl...I mean what the hell have you gotten yourself into?" she says with a hint of empathy around the edges of her voice.

"Don't." I move toward her and she flinches, concern furrowing her brows at the walking stick in my hand. "Don't pretend you give one fuck about me. I haven't gotten myself into anything. I didn't do that to Quinn, you douchebag," I say and lean the walking stick against the wall, still close enough to reach if I need to.

"You know her?" Sam's self-righteous tone grates at my flesh like a micro zester and I feel myself getting flustered.

"Yes I know—knew her. I was trying to help—" I stop myself, start to pace. "I don't know what I was trying to do."

Sam stands and walks to the kitchen. She opens the cabinets and finds most of them empty. She looks in the sink and flips the water on, scrubs two glasses and turns to me as she dries them.

"We're going to play a little game of twenty questions," she says and takes the half bottle of Jameson off the counter where I left it, open and lonely.

She comes back to me, pressing my glass with Hamburgler on the side into my hand. "Drink this." She takes a gulp from her own glass. It goes down easy and she says, "I'll start. Who's the girl in Inman?"

Shivers crawl over my body as I take a swig of whiskey.

"I don't want to play your games, Sam," I say and stand up straighter, staring into her eyes, trying to pull some information from the depths there before they start swimming in front of me. I get nothing but her lashes growing wetter and her firm chin jutting out further in my direction. My email dings. She touches me then, softly and with trepidation, the pads of her finger tiptoes along the cut under my eye, pushes a little. It hurts, but I don't back away. The whiskey is warming my muscles, urging me to relax and Sam's face is soft between the slight lines near her mouth where stress has embedded itself. I haven't been touched since her fingers. It's been a year, two, maybe more. I've lost track of what day it is. Gooseflesh swarms my arms in waves and I don't know if it's a warning or my own insipid wanting.

"You stole my life," I say and take a step back from her, like my words might just cause her to hit me.

She smiles at me and her lips are dripping with pity as she says, "You didn't want it, Scar. And you sucked at it. Your intentions were all the fuck over the place." She is quiet but firm. I take another gulp of my drink. My email dings.

"You need to get that?" she asks, motioning to my computer.

I shake my head and don't even look at the computer. "Just tell me what you want and then get the fuck out. Get whatever you need to get off of your conscience so I can get back to dealing with the fucking shitball of chaos that's devouring me right now and you can leave."

"I'm not leaving."

"The fuck you aren't," I say and down the rest of the whiskey. "I've been looking for you for a year and a half."

"Why?"

"For a lot of reasons," she says and sets her glass down on the coffee table and refills mine. "But right now, why don't you tell me what kind of mess you're in."

"I'll make this quick," I say, pouring a splash of whiskey and downing it in one. She moves the bottle away from me. "I've been waiting tables at a crappy restaurant where I'm groped every day by the greasy cooks and where the general manager, who happens to be the governor's son, jacks off in the office every morning to bad porn and the other night, because I was desperate to fucking matter again, I rigged a camera in the restaurant. Only instead of capturing someone way over-abusing the three-second rule, I managed to get three guys gang raping the girl who is now dead in her shitty studio in Inman. I didn't step in because I'm a coward, and now this bus boy, this really nice, kind, sweet guy who is the antithesis of everything that you are, stepped in, got beaten to a pulp, and was arrested for breaking and entering when the cops showed up. Now Quinn's dead and it was those dbags—I fucking know it was them—from the restaurant because why would a nameless black girl or a lowly bus boy ever get any justice in this fucked up piece of shit we call a world. I mean how am I supposed to fight the new governor and his legal team? Who the fuck would believe me—"

"The governor?" Sam asks, concern darkening her face.

I nod, pour more whiskey, and throw it back.

"Jack Marino?" she clarifies. I nod and close my eyes as the whiskey burns my insides. "Tell me that you—wait. You recorded it?" she asks. Now the concern turns to disgust and I can't blame her.

"I didn't have any options. I was hiding and waiting for everyone to leave and then it happened and I had no options," I repeat.

She breaks eye contact and I know that she doesn't think that it's a strong argument. I'm starting to doubt it myself.

"What did you do with the footage?" Her voice sounds like she just walked through a dust storm. My eyes flick to my Macbook, but I don't answer her. Her eyes land on the computer screen and most of the color drains from her face. She says, "Scar, you didn't?"

I down the rest of the glass and shove Sam hard in the chest as I walk past her to go to the bathroom. The air is still and quiet. I don't have to pee. I just need to breathe. I don't stare at myself in the mirror. I don't look at the bloody carcasses of the oranges in the bathtub. I just wait and contemplate stepping out the window above the toilet. I sit on the toilet and sway a little, lean into the wall and then stand because the act of sitting on the toilet tricked me into needing to pee. I clumsily yank my pants down and sit again. It takes forever, just enough time to face her again.

"Who did that to your face?" she asks when I come back into the room.

"I did."

"Scarlet." I can feel the pity in her voice. It makes me want to punch her or kiss her. I can't tell the difference anymore. She stands and moves to me. I don't back away this time. I need someone to feel sorry for me, if only for a few seconds. She touches my eyes with the soft pads of her fingers. She pushes again, like she wants to pluck my eyes out with her thumbs. I can feel her hot breath on my lips. From the darkness behind my eye lids, she whispers, "Tell me you haven't shown the video to anyone."

"I've shown it to everyone," I say, pulling her hands from my wet eyes. I move to my laptop and hit the space bar. My YouTube video screams into life on the screen and Sam stares at it with sad eyes. She sits on the couch and runs her fingers over her eyes like she's trying to rub out the images and simultaneously wake up to the reality of what she's seeing. She hits the space bar too, pausing the video with Jack's hand on Joe's shoulder. She refreshes the page and I try not to look at the hits, but I'm enticed when I see the digits are already hitting five figures.

"Je-sus," I say.

"27,959 hits. That's a lot. When did you post it?"

I glance at the digital time on my laptop. "An hour ago."

"Fucking hell," she says and stares at me for a long moment.

"What?"

"They'll find you by morning."

My email dings again and I shake my head. We glance at my email together and see that I have 79 new messages forwarded to me from the new account, mostly re: Topsail Video, with a few scattered Eversource reminders that my bill is late and two from Oprah and Chopra, asking me to sign up for their new 21-day meditation program.

Sam stares at the screen as if the answers to all of my problems reside there in between the lines of the emails. She's not looking at me. She is wringing her hands between her knees as if trying to work something out. She glances at me, but looks away as soon as my eyes meet here. She stares at the wall, searching for something, an answer, the right words, an easy way out, anything. She looks at her phone. She has a dozen text messages, but she doesn't answer. She swipes the screen and her thumb hovers. She looks at me again. This time she doesn't look away. She's sitting in her disgust. At least that's what I feel in that moment before the liquor starts a fire behind my eyes and have to blink. Sam finally makes a decision; she pushes the Jameson toward me. I pour another shot and drink it.

"We gotta get you out of here," she says.

"I'm not going anyshwhere with you," I try to say. Sam stands and starts to pace, ignoring me.

"Come to my hotel," she says.

"Whatever-the-fuck would we do there, Sam?" I ask and reach for the bottle.

"You'll be safe there," she says and I laugh until whiskey burns my nose.

"Not safe. Least with you," I attempt. *Fuck. Here we go again.*

"Don't be naive," she says and starts to move around my studio with purpose. She finds my old Showtime promotional bag and starts stuffing it with whatever clothes she can find. She winces at the smell of my restaurant clothes and I know she's inhaling the GMO-riddled fry oil scent that never leaves the cotton, even after it's been washed, which it isn't now, and hasn't been for three days. Embarrassment hits me as I watch Sam open my underwear drawer and stuff my practical department store boy shorts in the bag. They're not colorful. No print or lace. Just plain black cotton. She comes back to me and quickly disconnects the drive on my computer with a few deft swipes on my track pad, closes the laptop and puts it away in my busted laptop bag. I'm leaning heavily into the couch now and my eyelids are failing me.

"Do you need anything else?"

"Yeah. For you to get the fuck out of my life," I say with clarity, though my legs feel like they're going to give out any second. I would sleep for two whole days if I could.

"I can't now," she says and stops in front of me, "I'm involved." Her whole demeanor has changed, as if in the span of the past five minutes, she's made a whole new plan for me, for us. "Did you call the cops?" she asks.

I just stare at her.

"Scarlet!" She snaps her fingers in my face, "Focus! Did you call the cops? Or anyone? Does anyone know what you've done?"

I shake my head, my eyes narrowing with intense hatred and the overwhelming feeling of wanting to rip her clothes off and fuck her silly on the splintered hardwood floor beneath us. I push her away from me again, but she doesn't move far. I've lost my strength. Soon my eyes will close.

"My quilt," I slur and watch her pick up the quilt, folding it into a square and putting it into the bag. I sit up suddenly and remember Sean's card on the coffee table. I grab my head. It's pounding. Then she's standing in front of me with a glass of water and a pill. I don't know where she got it. I threw back the last ibuprofen I had yesterday.

"What is this?"

"For your head, so you won't wake up with a raging headache." She pushes it through my lips and holds the glass up to my mouth so I don't spill it. I swallow hard and water quells the fire in my gullet.

My fingers crawl to Sean's card around her legs. I get a grasp on it and hand it to her. "Good guy," I say.

She inspects the card, nods, and pulls out her phone. "Hi, Sean. My friend and I need a ride if you're available." Sam starts to give Sean the address. I am toast.

The last sound I hear is the incessant dinging of email notifications on my phone and Sam making a second call to someone named Mark, I think.

"Going to be late." These are the only words I hear her say before she hangs up and then she has my head in her cool hands, and says, "I'm sorry, Scar."

I hit darkness hard.

CHAPTER 14

I awake to the sound of gulls squawking from what seems like the inside of my brain. Sulfur and hot metal scent the air of a slightly swaying world. The air is cold, crisp and clean in my lungs, and I immediately want a cigarette to dull the severity. I start to roll out of bed but find myself bound. I have no arms. I roll hard to the right. A cold metal frame catches my shoulder before I go down face-first on frigid concrete. Reflexively, my arms move to shield my head from the fall, but they get caught on the zipper of the sleeping bag I've been stuffed into. The bright light from the fall almost evens out the pain pulsating behind my eyes from last night, but then my whole head is in a fit of bass against my temples. Beyond the shocking pain of my beaten face and now smashed head, I am starving, ravenous, the emptiness in my stomach feels like an emaciated junk yard dog is eating at the lining of my stomach while clawing its way out.

Where am I?

What have I done?

I squint into the broken sun to my left. A dusty cracked window fragments the light and makes me bleary-eyed. I squint, but my eye is swollen still from last night's orange fight. *Last night? Was it last night?*

The bruises feel like they're on their second or third day of healing, like I've come to the place where my skin is stretched tight and the deep purple of the hematoma has turned the bilirubin bile yellow and the stiffness is way worse than the first day, a reminder to me that I've fucked up again and that I should remember this pain the next time I want to beat myself up. I try to focus, but everything is grey: grey walls, grey floor, grey ceiling. Concrete, like a tomb. *Is this a basement? Jail?* My pulse quickens and my cheeks flush as anxiety takes me over. My hands shake next. Here we go again. I look for something, anything to tell me that my squirrel brain is wrong. I am not, in fact, incarcerated. I know this because I next find my provisions. I vaguely remember Sam packing up anything I would need before leaving my apartment: a couple duffle bags of clothes, all of my computer and camera equipment, an assortment of crackers, dry goods, cheese, and peanut butter from my cabinets. A few bottles of water. Some books.

When I sit up my head swims, dots of light playing at the edges of my vision. I poke my hands up through the zipped sleeping bag, stabbing myself in the neck a few times before my hands are free. I grab a box of crackers and rip it open, stuffing a handful of Agent Orange squares in my mouth. My fingers find a bottle of water and I guzzle it, so happy to feel the clean, cold liquid in my mouth. I stop, lean into the cot, breathe. There are new things, things I didn't own before: the cot, the sleeping bag, a camp stove, small portable pans. Brand new, waterproof hiking boots. Sweaters with the tags still on them. Bandages for my cuts. Underwear. Thermal underwear too. Two new polos, one red, one black. Beyond the walls I hear water, lapping water and cars, the air breaks of buses, and beyond that, a heavy silence that only the ocean can perform. Then I smell the salt and this dry, crisp air soothes me.

Sam. This is all Sam. She did this. I have a snapshot in my brain of her dragging me through the sporting goods store and slapping down a black card at checkout while Sean waited outside, smoking. My stomach tightens with anger and unfortunately a hint of gratitude. Owning new stuff feels good. It reminds me of my old life. I unzip the sleeping bag further and find that I am wearing a full set of thermal underwear and thick wool socks. I climb out and stand, stretching, reaching my face toward the light from the window. My breath is in the air and there are snowflakes frozen on the small window in front of me. The sun hits them and diffuses the light in the room. It's magical, almost unreal. I wonder what will become of Quinn's cat. I glance in the corner and see my messenger bag. Digging inside, I see all the things I need, my last cigarette, but no lighter, my tiny button camera, and my notebooks. I breathe a heavy release and hear thick wood scraping against concrete behind me. I turn to find Sam, with a tired smile on her face, entering the room from what looks like a barn door, holding two steaming cups of coffee and an armful of newspapers. Beyond the door, I see a wall of dusty windows and the open empty space of what seems to be a huge warehouse.

"Morning," she says and drops the papers next to me. I take the cup she offers. "Light cream and one stevia, right?" she asks.

I nod. "Thanks. Where'd you find this place?" She's staring out the window, maybe contemplating our battlements.

"I told you yesterday. I secured it for *TRRL* last month."

"Why isn't production here?" I ask glancing around for the obvious signs of production like camera equipment or lighting rigs. There aren't any in this room, which is starting to look more like a garage, now that my eyes are focusing.

"They just want to shoot interstitials here, but the owner said the only way he'd do it is if we agreed to a three-month lease and hired someone to clean out the asbestos," she says and sips her coffee, her long fingers wrapping the cup in an embrace. I have a millisecond of a remembrance of those fingers and feel heat rushing to my chest. I'm ashamed to admit that I don't know if we fucked last night or not. I hope not. I'd want to remember that. I look away and out the window to her view.

"Lucky for me, I guess," I say and stare at the pier running along the side of the building. It is long and secluded. We're on the waterfront, but it can't be downtown. It's too quiet. There's too much rust and debris. I can see oil barrels littering a sand lot to the left of us where it looks like a construction project was abandoned months ago. It's surrounded by chain link, caution tape, and inhabited by a family of fat geese now. I can't hear people anywhere. To the right is an old brick building with a giant, rusty metal fish on top and it hits me that we're in the abandoned shipyard in East Boston. No one will find me here.

The cold air breaks through the flimsy, old window seal and steals my breath again. I love it. It feels like new beginnings and clarity. I glance at Sam and she gives me a harried smile before turning away from the window. Then it hits me: the video I posted is out there in the world.

"Extremely lucky for you," she says and plops down on my cot next to the newspapers. She pulls an iPad out of her bag. "It's had 2.7 million hits in three days," she says and hands me the device and continues, "Go to Huffington Post. They seemed to have the first coverage of it."

My hands feel numb. Sam wraps the sleeping bag around my legs once I sit next to her and take hold of the iPad. When I open the HuffPo app, the headline reads "SON OF A GOV!" above a grainy screen grab of my video. Joe and Quinn are walking toward the camera before the chaos begins. The whole composition is grey, but

Quinn's pink shirt pops in the middle of the frame. I click the link and read:

"Massachusetts is reeling this morning as news of a rape caught on video at a popular restaurant in downtown Boston allegedly shows the new governor-elect, Jack Marino's eldest son and General Manager of the Topsail Bar & Grill, leading a group sexual assault on a young waitress who works under him at the restaurant. The assault occurred after hours in the kitchen of the Topsail and two other men, Donald McGivens, the Topsail Kitchen Manager and Nathan Marino, a cook, have also been identified, as well as Lucas Walker, a bus boy who was initially accused of and jailed for breaking and entering on the night in question. The younger Mr. Marino was arrested at his home in South Boston, while his father and lawyers looked on. Sources say that Mr. McGivens and Mr. Nathan Marino, a cousin to the accused, have yet to be located. Mr. Walker is under surveillance at the Suffolk County Detention Center Infirmary, where he was placed two nights ago after another inmate allegedly attacked him in his jail cell. Mr. Walker's condition is stable but serious and he is being monitored. THIS IS A DEVELOPING STORY. UPDATES TO COME."

A video is embedded just below the article and I click on it without further thought.

"TOPSAIL BAR & GRILL ASSAULT / MARINO ARREST - WGBH News 4," the screen reads.

At first, I don't hear anything as I watch the front door of a single family home in Southie, then there is a murmur as the front door opens. Jack stands in the doorway, his crisp, usually pressed white shirt wrinkled, his tie loosed. His stubble and haggard expression are real and present and the look of detestation on his face as Joe is led from the house in handcuffs is palpable. The block is full, the locals out in full force. Folks in the neighborhood scream and hold signs.

"Rapist!"

"I hope you rot in BLEEPing hell for what you did, pig."

"Are you ashamed of your son, Jack?"

"Did you know your son was a rapist, Jack?"

I can't help watching an older, light-skinned black woman stand stock-still in front of Jack's wrought iron gate. Her eyes are wet and she doesn't move, just stares through the bars at the governor-elect. Hatred drips down the lines of her cheeks. Her sadness overwhelms me. My face gets hot and my eyes well up. Sam sits up; her movements are slow and her spine cracks. I can't look at her.

Darlene Severson, the blonde reporter on the scene, speaks at the camera with a put-on air of seriousness as Joe is stuffed into a police cruiser feet first.

"We have been asked by the Boston PD to urge the shooter of the video to come forward, as their witness testimony can seal this case. If you are out there…" Darlene's blue tinted contacts are staring through me now, "please come forward."

"You can't," Sam says, straightening out the newspapers between us. I see the headlines. They are all me and this video.

"I think I have to," I say and hand her the iPad as the video on the screen cuts to my footage. I can't watch it again, but I know that if I walk out the door, it is all I will see, hear, taste, and smell. "I have to, right?"

She shakes her head, thinks. "I think if you do that, the Marinos will figure out a way to take the pressure off themselves by somehow pinning this on you. And you are nobody."

Her words sting, but I know she's right.

"I am nobody."

"You know what I mean, Scar. You're disposable. Don't think for a second that Jack Marino doesn't have just the PR team to take you down, ruin your life, and make you nonexistent. Not to mention, what you did is illegal. They'll arrest you—"

"What I did is hardly anything compared to rape and murder," I say. Sam hesitates, but then says, "Massachusetts is a two-party consent state if you record audio. You didn't get consent obviously. Plus, you walked away from the dead body of the rape victim and didn't report it. You're being naive."

"I did report it."

She swallows hard, but her stare never waivers. "What do you mean?"

"I called from a pay phone at the bodega before Sean dropped me last night."

She nods and puts her head in her hands. "I'd wondered who that was," she says. "The news has been playing parts of the call."

"I concealed my voice."

"They will arrest you and lock you up and you will be the fall guy." Her tone is matter-of-fact, devoid of emotion. "Or. They'll kill you and make it look like suicide or some shit," she says as if that's it, we're done. The gig's up. I stand and start to pace, my pulse beating a bass drum in my throat.

"You have to go to work today and tomorrow and the next day, until all of this dies down."

"And then what? I just wait for it to get quiet and say, 'oh hey everyone, it was me. I shot that video'?"

"No. You tell no one," she says and takes a sip of her coffee, staring at me over the rim. "Unless that's what you want."

"Want what?"

"To be Internet famous for a few minutes like all the rest of the video junkies out there, shooting footage of people dying in the streets or homeless people getting beaten up. Is that what you want?"

"Fuck no. I want the truth out there."

"You are not the truth. The video is," she says. After a thoughtful pause, she adds, "I'm glad you said that. I was about to leave you here to wallow in your click-porn quest."

"Fuck you."

She laughs.

"What?" I say, moving closer, my anger rising in my chest.

"Your face. You're pissed, aren't you?"

"Of course I'm pissed." I hold my hands up and look around. "I'm hiding out in some old warehouse, freezing my ass off, and I can't tell anyone who I am or what I did because I might go to jail or die! You're goddamn right I'm pissed. Wouldn't you be?"

"I am." She takes another sip of coffee. "I'm pissed that this happened. I'm pissed that I'm part of the reason you were in that restaurant to begin with."

I roll my eyes. "No. You're not. You got what you wanted."

She nods, thinking about this. "Yeah. I did and I was sorry about it every day after you left."

"I didn't leave. I was fucking fired, Sam, because you lied," I say and neither one of us looks into the other's eyes.

"I did," she says. "I've spent a long time looking for you though, Scar. When I heard we were going to be shooting in Boston I leapt at the chance, thinking I might finally find you. I might finally get an opportunity to say I'm sorry. I'm doing that now."

I study her. She looks remorseful. And sad and tired, like life has taken her by the balls and thrown her for a loop. Then I remember what seemed like another sincere apology last night. Maybe she really means it. I smile and wave my hand in the air, like I'm pushing it all out the window and into the water. "I have to get ready," I say.

She nods and stands to leave, but turns back and grabs me. My coffee splashes through the sip hole and onto the back of her leather jacket as she holds me tight to her and says, "Believe me."

It takes me a minute, but my hands finally find it in themselves to forgive her and I hold on for dear life.

"Go to work. I'll meet you back here after your shift for dinner. We'll make some kind of plan. There's a bathroom on the other side over there. Stretch out. Use the space. Do some yoga or something." She nods beyond the door before she lets me go and turns to walk away, disappearing into the darkness of the warehouse.

The air is still again after the sound of the loading door coming down on the concrete. I close my eyes and breathe in the sea air and something I haven't felt in a while: myself. Power and myself. I stare at the newspapers on the floor and pick up the Times from the top. A screen grab of my video is on the front page. *I've been published in the Times*, I think, then toss it back on the floor, stripping my clothes off as I do. When I'm naked, I see all the bruises. The pain floods back. There's probably nowhere to shower here.

I slide the wooden stall-like door open and look out into the depths of what must be about 9,000 square feet of cold nothingness. Then I run like goddamned Alex Owens through the space, doing my own flash dance. When I get to the other side, I am out of breath and freezing from the sheath of sweat all over my body. I find a room marked "WC" and slowly open the door. On the other side is a clean bathroom, with a shower stall. It smells of lilacs. Sam or one of her PAs must have cleaned it for me. There are fresh towels and a big shower that I step into after turning on the hot and cold. The water pressure is just the right amount of perfect to wash away what has been. And then it hits me. Sam said 2.7 million hits in three days. I've been here for three days. I don't remember a thing.

CHAPTER 15

The air outside is dry-cold. My lips chap as soon as the wind touches them. There is a pulse to the city right now. I feel everyone talking. They don't even notice me. They are on their phones, tablets, and newspapers like nothing outside exists. I float through them and hear them talking about me. *The Shooter* they call me—the Topsail Shooter. I don't even need to look at Twitter to know that #TopsailRape and #TopsailShooter are trending. I can feel it in my bones. I feel exhilarated and immediately hate myself for it. This is disgusting. This is just what celebrity feels like.

When I turn down Newbury, I hear the sounds of the attack all around me, bouncing off the concrete, hitting the glass off store windows in front of me, jumping out of people's tiny speakers on their phones, muffled by earbuds. People twist their faces in disgust, but are unable to look away from their devices. Quinn's screams pierce through the noise, the rest—pots and pans and Joe's guttural words—are mush in my ears. I only hear Quinn and an emptiness fills my gut. I want to puke again, but I swallow it down, put my head into the wind, and keep walking. A crowd stands outside Starbucks, all staring at their devices. I hear, "If anyone has information about the shooter" and "…has not been identified, though sources claim the BPD is using 'any means necessary' to uncover the identity of the Topsail Shooter." This last one gives me anxious pause and I step into line, immediately allowing my brain to fall down the black hole of conspiracy where the cops have bugged the warehouse and they've been following me this whole time. I glance over my shoulder and find the twisted mess of a copper-colored chest length beard and the bleary eyes of the hipster behind me and think, there's no way this guy's a cop. The patchouli essential oil and the Cosby sweater are a dead giveaway. My breathing rights itself.

Next door at the Topsail the windows are blacked out with visqueen. This can't be a good sign. Will anyone even be there when I get there? I've missed a day of work already and I haven't figured out a good excuse. They're going to know it's me. Everyone here surely knows it's me. I look around at their faces, doughy under the chin, a scroll of images reflecting life in their eyes as they swipe up on their devices. I realize I'm the only one not looking at my phone. This will surely give me away. I want to stand on the tabletops and scream it to the crowd of sheep next to me: *I'm the shooter! I did this. I'm the reason she is dead!* But I bend my neck and force my spine to curve a little more, just like everyone else. I have to blend in. I have a new text.

(323) 684-7979: Did you make it to work okay? Not trying to be a mother hen, just worried about you. 8:12am

I open the contact, change the name to *Sam Martin*, and go back to the messages. I see a bunch of new ones, most of them from Margie, mostly from Wednesday, two days ago. I have four phone notifications too.

Margie: WTF? Have you seen the fucking news? 7:57am

Margie: Scar? Pick up the fucking phone! 8:09am

Margie: I'm sure ur prolly sleeping one off but you gotta see whats happning at Topsail. TURN ON THE NEWS 8:10am

TopsailCOOKIE: Every1 pls report to work for your shifts. 8:11am

Margie: RU going in I dont think we should. new Joe was a dbag. 8:11am

Margie: K well I guess I'll see you later call me when you get these we gotta talk. 8:14am

TopsailCOOKIE: Sev of u missed ur shifts. We get it. Its real important you stop in sowe can tell you wats up PLS come between 10-2p thur-sat

I listen to a voicemail from Tuesday, (212) 986-9979. 2:17a.m. It's twenty-seven seconds of silence and slight breathing and then a light, boyish voice says "It's her," as they close the call. The other three notifications are unknown numbers and hang-ups. My pulse quickens and my cheeks start to flush. I can barely breathe. My throat is constricting, my flesh prickling. I look back at the bearded hipster behind me, but he's still vacant. No one notices me. No one is staring at me over the rim of a newspaper. No one is watching me through dark glasses, whispering orders into the sleeve of a black suit. No one knows I exist, except the person who just left a voicemail on my phone. It's her. *It's me. They're talking about me.* My body is pulsing. If someone touches me, they'll vibrate. I squeeze my arms to my sides.

I start to light a cigarette, but stop when a woman walking by looks up from her phone long enough to scowl at the cigarette hanging from my lip as she heads to the cream and sugar station. She stops in her tracks and I blink. Fuck. I'm inside. I'm inside and about to light up. I've lost my mind. I take the cigarette out of my mouth and put it back in my pack, hold my hand up to apologize, and wait for her to walk away. I need to get a hold of myself.

I stare at a dissected *Boston Herald* resting on the creamer station and see Quinn's Harvard graduation photo staring back at me. I look away from her eyes and to the other stories: a homeless veteran in Copley opened fire on passersby, wounding two; the Dow plummets again; REI on Newbury was robbed; No indictment for North Carolina cop in the shooting death of 13-year-old Dante Marshall; Topsail Bar & Grill to remain open under interim management; Quinn's mother collapsed when she saw the video. I push the paper into the circular receptacle and find a *Boston Globe* waiting underneath. This time, I'm staring at a front cover photo of Quinn's apartment. Police tape crosses the doorway where I stood three nights ago and stared in at her lifeless body. The headline: TOPSAIL RAPE VICTIM FOUND DEAD and a byline that reads, *the woman at the center of the alleged rape at the Topsail Bar & Grille was found dead in her apartment with what police say looks like self-inflicted wounds and high levels of heroin in her bloodstream.* I step back. I walk out. My hands are shaking profusely when I finally light that smoke, standing next to the railing of the outdoor patio of the Topsail. The patio is full of reporters. They look like high-tech chickens in a coop.

There was no heroin. Quinn was a just a kid working off her student loans at a crappy restaurant and then she was raped. She was just a kid, a Harvard kid. She didn't kill herself. She didn't—

"Need an escort in, ma'am?" a deep voice behind me says. His hand is on my arm and I wrench away before looking up and into the eyes of a police officer.

The reporters systematically get quiet as the cop, who looks like he's still in high school—albeit as a fifth-year senior and the biggest linebacker on the football field—stares at me quizzically. He wears a smile on his Boston Irish face. I glance at his nametag and see that he is called Johnson, so maybe I'm way off the mark with my first impressions here. I smile at him. I really had no intention of doing that, but my body is sometimes smarter than my brain. I have to get past this guy or at least away from him.

"You work here, right?" he asks and I laugh nervously.

"I do. Sorry, officer, I didn't mean to just stare…"

"Understandable, ma'am. You guys have been through a lot."

"Just heading in," I say and turn to stub out my cigarette.

"I'll escort you," Johnson says and puts his hand near the small of my back. He doesn't actually touch me, but I can feel the heat from his palm through my polo. I can't run. Johnson's hand feels like a brick wall behind me. He holds the door for me.

When I enter the dining room, I see a smattering of uniformed officers, a few official-looking men and women, and about ten Topsail staffers spread out and talking in what looks like rounds of speed dating. Cookie looks alert, but nervous. His boobs are sweating profusely. Margie is still dressed (up) in street clothes and is cooperating fully with big-handed expressions. Pickles is hunched over his coffee like a wolf protecting his food, and a few of the kitchen guys sit with their palms tucked into their arm pits, glaring at the officers questioning them. Gary, who has a tattoo on the side of his shaved head of a bullet and the words "187 on an undercover cop", looks especially nervous. Johnson's hand finally touches my lower back and pushes me in the direction of a severe redhead in plainclothes. Her hair is the color of my hipster friend's beard and for some reason this unsettles me. I can only imagine what she's hiding under that tight ponytail.

"Detective LaChance, I found another one," Johnson says. LaChance gives me the once-over and nods but says nothing. She scans the dining room, unsatisfied.

"I'm Detective Betsy LaChance. What's your name?"

"Scarlet Battell," I say through sandpaper. LaChance raises an eyebrow as she scans a legal pad in front of her and checks something off—my name, I'm assuming.

"Here you are: Battell, Scar." She smirks at her own joke, but gets serious quick. "You were on the clock the night of?"

I nod, clear my throat. "Yes, ma'am."

"Good." She glances about the room again and then her eyes land on me, on my fading bruises, "That's a nasty shiner. You an MMA fighter or something?"

"Kickboxer." I smile through my lie and she smiles back, nods, checks out my body, looking for muscles. Luckily, I have some left over from my field hockey and American Gladiator training days. I flex my quads for good measure.

"I did one of those cardio kick box classes once. Kicked my ass. Literally. But man oh man did I feel like taking no shit after that." She closes the folder in front of her and sighs heavily. "There's no room in here for us. Follow me." LaChance turns and doesn't wait for me to follow, but I do even though my legs feel like they're going to melt. I don't want to go into the kitchen, but that's where we're headed. If I pass the threshold of swinging doors, Detective LaChance is going to know everything. The threshold will be a truth serum. In with the truth. Out with the lies. The words might spill out of me. Maybe that would be a good thing. Maybe I can be free of this, but then Sam's voice is in the back of my head saying, *They will make you their fall guy. You will go to prison for a very long time.*

We head to the office and I stand just outside the door. LaChance goes in, talking, saying something to me over her shoulder. When I don't respond, she turns back.

"It's okay. You're not the one in trouble here, Scarlet. We're looking for the scumbag who recorded that shit. We just need to ask you some questions so we can figure out who our guy is," she says. She's doing that thing the online people are doing: assuming I'm a man. Like I derived some pleasure from filming the attack on Quinn, just like a man would. But would a man? All men? I may cringe when Joe leers at me from under his dandruff eyebrows, but even I know he is not every man. He's not even those three men. That group is not all men, yet I must be one because I kept shooting. Only a man would keep shooting and put it online, right? Doesn't anyone stop to think I might have been doing it to help Quinn and Lucky when I could do nothing else. I could do nothing to stop— Here I go again, down the rabbit hole. I stop myself, worried that I might have said any of that out loud, like I'd done this morning while staring in the mirror after my shower. I hold great debates with the inside me these days, my inner child has become argumentative and likes to throw tantrums and I have to quell her blatty voice and get myself together. I just hope I didn't do it here in front of Lady Dick.

I'm staring at her. I don't know how long I've been doing this, but I don't move. I contemplate running, but the odds that I'll make it out the back door before getting tackled by a bunch of police officers is slim to none.

Rick Marino leans against the wall, scrutinizing me. I am pinned. But it's not Rick who's got me stuck to the spot. It's not Rick, or LaChance, or the twenty cops roaming the area all around me, or the swimsuit calendar on the wall, or the slight stench of old jizz in the room. What stops me in my tracks is sitting on the desk. Spread out atop the desk calendar are three items inside an evidence bag: my blue Bic lighter, my Burt's Bees lip balm, and Taylor's stolen Trader Joe's card. On the TJ's card are a couple of dark splotches. Blood. The side of my knee tingles and I remember scraping it on the metal of a bread rack. My blood. My blood on my TJ's card, next to my lighter covered in my fingerprints, and my lip balm with my saliva embedded in the wax under the cap. I swallow the ball of dust in my throat and try not to look at the bag.

CHAPTER 16

"Come on in, Scarlet," Rick Marino says, his caramel voice tinged with salt. If I don't cross over into the office, I might as well scream, "It was me! Take me away!" For the briefest stint in my brain, I think of the three meals a day I'd receive in jail, the bed, the camaraderie of the other women, the nightly sex, the safety being behind bars might bring, television, a library, maybe a gym, but these thoughts waver as I stare at my belongings and think even harder about the cage they'd put me in. The cage would make me crazy, all the freedom sucked out of my life like Thoreau taking down the woods. I have to be smart here.

I step into the office and Rick's brows soften, but he doesn't stop scrutinizing me. LaChance takes a seat at the desk. "Mr. Marino," she says without looking at him, "can we have the room?"

Rick glares at the back of her head and his left eye twitches slightly, but he unfolds his arms and walks toward the door.

"If you decide to charge her with anything, I want to be present," he says.

"You'll be the first to know." LaChance placates him with a smile. I'm too stunned with the idea of being charged to even watch him leave. I swallow the cotton ball of fear in my throat. I do not look at the lighter, lip balm, or Trader Joe's card. I do not look anywhere other than Detective LaChance's eyes. Mrs. Wright, my third grade teacher, taught us that the first rule of good, respectful listening is to make strong eye contact with the speaker. Whenever I need to show respect, I do this and I don't let go. Just last week I read that prolonged, unblinking eye contact is also a sign of psychopathy. I don't know what's real any more. I glance at my hands every five seconds so she won't think I'm crazy.

LaChance waits for the door to close behind me. I hear the sounds of the kitchen get quieter until they are gone and only the hum of the radiator whispers in the space around us. She is smiling at me and I'm staring into her eyes again like a psychopath. I smile back and it's toothy and awkward.

"Men. Amiright?" she says, the last three words rolling themselves together into one. "Always gotta have their noses in other people's shit."

I laugh too loud. She doesn't seem to notice, just takes a sip of her Dunkies. I get a whiff of hazelnut flavoring. My mouth waters. She turns to a manila folder on the desk and rifles through the paperwork inside. Video grabs and police stills of the kitchen from the night of the attack peek out at me. I can see Lucky's blood on the floor. His body isn't in it, which is a relief, but it's swept to the side like he was dragged out of it.

"You seen these?" LaChance asks, nodding to the photos. I shake my head.

"You mind taking a look? They're a little gory, but it might help us," she says and pushes the paperwork out of the way and in the process, nudges the evidence bag that holds my missing pieces.

"No. I'd be happy to," I say. She nods a *you seem like a good kid* kind of nod and I pretend to study the photos for the first time.

"So, you worked that night?"

"Yes. I was second cut."

"You left—what? Tenish?"

"Ten-thirtyish," I say. "I think I clocked out at 10:37."

"You left out the back door?"

I nod. In one of the pictures, someone has outlined three items on the floor near the bread racks and written: *This is where the shooter was standing when recording. These items belong to the shooter? DNA?* LaChance pokes her finger at the spot in the photo and says, "We found these back here." She drops the evidence bag on the photo. "Recognize them?" I shake my head a little too soon and to cover myself, I take another thirty seconds and study the items again and shake my head.

"Coupla folks said you were an ex-Hollywood Producer or director or something? What'd you work on?"

When anyone asks me this question, I go for the most recognizable show on my resume and say, "I was a story producer on *Most Dangerous Seas.*" To which the response is always, "Cooooool. Did you get to go on the boats?" and then I say, "Only when they were docked. Funny thing about the captains, they're terribly superstitious and they think it's bad luck to let women on the boats."

If I am telling this story to a man, he will usually nod his agreement and say, "Isn't that something" or "Very interesting." But if I'm telling it to a woman, like butchy LaChance in front of me, she'll shake her head, just like she is doing now and say, "Morons" or "Men! Still running around trying to convince everyone that *we're* the ones who fuck everything up!" LaChance has her eye brows all twisted up and says, "What a load of misogynist bullshit, huh?"

I laugh and shake my head with her, my laughter trailing off to, "It paid the bills. Until it didn't."

"Recession?"

I nod.

"What a bungle that was. I'm no Obama fan, but Jesus-H-Christ, he had a lot to deal with when he took over for that monkey in a suit."

We both laugh, nodding our agreement, and then LaChance says, "So…never seen this Trader Joe's card, huh? It's from a store in L.A."

I shake my head and say, "No, ma'am."

She waves it away and says, "We'll figure it out. Covered in prints I'm sure."

I slowly suck in air so I don't pass out.

"I mean, you're not the only Topsailer's been out to La La Land. Lucas Walker was out there too, as well as a couple of the Marinos." She closes the folder and sits back in her chair, studying me. "You clocked out at 10:37 and left out the back?"

I nod, trying to stay as matter-of-fact as possible.

"You take the T?"

I have to think for a second about the swipe record on my Charlie card or surveillance cameras at the Convention Center T stop. "No," I say. "I cabbed home that night."

LaChance whistles through her teeth, "That musta cost ya. What's it from here to East Somerville? Thirty bucks?"

"Usually twenty to twenty-five."

"Steep."

I nod and continue, "But quiet and fast."

She purses her lips and leans forward to write a note on a legal pad. "Which one'd you use? Or did you Uber it?"

"I used Green Cab.

"Fuck these Uber-assholes taking everyone's jobs. Excuse my French." She scribbles down *Green Cab*.

"Absolutely, and you never know who you're gonna get with an Uber."

"Some definite psychos out there." She looks at me again, "Use your card?"

"Cash."

"Remember your driver, by chance?"

I think for a long time and smile, saying, "I do!" I dig in my bag, pulling Sean's card out, and read, "Sean O'Toole, #11."

LaChance deflates. A motherfucking alibi. I know that if she calls Sean, he'll vouch for me. My soul is doing the running man. She won't call though because she knows it's a dead end. She drops her pen and leans back again, studying me further.

"Okay, Scarlet. Just a couple more questions."

"Of course," I say, adrenaline coursing through my veins after my tiny win.

"You ever witness Joe Marino acting untoward with any of the girls?"

"Does a bear shit in the woods?" I ask her, channeling my best Margie impersonation.

"We've been hearing that a lot. Do you own a GoCam?"

My mouth goes dry again. "A what?"

Her smile dips a little and her caterpillars become one above her darkening pupils. "For someone who's a big Hollywood hotshot like you, I'd think you'd know it's a video camera."

I shake my head and say, "Hmm. I'm not familiar. Is it a consumer camera? I only worked on shows with professional models, like the Red." *Fuck you, LaChance.* She smirks at me.

"Don't worry. No one here seems to know what it is. We assumed you would."

A knock sounds out behind me and Johnson sticks his head in the room. "Governor's here, Detective."

"Whooptie-fucking-do." She rolls her eyes at me, trying to share another moment of girl power. "You're good to go, Scarlet. We'll be in touch if we have any more questions."

"Should I stick around? Are we opening for lunch?"

"I'd head home if I were you," she says, not answering the question.

I turn to leave, but feel her hand on my arm, pulling me back. "You're at 41 Lincoln Street in Somerville?"

I nod. She smiles and moves me toward the door.

"Keep your phone on." She leaves me standing just outside of the office as she moves through the swinging doors. I stare at the evidence bag on the desk and contemplate making a go for it, but on the out swing of the kitchen doors, Rick Marino steps in, trading places with LaChance.

"Scarlet. Good. You're still here," he says and takes the same arm LaChance used to lead me out. He's turning me back to the office. "I would have been sad to see you arrested."

"I wasn't sure if I should leave—"

"I have something for you," he says and motions behind us with a wave toward the office. I turn to see Pickles and two of the dishwashers behind me. They're following us. They soldier into the office, looking just as nervous as me. Rick goes to a filing cabinet against the wall and leaves us with our backs to the desk. This is the only chance I'm going to have. I know this. I wrap my fingers around the evidence bag behind me, folding it slowly, trying not to make a sound, and somehow I succeed. I stuff it in my bag. Rick turns to us with an apologetic smile, and hands all four of us an envelope with our names on the front. "A little something from Corporate to ease the burden of—" He stops himself, searching for the right words. "Well we're not sure exactly what to call this yet. We'll all be transitioning for a while and we'll be in touch about scheduling."

"Scheduling what?" Pickles asks, staring inside the envelope, which holds a check from the Marino Restaurant Corporation for 500 dollars. "Five hundred bucks? Until when?" he asks. I can see Pick's jaw working and I know he's holding back angry tears.

Julio, the day dishwasher says, *"Que paso?"* and looks at Emil, the night dishwasher, for clarification.

Emil shakes his head and says, *"No mas trabaja."*

Julio's mouth opens and his eyes get wide. He turns to Rick and says, *"Hijo de puta."*

"Just until we get this sorted—" Rick starts, with his hands in the air, asking all of us to calm down before we erupt and cause a scene.

"So what you're telling me is that Joe, that pussy, rapes and fucking kills Quinn, and then gets his baby bro to come in here and pay us all off with five-hundred bucks until you guys are ready to schedule us again?" Pickles says, making the word "schedule" as prissy as possible.

"There's no evidence that Joe—"

"Oh fuck that!" I say, the words coming out of my mouth before I can stop them. Pickles, Julio, and Emil all turn to stare at me, nodding like we're all about to run into a rumble. I continue, "There's a fucking video showing what your brother did to Quinn and Lucky. That's all the evidence anyone needs." My tone is a little too defensive and my words are met with Rick's condescending smile. That smile is the same one the fifteen-year-old kid in Texas wore during his murder trial when he used Affluenza as a defense after he killed a family of five while driving drunk in a mall parking lot. That smile says we're all screwed.

"Until Joe's been found guilty by a court of law, all charges against him are alleged."

I shake my head and stare at the unopened check in my hands.

"It was a sick and twisted individual who taped that attack, Scarlet—

153

someone who gets off on seeing women raped. Someone who would especially get off on selling that footage online. That person is the one who should be behind bars, not my poor, addled brother."

Addled. Insane. Not right in the head. Incapable of making human decisions. *You motherfucker.* I close my mouth. I am not powerful enough to fight this. The media spin has already begun in this crusty office.

"He raped her because he couldn't get anyone else to fuck him and then he sucker-punched a dude who was already passed out. Your brother's a weak-ass faggot, Mr. Marino," Pickles says. Even though the word "faggot" makes my skin prickle, I can't help but agree with him on everything else. He stares at his check and I know he wants to tear it to shreds, but he can't. Quietly, he says, "I fucking trusted you guys. When you said filing the worker's comp would screw your dad and his campaign, I believed you. I tried to do the right thing."

"We took care of you, Robert," Rick says. The sound of Pickle's real name catches me off guard.

"Fuck you. You mighta paid my hospital bills, but I coulda taken this whole place down. That broken tile I slipped on? My friend at Public Works said the health inspector told you dickheads to fix it months before I fell in the pit."

"We did fix it, Robert. Your shoes lost their tread. You know that."

"After!" Pickles yells and it startles me.

"Pick, we should just go," I say, taking his burned arm in my hand. The skin in the crook of his elbow feels shiny. He rips it out of my grasp.

"Look at me!" he screams and it's louder than the last, his voice cracking slightly.

Rick holds his hands up and fans them like he's trying to put out a fire, but still that condescending smirk never leaves his face. "It seems like you have a lot of pent-up hostility toward us."

"Pick, shut up," I say as I hear the swinging door hit the wall in the kitchen. People outside are trying to quietly approach the office, so as not to interrupt.

"They're just gonna fucking get away with it again, Scar!" This time I really grab his arm as Johnson, LaChance, and two other officers lean into the room.

"Everything okay in here, Mr. Marino?"

"Robert's just a little upset that you guys are shutting the restaurant down for a bit."

Pickle's chest is heaving. His breath is rattling around his ribs and his hands are clenched into fists. LaChance nods and studies Pickles. Rick gives her a wide, determined stare, and with a slight movement, nods in Pickles's direction.

"Pick, come on, buddy. You're going to get in trouble if we don't get you out of here," I say quietly to him, but loud enough for everyone to hear. At the word "trouble", he breaks from his Hulk transformation and comes back to normal.

"I didn't mean to say faggot, Scar. Sorry," he says just to me. I squeeze his arm and lead him out. Julio and Emil follow us, heads down, not making eye contact with any of the people of authority as we part the sea of officers.

LaChance is still staring at Pickles, so I say, "He's just upset." Then add, "We all are," just to cover myself. She only glances at me and smirks darkly. I am no longer a person of interest to her, but Pickles is. I push him softly in the small of the back through the door to the front of the house. Everyone silently watches us leave. Margie, her eyes wide, mouths, "What. The. Fuck?" I respond with words that have no sound, "I'll call you," but I have no intention of doing that.

I smoke a cigarette with Pickles outside and discuss job options, then we part ways after a lopsided hug. I walk calmly for a block up to Mass Ave before turning the corner to sprint through a waiting bus crowd.

CHAPTER 17

I find some semblance of relief in the warehouse. On the way back here, I cashed my payoff from the Marinos and bought a few groceries, not a lot, but a few. I don't know how this ends, so for now, hoarding whatever money I have left seems the best course of action. Right now there's no rent to pay, unless Sam decides she wants something from me. The thought makes my thighs tense up and excited shivers trickle down my spine. I only have to pay my GoPhone and buy food. I can do this for a little while until we have a plan. Maybe she's going to get me out of here. Maybe I could change my name and start PAing again. Maybe no one will recognize me. Maybe I could have a whole new life, starting with nothing until it becomes something. But then the overwhelming thoughts roll in. What if I have a perfect, happy life, filled with love, and a home, maybe even a dog, a small one, like something French, some snorty bulldog that looks like a fluffy gargoyle that trots around behind me and loves me more than its own food. Maybe I'll have unconditional love and a passport to take me all over the world with my therapy dog. Maybe Sam will be with me…but then what if they find me? What if I can never shake the feeling that they're after me? What if I can never enjoy the new life I've built because the guilt of what I've done is so great that it eats me from the inside out and overwhelms my happy, meditative life, until I create scenarios where the cops are surveilling my apartment and listening to my voicemails, reading my emails, and then one day while I'm doing yoga in my home studio, there's a knock on the door, but before I can get to it, it's being beaten down by LaChance and her SWAT team? What if they want to take me away from my beautiful life? What if they want to crush the serenity around me? I close my eyes and take ten deep breaths imagining numbers one through ten in the darkness of my brain. My heartbeat slows and the color runs away from my cheeks. This is not then. This is now and I am here and I need a plan.

I'm hoping the drama that went down in the office will prove helpful. I'm hoping that the rules of deduction play in my favor, but I know I'm now on a short list of people who might have taken the evidence. The evidence sack stares at me from the folds of my bag. There are only four of us who could have swiped it from the desk. I kept my cool. Hopefully they don't think it's me.

I'm assuming that they haven't had time to run the DNA or track the Trader Joe's card. But even if the information *is* there, it would be in Taylor's name, not mine. Of course if they cross-reference at all they'll find me. If they do an image search they'll see pictures of Taylor and me in front of the Waverly when Gloricrux opened for Animal. The pictures will accompany a video blog Taylor did in which she and Gretchen get drunk on cheap wine and trash me for cheating on her with Sam (and Gretchen). If they really dig, they might find the pictures Gretch took of me while I was naked and sleeping in her rat-infested apartment that have been emblazoned with the words CHEATING WHORE across my tits.

I looked so different back then. I was clean. My eyebrows were threaded on the regular and facials were a part of my weekly regimen. I used to drink more bone broth, but I've replaced the gelatin from the broth with cigarettes and my forehead is starting to look like a ruled notebook where I scribble all my secrets. It might be hard to recognize me. I'm pretty convinced that my eyes have changed too. They've gotten darker where they used to be a bright sea color that you could sort of see gold sand through. Now they're Crayola Outer Space and just as dense.

The next thing they might see is a picture of Taylor throwing a beer bottle at me as I walk up my old front stoop. The beer bottle landed squarely in the middle of my chest and shattered there. Cal, her drummer, snapped the shot at impact, but not the one after, wherein I was bleeding through my t-shirt from tiny lacerations. This one might look more like me now: Bedraggled. Befuddled. Beaten. If they find these photos they will use them in an effort to discredit me, to publicly shame me, just like Taylor did within our small circle of friends after I returned from *TRRL*, after I'd lost my job for fucking Sam.

I kick my bag shut and text Sam. She hasn't responded to any of my texts today and that good ol' feeling of abandonment is starting to creep its way into my chest. I hate myself for it. Surely I don't need her to help me figure this out. Surely I am capable of doing this on my own, but then I think about her paying for the camp gear, the warehouse, the clean shower, and defeat and inability wash over me. I am hoping Sam will come back, even though all of the warning signs are there and they're screaming RADIATION. I should be able to do this on my own by now. I should be able to stand up for myself.

I glance at my phone and see no returned texts. I throw the phone in my bag. Every ounce of my being is screaming at me to go home. Just go home. I should be in my own place, my shitty little comfortable apartment where I pay the bills, no matter how far behind I am. That place where I live, where I breathe, drink, cry, beat myself: my own home. I pick up my bag and head out without thinking any further about it. It only takes me twenty minutes to get back to East Somerville. The bus drops me at Franklin and Broadway and I breathe, but when I turn down Lincoln I see two police cruisers sitting several cars down from my place.

I pull my hoodie up and keep walking past Lincoln. I grab another bus, cursing my stupidity. I'm not free. I pull the hoodie down over my eyes to shield my forehead from the cold window. I'll return the camping goods to Sam. I'll say thank you very much and go home, no matter how many cops sit outside my window. I glance at my phone. Margie has been texting incessantly but I ignore her. Still no message from Sam. That's probably for the best.

I step off the bus and walk right past two police officers. They don't even look my way even though I'm wearing a hoodie. I'm not black enough to cause suspicion I guess. I don't fear death under this hoodie. In fact, I hide under it when I enter the ICU at Beth Israel and head down a long, circular corridor filled with humans hanging on to life. I smell old age and urine, vomit, decaying skin, infection, but I keep walking until I'm standing in front of the sliding glass door of number seventeen. I stand outside for a long time and stare at his feet pointing to the ceiling, tucked tight by a hospital-cornered sheet. A curtain cuts him off at the knees and I remember my Gramps.

Gramp died in a bed just like this after living in a coma that didn't allow his eyes to shut. I remember leaning over to kiss him on the cheek and feeling the crust of his tears on my lips. I remember gently dropping Visine in his eyes to keep them moist, so they could loll around in his skull, taking in everything around him. He was unable to communicate what he saw, what he felt, what he wanted. I know what he wanted though. He wanted to die. It was on his chart. Do not resuscitate. Do not keep on Life Support. But there he was, taking in everything, unable to leave even when he wanted to.

That was my mother's fault—his prolonged, eyes-open coma. He had been in cardiac arrest while she was in the room and she flipped out, screaming at the doctors to resuscitate him, to not let him die. The nurses held her back. It took three of them, two females and one male. My mother couldn't let him die. He was the only one who liked her still. He was the only one who called her pretty any more. So she screamed and threw punches in the doctor's direction and he slammed my Gramp's chest with the paddles.

I imagine it must have been like the snap of a bungee cord. My Gramp taking a stroll through the tobacco fields, sun on his face, youth in his muscles, holding Gram's hand on one side and mine on the other. We're all young and happy and sun kissed. On the other side of the field waits a picnic on an ancient wooden table, biscuits and gravy, thick sliced beefsteak tomato sandwiches slathered in Cains Mayonnaise, a pitcher of sun tea, and a circle of friends with guitars and backed up by Cleo on the spoons. I can hear him humming. I can feel his smile radiate from his lips all the way down his arm and into the hulking paw of his hand, vacant of liver spots, wrapped around my own tiny one. I imagine that Grampy is living for seconds in a world where his granddaughter hasn't been beaten, hasn't been raped, hasn't lied, cheated, or stolen from anyone, hasn't been tainted at all. He lives in that space for nanoseconds, maybe even years. This is the one where she grows up and becomes a Contender on *American Gladiators*, or a best-selling memoirist, or an award-winning filmmaker. He smiles down at me and in my kid face, he sees all the potential and possibility in the world. And when he looks up, fresh tobacco leaves, his beautiful wife, and sunshine. But out of nowhere, a giant hook moves in and jerks him off-stage. Electricity sears his veins. He's flying through darkness and his eyes flash open and never close again until he dies three weeks later, an all-seeing, all-knowing vegetable.

I almost run then, at the memory of my grandfather's plagued eyes staring at me, begging me to help him close them on the world, but I know that I must go in to this sick room. I cannot run from this. I am responsible for this. I take a step in, no longer following a blue line on the floor. I am veering off the path and going against what sanity tells me as I step closer to the bed. His hand is resting at his side. A drop of dry blood has formed a tick-like bump near the needle where intravenous fluids pump into him. His hands look soft despite the work he does. I want to hold them immediately. We haven't shared more than fifty words together, but I feel closer to him than anyone in the world right now.

This silence suits us. I walk around the end of the bed and find a chair on the other side. I don't look at his face until I'm seated. The injuries he sustained from the three men who beat him have caused bleeding in his brain. The newspapers say he'll recover, but still it sounds horrible. Brain bleed. Blood on the brain. I imagine it, blood traveling like rivulets through the grey matter, getting stuck in a memory here and there, clogging up the ability to tell his fingers to form a fist around shoelaces he doesn't remember how to knot. Blood on the brain. I can understand this almost. I can understand being lost in the blood.

Lucky's face is a mess of colors: blue, black, purple, yellow, brown. His thick, blonde hair is matted on one side with what looks like molasses and a bandage covers the rest of it. He has a patch over his left eye and a cut, or more like a breaking open of the skin, running into the hollow of his cheek beneath. His lips are swollen and broken.

His chin is more purple than white. I want to kiss him like he's the princess in my fairy tale. I want to make the discoloration and deep cuts disappear by touching my lips to his, but I know that fairy tales are bullshit and I'd probably just trigger some alarm that goes off when his heart races with fear. Instead I wrap my fingers around his hand and don't say a word.

Tears come and they make me angry. I wipe them away before they can spill down my cheeks, but my efforts are futile. Before long I am resting my forehead on the sheet next to his hand and I've dampened the whole thing.

"I'm sorry, Lucky," I whisper and touch my lips to the back of his hand. It doesn't move. Nothing changes. "I should have helped you." I drop my eyes and retreat into my hoodie as a nurse walks by and stops to stare in at us, a misstep in her rounds. Her brow furrows and she makes a note on a chart before moving on. When I look back at Lucky's face, his eyes are open.

"You," he says through gritted teeth and dry, cracked lips. I stare into his eyes and say, "I'm sorry," again. He blinks and a tear breaks through his long lashes, splashing his cheek. My email dings and it's like an alarm telling me to stand.

"I'll come back," I say, but know that I am already lying. He nods, but the look in his eyes tells me he doesn't believe me either. Before I can turn to go, he squeezes my hand hard and says, "Coffee."

I don't know if he needs coffee now or if maybe sometime in the future we could have coffee together, but it feels like a proposal. I smile and I mean it. I nod, squeeze his hand in mine again and slip out seconds later, heading into the night, back to the safety of the buses. I catch one heading toward Eastie and stare at an email from someone called Cae Terus. I click on the email, subject line: we know who you are. My cheeks burn. I close my eyes hard and then open them to make sure it's real. It is. There's an email. I read the first few lines: "Scarlet Battell, you may know us as Never There, Anonymous, Anon. But we are Caeterus. We know who you are and we are protecting your weak attempts at veiling your identity FOR YOU so that the authorities don't track your silly IP address and arrest you on the spot at your apartment at 41 Franklin. Don't tell anyone you shot the video of the Topsail Rape. We are deleting the YT logs as we type this. You might want to stay somewhere else until this blows over. Your apartment is not safe. Act NORMAL. We'll be in touch. You're welcome."

My heart takes up near regular beats again and I am acutely aware that the man sitting next to me is too close for comfort. Did he read the email? I glance at the others, many of them are staring at me. I hit the stop strip. I squeeze past the old man sitting next to me and walk to the door before the bus stops. As soon as the doors open, I push through them. My phone rings. It's Sam.

"I need to show you something," I say before "hello."

"I was just calling to tell you that I'm on my way. I can bring food. Any special requests?"

CHAPTER 18

Sam shakes her head, stares down at her feet. Every move she makes causes a nervous tingle to run up my spine. The relief I felt when I saw her was a betrayal perpetrated against myself. She'd been stuck in production meetings all day. That was all. But now she is here. With food. A glorious spread, a charcuterie of sorts. Food I haven't eaten in a year. Delicious fatty cuts of organic grass fed meat, and the stinkiest cheeses. Fresh fruits and thick, heavy, and nutty breads. Cultured butter. I have missed the butter. And wine. Something red. It doesn't matter. I want it all.

"I have to tell you something," she says as I start eating like a ravenous homeless child.

"That this whole situation is fucked and I have no out?" I smile and sit cross-legged in front of her, meat filling my cheeks.

"The real reason I told Cass about our…about having sex with you is because I was afraid you'd out me."

"That's bullshit." Anger builds in my chest and I swallow a lump of Soppressata. "Why would I out you? Why would it have fucking mattered anyway? No one gives a shit, Sam. Three-quarters of Hollywood is flaming. We're all fucking gay, so who gives a shit about your sad little ego?" I shove her in the chest. I don't know where it comes from, but it comes hard and fast and I can't control myself.

Again, she shakes her head. "No."

"No?" I say and I come at her again, but this time she grabs my wrists to stop me from pushing her. She is stronger than me by a long shot and her force stops me in my tracks. "No, what?"

"No. Not my sexuality."

It's my turn to shake my head and I try to take a step back, but she holds my wrists up in front of her like a shield and I don't know where to go.

"My body," she says quietly.

"What about your body? Say it," I say the words with a force that must seem angry, but it's not. It's anticipation. I am trying to find a reckoning. I'm on the edge of a cliff. I'm about to feel rectification. I am about to rebuild. We are about to rebuild. I can hear it coming from her. I can feel it vibrating in my own body.

She releases my hands and I can see she is shaking, not out of fear, not like a dog with too much energy that needs release. This is from her core. This started somewhere deep in her solar plexus and is reverberating like a boulder thrown into the middle of a lake. Her lips are quivering; her teeth chatter. She closes her eyes, I assume, to talk to the quaking, to tell it to simmer down. When she opens them again, she stares straight into me, locking on me, and begins to strip off her jacket. My hands move to help her, but she won't let me. She softly pushes me away and continues. This reminds me of how she pushed me away the night of our fuckery before Cass fired me. She stands. I follow her lead.

I shot a documentary once about cancer survivors who had undergone double mastectomy surgeries, how their lives had been forever changed by the removal of their breasts, how these women had completely reclaimed their flesh. They'd reclaimed their power by tattooing themselves or finally going topless in the summer. They'd taken back their bodies from science, from disease, from the harsh restrictions we as a society had placed on their skin. Day after day, I would go into a house, or a cabin, a hospital room, a tattoo parlor, a church, a bathroom, a women's only gym, and they would strip for me; terrified, proud, at ease, laughing like someone was tickling them, and I would film them without words, letting them tell their stories with their skin and scars. This is what it feels like with Sam in front of me now. I stand back like a camera lens and let her tell me her story.

She is slow and soft and terrified of me. When she is only in her t-shirt and jeans, it's hard for me not to stare at her breasts: perfect, firm, and round. I watch her t-shirt fall like a feather. The air around me is still, save for the sloshing of water against the dock outside. Sam hasn't blinked. She stands before me in her bra and jeans and our breath mingles in the distance.

"It's okay. Show me," I say.

Lips quavering, she reaches behind herself and unclasps her bra. It is nude in color and nearly matches her milky skin. She has a beauty mark where her shoulder meets her clavicle, a light, nearly perfect dot, which reveals itself when she pulls the straps of her bra away from her shoulders and lets it fall to the floor. My eyes move from her clavicle to her eyes and I find that they are wet and brimming with tears, but her jaw is set and determined. I move closer, my hand reaching out to touch her, but she holds her hand up to stop me and that's when I see the scars. They are tiny, dimpled, old scars and they stretch below the soft tissue of her breasts where she holds them in her palms.

"Don't. Okay? Just let me…"

I nod and don't move from where I am standing.

Sam continues and a lump forms in my throat. My stomach aches like I haven't eaten in days. My eyes tear as she stands in front of me, topless, for what seems like several minutes.

"You're beautiful." I don't mean to compliment. I don't mean to placate. I don't mean anything more than actual fact. "Beautiful" seems silly, so trivial, yet it's what I have and I mean it. She shakes her head.

"Shut up," she says.

I do. I take in every inch of her. Her hand rests on her abdomen, just above her jeans, almost like she's shielding it from an attack. I think she might be measuring her breath. I allow my eyes to move from her hand up through the valley of her ribs and tensing abdominals, to the gap between her breasts, to her strong jaw, her high cheek bones, and then finally back to her eyes, her eyes like the ocean floor, if the ocean were speckled with flecks of gold. She is no longer crying. She looks angry, defiant, like she's about to tell me to fuck off. I hold her eyes while she unbuttons her pants; the ripping of her zipper in the quiet space around us sounds like flesh tearing apart. Her eyes are dark.

She pushes her jeans down, steps out of them. I don't look. Something tells me not to look, as if this beautiful facade will explode. I have a remembrance of her hands on my wrists, holding me down in my Four Seasons bed. I have a dream in the nanosecond before she speaks, of her swatting my hands from her jeans and pinning me to the bed before she kissed my hands away.

"Look at me," she says, deep and forceful, her eyes clear and focused on my own.

"I am, Sam."

"Fuck you, Scarlet. You're not really. Look at me. All of me. See me for what I am."

I shake my head, tears finally coming to my eyes and I say again, "I am."

She rushes me then and kisses me hard on the mouth. I taste blood and my body feels like a sack of flour. She grabs my wrist and shoves my fist into her crotch. I do not break eye contact. I do not give in.

"Touch it," she says with a mouthful of disgust and I do.

And then her fingers are digging into the flesh of my shoulders and it's hard, too hard, I pull away from her and sit up, but it's dark and nothing is right. Sam is standing over me, her brow furrowed. She looks exhausted and fully clothed.

"Wake the fuck up," she says.

"I am—I." I look down at my lap and see that I am clothed. Fully. She is also clothed, but it was so real, this dream. Blood rushes behind my eyes and without another thought I reach out quick like a snake. I strike and grab her hard between the legs. She grabs my wrist, but doesn't remove my hand from the mound of flesh under jeans. There's nothing there, nothing substantial anyway. I want to move my fingers inside of her, but the jeans are there and there's her hand. I stare into her eyes, angry yet egging me on.

"What are you looking for?" she asks.

I just shake my head, can't actually say the insane words. There's nothing there.

"I thought you were someone else."

"Lucky?" she asks and I pull my hand away fast and shove her away from me.

"What happened?"

I shake my head, pull the evidence bag out of my bag, and throw it at her. She catches it and stares at the contents.

"Where did you—Is this from—did you—?" None of the questions seem to be the right one. She actually looks over her shoulder to see if anyone else is there, but there's no one obviously.

"They found it at the restaurant. It's all mine, even the blood."

"But that doesn't mean anything. You work there."

"They had a crime scene photo and all of the items were on the floor right where I was standing when I shot the video and they were all circled and there was a note that asked, 'Do these belong to the shooter?' So yeah, it means something to them," I say and start to pace. Sam stands back from me, staring at the contents of the bag. Her toes touch a black spray painted tagline on the floor, it's the only bit of graffiti in this room, unlike the rest of the space. I get the feeling she doesn't want to cross it. It separates us and she probably thinks that if she goes further, she'll be too involved. She's probably right, "Listen. Maybe you should let me handle this on my own," I say and can't for the life of me understand why I would want to protect her, but the old guilt is starting to surface.

"No," she says.

"Sam, if they find me, you might be in trouble too."

She shakes her head and chucks the evidence bag on the bed, "For helping a friend? Nah."

"I never said we were friends," I say.

"We were."

"No. I was your boss."

"I was the only person you even remotely talked to or confided in, Scar. Don't rewrite history. We have too many secrets together. We like each other. We were friends," she says, but drops her head to her chest. My email dings into the hollow space around us.

"Something else happened today," I say, rescuing us both and then I hand her my phone. I have another email from Caeterus. She reads. I grab my laptop and open it, sitting on the cot. She sits too, but keeps that line between us. For a second, I wish she would get closer. I wish we could sit against the wall, shoulder to shoulder with a nice charcuterie and drink some wine and talk like normal human beings. I Google Caeterus and we both stare at the screen. A Wikipedia entry comes up and we read about how Caeterus (also known as CXI) outed Martin Stretcher, the cop who shot Terrence Pepperman in the back and then tried to plant a Taser in his hand. They brought down Charles Seymour III, the high school football player in Texas with a senator for a father, who shared a snapchat of a drunk fourteen-year-old being gang raped at a homecoming party; Caeterus hacked Seymour's pimped out phone after he made some inflammatory remarks about the slutty fourteen-year-old and how there wasn't any evidence against him and his friends. They warned him they were going to do it, but Seymour and daddy thought they were above the law. Caeterus have also been responsible for several DDoSes, or "distributed denials of service". One in particular, the DDoS that disabled the Westboro Baptist Church website, really got them some press, but they don't seem to want exposure unless it helps the victim of a crime.

I pull up the website on Caeterus and read that the organization promotes access to information, providing national security intelligence to the people and offers platforms for free speech to those without a voice in the world. The organization boasts a deep financial underbelly and hires and trains agents several—

As we're reading, the page goes blank and is replaced with a black screen. A gif is embedded in the middle of the page. The title card reads "Caeterus11: The Truth" and that fades to a logo. In the middle of the screen floats the letter C and a roman numeral XI centered inside the letter's curve. Words emerge in line with the C: *with others held constant*. This card too fades, to be replaced by: *The way. The truth.* All at once I'm overwhelmed by fear that the NSA is watching my online strokes to see that I'm looking at information about Caeterus. I x out of my Firefox tab and stare at Sam. Her brows are raised and she takes a deep breath.

"That's probably a good thing. They sound like they want to protect you," she says.

I nod, but am not totally convinced.

"What do you think they want?" she asks.

"What do you mean?"

"Well, they have to want something in return." She smiles at me like she's explaining something simple to a small child.

"They want to give a voice to the voiceless," I lamely summarize.

Sam shakes her head. "They'll want something. Maybe they think you're still connected. Maybe they want you to be a vigilante for them."

"A vigilante?" The word sounds goofy coming from my mouth.

"Yeah, like a digital vigilante, like maybe they want you running all over town with your GoPro, capturing big people doing the bad things to little people."

"That's ridiculous."

She shakes her head, "I don't think so. It's happening a lot right now. This 'citizen journalist' thing is really popular."

I think on it, allowing myself a moment to imagine myself in stealthy black clothes, some kind of leather, or lycra, like a superhero. I'm strapped all over with GoPros and perched atop the Pru like a lithe cat. And then I shake it off, embarrassed that I even entertained the thought.

"I'm not a vigilante. I'm just fucked up." I wait for the right words, but they're never going to be right. "Sometimes I think I did it to make myself important again, like I was when I was story producing."

She nods and it stings that she agrees like she's already thought of this.

"But at the end of the day, they were shitty people and no one was going to stop them from taking advantage of people. When Joe and Quinn walked in, I knew what was going to happen. I also knew that I couldn't put the camera down. I needed evidence and—and maybe I knew, maybe somewhere deep down, I knew that this would do it. I could be important again. I could do something meaningful, but after this, after all this shit, I don't want to be important. I want to disappear."

"I don't think you do," she says, "I think you want to tell the truth again, show the reality of our existence."

Laughter escapes me in a burst, "The reality of our existence? Drink the KoolAid much?"

"I'm serious. This is what reality television is supposed to be, not some watered down club scene where two idiots fuck in the bathroom," she says and my skin crawls and my head starts pounding just like it used to. She's studying me, but I can't let her see this.

"Scar, I didn't mean to—" She cuts herself off. We're both getting sick of hearing her apologize. "Come here," she says and I turn to see her standing again. She holds her arms out. I hesitate for a millisecond before walking into her arms. The feeling of her arms around me, holding me tight to her chest like I'm in a cage, causes some kind of tremor in me, like my body is a muscle that has been tensed for a long time and a massage therapist is trying to stretch it out, to lengthen it, to knead it with the soft butt of a palm. The muscle is my quadriceps and they attach to my psoas and my psoas clutches my hips and my pelvic floor and when it's tight, when it hasn't been loved in a long time, it causes my legs to pulse and jump and this sick feeling swells, this feeling that hollowness is going to take over and I'm going to implode through my lower abdomen. This feeling that thousands of beetles are scurrying around in my legs and my cunt and stomach.

This is what happens when she hugs me. She feels like she's resisting it too, like her arms are fighting the rest of her.

She tilts my face up to hers and she kisses me and I know it's going to happen for real this time on this shitty floor with the black line that I've crossed. When she pulls my clothes over my head and down my legs, her fingers are steady on my thighs, my stomach, holding onto the valley between my breasts. She undresses herself this time and finally I see her in the amber light of the room. She is milky white and speckled with dark freckles, curved and dipped, with ash blonde nests of hair hiding the spaces I've not seen before.

We stand for a long time just looking at one another. She even pushes me back to get a better look. It takes an hour—at least it feels that way—for us to study each other, and then I am crawling back to her on my hands and knees, crossing back to her and burying my face in her stomach, breathing in the sweet, musty smell of her sweat. My lips come away salty and she kneels before me and pushes me back onto the concrete. I convulse as her tongue touches me and her fingers dive inside. I grab her head, her shoulders; hold her there. I'm surrounded by blackness and the incessant dinging of my email as I await my turn to fuck Sam.

When I wake, hours later, wrapped snug in my sleeping bag, Sam and all evidence of her are gone again. This is too familiar.

CHAPTER 19

The air is cold and lonely.

I can only do a few things right now: obsess over the news (and Sam), occasionally eat, and very rarely sleep. I've found a strong Wi-Fi signal named "ShareYoWeed" and it keeps me on the rat wheel of information. My brain is going to shut down soon. I can feel it. When I do close my eyes, I see everything wrong I've ever done. I see Taylor in a rage, throwing the cat at me, calling me a fat coward. I see boys, so many boys, the disappointment on my mother's face. I see all the bills I can't pay and the threatening student loan Nazis trying to track me down. I see two redneck Texas cops slamming my shaved head into a cruiser when I was nineteen, pointing at my bumper sticker and informing me that "Some people deserve to be hated." I see Alex, my first real boyfriend. I see his eyeball peering at me through the crack in a barn door as I make out with Hanna, our best friend. I feel the lumps of dinner rolls stuffed into my apron that I stole almost every night from the Topsail when I first started working there. I see my car repossessed and I try to imagine where my cat, Doodle, is. I see myself, standing on the roof of a building in the middle of Bushwick, Gretchen's apartment, and I hear the words *just do it. Just jump* rattling around in my brain. I lean over the edge and a gust of wind pushes me back. I see my Gramp sitting in a tree next to the building. He's crying. I see myself falling, but know it's a dream and then I feel the crush of the orange, taste blood spattering my tongue. The effect is something like ecstasy. My breathing calms itself as the blood crawls its way back into my system. I see myself producing porn. I see reality. I see Quinn's dead body. I see Lucky in a pool of blood. I see myself running. I see myself fucking Sam again.

I squeeze my eyes shut and open them to drown myself in the blue light of my MacBook. Right now it's the only light in my warehouse stall. I'm cold. I've yet to light the Coleman stove or the space heater Sam bought me, or put wool socks on. Fall is flying at me and I can't outrun the drop in temperature. This is all unraveling. I can feel it. I click on Huffington Post. I click on Mashable. I click on Reddit. I scroll Twitter. I go to Wiki, Alter, Reuters, and DailyKos. The *Globe* is pissed. They're trying to be unbiased, but they really want my head on a platter. They just need to know. Everyone needs to know who the Topsail Shooter is. Who am I?

So I walk. I walk all over the city and watch everyone process what's happening around them. I walk and I stop at a Dunkin Donuts or a Starbucks and I eat shit food product behind cool glass and drink coffee sourced by overworked, underpaid migrant workers. I swallow my shame. I fight back screams. I watch. It's been nearly eight days since the video went out and they don't know who I am or where I'm hiding. Sam says that if we get past two weeks, I might be in the clear. I might be able to go home. But I think even she's tiring of me and my incessant anxiety. She hasn't called in three days. The last time I spoke with her, she just told me to lay low, stay inside, work on my memoir or something, but I can't be caged. I stalk my apartment like a jilted lover every other day and find that it's still not swarming with police. Caeterus is apparently doing what they said they would, but what if Sam's right? What if they want something from me? I don't have anything left to give. I don't even have a real bed anymore.

I've stood outside of the hospital on more than one occasion, but I'm too afraid to go in again. The news says Lucky is awake and he's being hailed the hero, just like I thought he would. Maybe someday, when this all dies down, we'll be able to have that coffee like two normal people.

I started walking this morning at nine and have wound my way like a constipated shit in the bowels of this city to my favorite Starbucks, the one in Central across from O'Hearns. I use the Starbucks window like a television. My phone's charging on their powermat and I have a stack of newspapers next to my laptop. There's some part of this that feels like real life again. I could be the college kid behind me checking their Facebook, or the old guy and his wife not talking over their newspapers. But I'm not. I never will be. I've deactivated my Facebook for one.

Directly across from me, O'Hearn's Electronics, an old neighborhood store, still sells televisions. They've got a window of them, stacked on top of one another, from every decade since the first, all switched to different channels. Occasionally passersby stop to watch, but they're usually older folks. The kids and urban professionals don't recognize these kinds of screens.

But several of them are stopping in front of O'Hearn's now. It's a weird mix: MIT kids, suited men, women juggling their lattes, phones, bags. They stop. I see soap operas, the news, the Topsail video, game shows.

And Taylor.

Taylor dressed in what looks like an off-the-rack McQueen midi dress, sitting in a director's chair, hair and makeup camera-ready. She is being interviewed. Her face reads like a self-righteous yet neighborly glam prom queen. I can't hear her words, but I see her "I told you so" smirk and my stomach aches. I swallow her words like *coward, pussy, talentless* and open my MacBook. I Google her name and at the top of the search, see a headline that crushes my solar plexus: "Ex-girlfriend identifies TOPSAIL SHOOTER, others come forward to identify and solidify claim."

There I am in a red carpet still. Me as a Glamazon. No one would be able to see the resemblance now.

"Holy shit," a guy next to me says and I glance at him through the curtain of my hair, around the side of my hoodie. "Sorry. I didn't mean to read over your shoulder, I just…fuck, right?" he says and continues to read the screen. "The Topsail Shooter. It was a chick," he says with disdain and glances at me, like he might have offended me with his shock. I look away from him and at the video on my screen of Taylor. I can't help it. I press play and then a crowd grows behind me, watching over my shoulder.

We're over a reporter's shoulder, staring at a medium close-up on Taylor as she sits in a tall director's chair. She smiles and in that smile, she wants the world to know that she was an innocent victim of a madwoman.

"I'm sitting here with Taylor Blakeley, ex-partner of reality show producer-turned-waitress, Scarlet Battell, whom Ms. Blakeley, as well as others who know Ms. Battell, have identified as the Topsail Shooter. Taylor, thanks for taking the time to speak with us. I know this must be difficult for you."

"Of course. Anything I can do to help."

"Let's start with how you recognized Scarlet Battell and eventually contacted the police to identify her."

"Sure. Well, that REI surveillance video has been all over the news and it caught my eye one day on a friend's wall, so I watched it and I immediately recognized the woman on the video as Scarlet. There was something about her walk. She just seemed shifty. I *felt* Scarlet. So I contacted the Boston Police Department."

"You were in a relationship with Ms. Battell for about four years, is that correct?"

She nods, chooses her words carefully. "Yes. Unfortunately, we were engaged to be married, but thankfully that never happened."

"Feel like you dodged a bullet there?" the reporter asks and Taylor nods, smiles, and mocks wiping sweat from her brow.

"Can you tell us a little about who Scarlet Battell is?"

Taylor takes a long time to think on this as if the words *pussy*, *coward*, and *nothing* aren't playing through her brain on a loop. "Look, Laura, Scarlet's a chameleon. She isn't who she says she is. She's a liar. A cheater. A bottom feeder, really. She uses her history of abuse to try to get people to feel sorry for her, but really, she needs help. When we were together, I spent years trying to help her be a better person, but eventually, you just have to stop taking from yourself and focus on your own health, you know? I left her eventually. It just got to be too much of a head trip and she was dragging me down to a place where I didn't feel comfortable or safe anymore."

"That sounds pretty abusive, actually," Laura feeds her.

Taylor nods, stares down at her hands, and works herself up until her eyes are brimming with tears. Laura hands her a tissue and I feel a knot in my stomach tighten as the people behind me close in. I don't understand how this is happening. *What surveillance video?* And then my throat constricts, *what if there are cameras near Quinn's apartment?*

"Do you have any idea where Scarlet might be?"

Taylor shakes her head and dabs her eyes, careful not to smudge the professional mascara on her lashes.

"She could be anywhere, I suppose. Has anyone checked the homeless shelters? She was evicted from her apartment here after she was fired and from what I heard, she drove home to Boston and has been there ever since," Taylor says and stares right into the camera, into my soul. I sink lower in my hoodie and hope that the people around me can't feel my breath quickening. I need to get out of here, but I can't make a scene. I need to get in touch with Sam. I need to figure out my next move. I can't breathe.

"Thanks for sharing what you can with us, Taylor. And thanks for being strong enough to tell us your story of abuse at the hands of one of America's most sought-after criminals right now." Camera Two cuts to Laura in a medium close-up. Straight to camera, she says, "Taylor Blakeley is the lead singer for the New York City-based band, Gloricrux. Their newest album just dropped last week and can be found on iTunes, Amazon, and anywhere music is sold. Taylor tells us that some of the harder tracks like "Gloryhole" and "My Downfall" were written in a cathartic state of healing after she broke up with Scarlet Battell, the Topsail Shooter. Joining me now is another person who has had an intimate relationship with Ms. Battell."

The camera view changes again and I slink even further into the seat back, my breath seeping out of me like air from a dead balloon. The heat on my shoulder from the quiet crowd behind me makes my skin crawl.

Sam sits in a director's chair next to Taylor. She looks annoyed and stony.

"I'm also joined this morning by Samantha Martin, who has a very sordid history with Ms. Battell. As I understand it, Ms. Martin, you were sexually harassed by Ms. Battell when she was your superior at Edwards Entertainment, the entertainment company responsible for hit urban reality shows like *KDX* and *The Real Real Life*?"

Sam nods and says, "That's true. I knew Scarlet only briefly, but in the few weeks that I worked under her on the show, she often sexually harassed me, berated me, threw a coffee at me once, and eventually coerced me into a sexual encounter. I feared I'd lose my job if I didn't comply with her demands. I—I thought we were friends, you know. She said she was my friend, but at the end of the day, I just had to come to terms with the fact that she was my boss and what was happening was inappropriate."

"That's horrible," Laura says. "And you too went to the police after seeing the surveillance video?"

What surveillance video? What are they talking about? My cheeks flush. I'm going to have a heart attack. *Why is Sam doing—*

Sam nods, tears welling up in her eyes.

"Can you give us any insight as to who Scarlet Battell is?

"I can tell you that she is very disturbed and I feel sorry for her," Sam says. Taylor shakes her head in a "what a waste" sort of way before smiling for the camera. "I haven't seen or spoken with Scarlet Battell for two years, not since the night she, the night…" Sam says, wiping at her tears. I can't swallow. I blink long and hard and open my eyes to find that it's all still there and it's still happening. Laura nods and then the camera pulls back even further to reveal a third woman.

Laura says, "And next to you is your ex-Executive Producer Cass Edwards, who, in fact, fired Ms. Battell when you accused the former reality show producer of sexual coercion." Cass nods. My coffee clogs my throat. I close the laptop to the groans of the people behind me and stuff it in my bag. I keep my face hidden as I turn and try not to fall off of the high stool I've been sitting on in the window bar. I push through the crowd, which is now gathering around someone else's laptop, and before I leave the café, I hear Cass say, "Listen, we're talking about someone who is a very disturbed individual, who can't even keep her hands off of her subordinates. It's obvious she got some kind of sexual pleasure out of taping this rape. I just hope she knows that she's totally and utterly responsible for the death of a kind, hard-working, Harvard-educated young black woman, and I also hope she rots in hell for what she's done."

I stop at the door and take these words in. Behind me someone says, "What a wicked fuckin' sicko." I push the door open and leave. I want more than anything to run, but know I can't.

When I finally get back to the warehouse, I flip open the MacBook and try to figure this out. I click on *Huffington Post* again and see my face staring back at me from the front page headline, the shot of me in front of the Wilbur from the Bitch & Animal concert and in the split screen, the front-page tabloid of me getting hit with a beer bottle. All the moisture has left my mouth.

BATTLE SCARS: TOPSAIL SHOOTER IDENTIFIED
SCARLET BATTELL, an ex-reality television producer currently listed on the payroll at the Topsail Bar & Grill in Boston, has been identified by Boston police as the person responsible for recording the brutal rape of now deceased, Quinn Franklin, and the beating of Lucas Walker by Topsail General Manager Joseph Marino, eldest son of Massachusetts governor-elect Jack Marino. Joseph Marino suffers from a form of Asperger's Syndrome.

The rape and beating happened on May 16th and three days later, the REI on Newbury Street was robbed. Ms. Battell was identified when her ex-lover, Taylor Blakeley, lead singer of the band, Gloricrux, notified police in Boston that she recognized Ms. Battell as the Newbury Street REI robber. Ms.

Blakeley saw the REI footage of Ms. Battell when police released grainy surveillance of the robbery to the public.

The video of the robbery is embedded below and shows Ms. Battell, who allegedly gained access to the REI by hiding out in the bathroom until the store was closed, proceed to gather camping supplies and clothing and, in a move that may signify Ms. Battell's mental state, stopped by the cashier's counter and appeared to check herself out, engaging in a conversation with herself. It appears on the video as though Ms. Battell thought she might have been talking with an REI employee, but upon inspection of the surveillance video and entry and exit key codes on the building, REI informs us that based on the footage, there was no one in the store with Ms. Battell at the time. After robbing the store, Ms. Battell then hid in the bathroom until a cleaning crew disarmed the alarm on the door and she was able to sneak out.

Ms. Battell's whereabouts are unknown and sources say she has no family in the area. "Once the connection was made that she'd broken into the store and worked at the restaurant, we were able to trace her IP and crack the encryption on her YouTube account," says forensics investigator Curt Schemple of the Boston Police's Internet Fraud Department. "It's obvious that Ms. Battell knows a thing or two about computers, or she's been helped. We had a tough time breaking the encryption and when we did finally, we found most of the upload logs deleted. Now we're seeking any and all information as to Ms. Battell's whereabouts, and information about who might be helping her. We've left her account up for the time being because she's posted a series of videos in the past eight days and we're hoping someone might be able to identify the location where the videos were shot."

The BPD is urging anyone who knows Ms. Battell's whereabouts to contact the BPD with any and all information they have. Ms. Battell's YouTube Channel is http://www.youtube.com/BattleScars and we must warn you that the videos on the channel are NSFW (including sex and violence) and shouldn't be watched by anyone under the age of 18.

The Marino Family has yet to make a statement about this new information.

Joseph Marino is awaiting a bail hearing on Friday, the 8th and his lawyer, Rick Marino of the law firm Marino, Mueller, and Best; says that he expects his brother will be out on bail by the weekend. Donald McGivens and Nathan Marino are also awaiting separate bail hearings, after being apprehended in Rhode Island over the weekend.

This is a developing story and we'll update as we know more.

I lean over the cot and throw up, right into my collapsible pot. Then I call Sam. She answers on the third ring, but the voice on the other end isn't hers.

"Yeah?" some kid, some guy, who sounds like I'm interrupting an intense session of Call of Duty says in my ear.

"Is Sam—May I speak with Sam Martin please?"

"Wrong number."

"Samantha Martin."

"Who's Sam?" His voice is eerily familiar, but I can't place it.

"Mark?" I ask. I have a moment of inspiration. She'd said the name Mark before. That night she took me from my apartment. *Mark*.

"No," he says and hangs up.

I hold the phone to my ear as if he might change his mind and call back, but it doesn't ring. I want to snap my phone in half. I open my text messages. Just this morning she texted me and said: *I'll be by tonight. I've missed you. Be safe.* But when I open my messages, our conversation is not there. I page through. There are no conversations with Sam. The last text I received was from Margie three days ago asking if I wanted to get a drink. My brain is buzzing and the sensation is traveling down my spine and I think it might paralyze me.

I type in the same number I called and write: *What is going on, Sam? Why are you on tv saying I robbed REI?* I hit send. A message immediately dings back at me, from AT&T: the subscriber you are trying to message has message restrictions. Your message has not been delivered.

I call the number again. It rings, but goes to voicemail with an automated message. I hang up.

My brain whirs, tries to start itself again, like a faulty beater of a car. I rip at my cuticles with my teeth and then I call the Four Seasons.

"Four Seasons Boston. How may I direct your call?"

"Sam Martin. Room 1013," I say, my voice is weak and jittery. I wipe a vomit splash off my chin and close my eyes, try to control my breathing while I wait to be transferred.

"I'm sorry, but we have no guests listed under that name," the receptionist says. The dry lump in my throat drops into my chest and plunks into the space where my heart used to beat.

"Samantha," I say, "Samantha Martin."

Typing keys on the other end.

"Mmm. No, ma'am. I'm sorry."

"When did she check out?" I ask, opening my eyes and focusing on a crack in the concrete wall in front of me.

"It doesn't look like we've had a Ms. Martin stay with us recently—"

I hang up without letting her finish. I shake my head of the still image of me by myself in the store. Maybe this will restore my reality. I look down at the story on my MacBook and click play on the video. There I am, walking through the store, picking up the Coleman stove and throwing it in the cart. I'm not steady on my feet. Several times I stop and rest my head on the handle of the cart in front of me. I grab the sleeping bag, the socks, the thermal underwear, the water, the boots. I open a bag of what looks like trail mix right in the middle of the aisle and start eating out of the bag. I hold out the bag to someone who isn't there and speak to the person, though there's no audio. I close my eyes and try with every ounce of my being to recall that night and can't. There's a cave in my brain and an avalanche has filled in the memories with rocks. There's no way out or in. My fist is clenched so tight that it feels like my knuckles are going to burst apart. I press the knuckles of my fist into the bridge of my nose and push hard, willing it to break. What have I done?

I open my eyes and keep watching. It takes me fifteen minutes to get through the store and then I head to the cashier, who is not there. But more importantly, neither is Sam. I gulp water and fumble for the laptop. I have nowhere to go. I close my eyes and when I open them, I see myself again on grainy surveillance standing at the counter of the REI, my head slightly turned to speak to someone who isn't there.

Then I cry. I cry like a child. I cry like my grandfather just left the earth again. I cry like I did in that basement all those years ago when those boys passed me around like a blowup doll. I cry like I did when my mother saw the blood and the cuts and the bruises and she looked away and told me to get the laundry done instead of asking who'd hurt me. I cry until I am dry, until there is nothing left of me and I am the skeleton of a human being, if I am even that any more. When I am finished, I stare at the orange resting next to an apple and a banana I picked up from a 7-Eleven two nights ago. The fruit sits in a ceramic bowl that my best friend Brandy made in art class in sixth grade. I take it with me everywhere. It holds the fruit. It holds that orange that I want to crush against my cheekbone, but the bowl is like a shield against me. I stand and start to pace. I stay away from the fruit.

I pull my phone out of my pocket and spin the email lever until it lands on the one from Caeterus. I should have listened to them. I open the email, hit reply, and type: IN TROUBLE NOW. PLEASE HELP. I click send and hope that it works.

I have to figure out a way to get in front of this. Do I turn myself in? Do I run? Who do I call? I think of Sean, but I don't know if he exists. I put on my wool socks and tie myself into my stolen sleeping bag and I wait. But if Sam's not here, then I'm—I'm what? Fucking crazy. That's what. If Sam isn't here, if she is truly not here, in the flesh, here in Boston, then I've done all of this on my own. I've created this warehouse. I touch the cot beneath me and it feels real. I put my hand against the wall and it feels cool to the touch. I'm not in my apartment. Maybe I'm in the basement of my apartment? No. I stand up and drop the sleeping bag. On tiptoes I peer out of the dirty window and hear the sea and smell the fish. I'm in East Boston. But how did I get here? And then the thought again: *I did this all on my own.* It envelops me in warmth, a strange sort of pride washing over me. It's all I have right now.

My email dings. The notification tells me it's Caeterus. Their message is simple: *Turn your location services on and we'll contact you. Stay where you are.*

I'm a prisoner. This time I can't leave. I open my YouTube app and pull up my account. What I find there goes beyond any reality I understand.

CHAPTER 20

I think of parallel universes a lot.

I think of the exact moment that your life changes in front of you. There's always a crossroads and you choose a direction and you go, without doubt, down that road, but what if it's universally wrong and part of your soul knows that, so part of you, this ethereal doppelgänger trots off down the right path and you split?

I had this moment on the floor of my old bathroom in the apartment I shared with Taylor. I had been evicted. I had nowhere to go other than my car, but it was winter. I'd been hopping couches with whomever would take me and my cat. Finally, I ran out of options, but I'd found temporary work, a day gig as a PA on commercial about tampons and it would be enough to give me a deposit and first month's rent for an apartment or enough to leave. I begged her to let us stay, just for ten days. Just the length of the job. When I knocked, she blocked the door at first, but I looked like I was going to pass out. I'd lost fifteen pounds in three weeks. I think that's why she let me in. I'd been taking showers at the local Equinox, where I still had a membership, though the auto-payment was overdrafting my account every month and I was surely in the running for a shutdown of all traditional banking soon, adding it to the pile of collections that were stacking up against me. I only hoped they could all wait the ten days I needed to make some money. Though I had no idea how I would cash the checks they'd give me. I couldn't use my bank. The money would evaporate. I imagined this is what new immigrants felt when they finally managed to find gainful employment. It was terrifying. I was on the cusp of something disastrous. Taylor knew it. She agreed to let me stay while I worked on the commercial as long as I could pay for the ten days. I had exactly three-hundred and nineteen dollars in cash. She said that was the right amount, but interest would come in the form of abuse for the next ten days.

When I wasn't working, I was chain-smoking through a verbal onslaught of things I wouldn't even say to my worst enemy (Sam, at the time). She never stopped. She never took a breath. I'd be so happy to leave at the crack of dawn for set that I'd walk into the cold streets with tears stinging my cheeks, but smiling. One time I came home after a particularly grueling fifteen-hour shoot day on a bridge in SOHO, to find that someone had forgotten to close the door to the apartment and through the crack, I could see a small group of people who used to be my friends: Gretchen, Kevin, Chris, Amir, Erin, and Taylor all sitting around a dead game of Rock Band, smoking a joint. The conversation consisted of brainstorming how to kill me, with a side of revenge porn for good measure.

I waited in the car for them to leave and when I finally let myself in, Taylor informed me with a vicious smile that someone had accidentally left the door open and my companion of sixteen years, Dixie, my cat, must have wandered out. I locked myself in the bathroom and cried until I knocked my head on the wall and passed out. I awoke to the stench of hot salsa piss and Taylor sitting over me on the toilet, shaking her head at me in a pitying sort of way.

"I've changed my mind," she said reaching between her legs. "I don't want you here." Then she pulled a bloody tampon out of her snatch and held it over my face for a second before chucking it into the trashcan. I closed my eyes and tried to breath. She stood up and flushed. "You need to be out tomorrow," she said as she stepped over me, her heel pinching the flesh of my arm and then my inner thigh, "And I'm keeping the money. Think of it as a tax for being so pathetic."

The door closed behind her and I lay there, a corpse.

And then I made a choice. I chose a path.

I had two options: 1. Reach for the razor resting a foot from my head on the side of the tub or 2. Get up, pack up what I had taken out of my little bag, get in my car, and drive home to Boston.

Now I wonder if part of me is gliding along the slippery slope behind door number one. Part of me wonders if I ever got out of that bathroom. But the other part of me knows the truth.

CHAPTER 21

I watch myself, a bird's eye view of my reality, a camera rigged in the corner above me, that Fictional Depersonalization Syndrome angle, but this is the real deal. There I am, tied into the sleeping bag, my face busted, sleeping, passed out, three days after escaping my own apartment. I awake with a start and fall to the concrete on the little screen in front of me.

I touch my temple as the memory of that jolting pain sears through my skull. Maybe this is the moment when I really started making it all up. I look up and see that there's no camera above me. I check the other corners, the window frame, the old wooden shelf and know that I won't find any cameras. The cameras that I placed are all packed in my bag, they have been on my person all day. I must have taken them down. I must have had an inkling that it was all falling down around me.

I watch the grainy video on my screen and wish that I'd used a better camera than my button camera, so I could see more detail. The me on the screen turns abruptly and glares toward the door, but there's no one there. There was never anyone there. I move onto the next video. There are ten in all ranging from 15 seconds to 15 minutes. I am the star of every single one of them. *Battle Scars. Reality.*

In this first episode, I am sprinting across the warehouse, naked, dancing, running for the bathroom. Acting like a lunatic.

Episode two: I'm cornered by the evidence bag. I'm sitting on my cot with my laptop, in the same spot I'm in now. I'm quickly moving between texting on my phone, calling someone and hanging up, staring at the bag, and frantically searching my computer. And then I'm up and pacing. I stop and stare right into the camera and smile. And then I'm putting on my coat and leaving. Cut to, me back in the cot, writhing around, dreaming of fucking Sam. My hand is jammed in my pants and I'm working it. The sound isn't great, but I'm moaning. I'm moaning and I'm in agony.

My stomach flips. I wait for the door to slide open and for Sam to walk in and wake me, but it doesn't happen. She was never there. The video cuts and I am awake and staring at the ceiling. There is no reality in this. This cannot be real, but as the videos go on, I can't even disbelieve it. I've lost my mind. It's clear. I get up and pace again, mumbling to myself. Then I sit on the cot and pull my laptop open. I'm looking for information about Caeterus. I am alone.

"They want to give a voice to the voiceless," I say, my voice petering off, talking to myself. "A vigilante?" I ask and then laugh at myself. "That's ridiculous. I'm not a vigilante. I'm just fucked up. Sometimes I think I did it to make myself important again, like when I was story producing. But at the end of the day, they were shitty people and no one was going to stop them from taking advantage of people. When Joe and Quinn walked in, I knew what was going to happen. I also knew that I couldn't put the camera down. I needed evidence and—and maybe I knew, maybe somewhere deep down knew that this would do it. I could be important again. I could do something meaningful, but after this, after all this shit, I don't want to be important. I want to disappear," I say and my laughter bursts. An abrupt cut has me on the floor, naked and on my back, near the door. My hands are out of frame, but it's obvious what I'm doing: fucking myself. I squeeze my eyes shut and shake my head, like I'm scrambling an etch-a-sketch. I close out the video and with trepidation pull up the next one.

Episode three is my face in the bathroom mirror and I'm talking to myself again or mumbling to myself. I'm staring myself dead in the eyes and therefore the whole world, dead in the eyes, and saying, "Digital vigilante. Battle Scar, the digital vigilante. She shows you what you don't want, but need to see." I smirk at myself and then say, *"Pew, pew!"* roll my eyes and my face goes dark again. I shake my head and say, "You're an asshole, a gutless coward. Maybe you should fucking die." The video cuts abruptly and then I am picking at my infected tooth with a sewing needle.

I can't bring myself to watch the rest. I don't understand what I've done. In fact, I'm wishing I'd swiped the gun from Quinn's apartment. I'm wishing I could put the cold steel in my mouth and pull the trigger. Instead, I toggle to the dock and find the Final Cut Pro app. I open it and the first project that opens is the episode 15 of Battle Scars. I run my hands over the keys, not pressing any, just feeling, remembering. I close my eyes and have a visceral image of editing the clips. There it is. I remember piecing it together. Or at least I think I do. I slam my MacBook closed and toss it aside on my cot. I walk out into the open space of the loft to search for cameras, tearing the place apart; boxes, crates, debris, I destroy it all. They have to be here somewhere, but I find nothing. I'm good at hiding from myself.

CHAPTER 22

I stopped looking at the news hours ago, after FX dug up my mother, who is living in some redneck commune in Oklahoma. She said the news about me didn't surprise her. I was always a little too far from Jesus to be right. The news volleyed between tearing my psychology and past apart and exploring the depth of my ineptitude as a human, how completely not worthy of life I am.

Joe is still under scrutiny and the talking heads are ripping him to shreds too:

He looks like a serial killer, like Adam Lanza's awkward Italian cousin.

That nose. Has Jack Marino had a blood test done to make sure he's really in the family?

I guess he felt like he had to rape her. How else was he going to get a girl?

Or maybe he didn't know what he was doing. Can a person really be blamed for a crime if they're...not all there?

Joe is not a poor, simple, addled fool. Jack's PR team has made the world think that his son is sick, but somehow they think I'm worse. In three hours the media has managed to completely discredit me as a human being. I am the sicko who got her rocks off shooting a rape video just so I could show the world. I didn't put an age limit on the video, so thousands of kids have seen it. And now it's snuff. I also, allegedly, offered the footage to TMZ first, but even TMZ wouldn't stoop that low.

Caeterus contacted me and told me to wait on the roof, so that's what I'm doing.

I've packed up everything, carefully separating the REI items from my own. I left the folks at REI a note of apology and I truly hope they accept it. I didn't mean to do it and that's the truth. What's left isn't much: my phone, MacBook, walking stick, Brandy's bowl, my cameras, some clothes, me. I am left. My body. It's mine finally. I am left with my body, my mind, and my soul. All of my possessions are piled around me and I'm awaiting a what—a helicopter? Someone traversing the side of the building? A ninja?—I don't know what to expect from Caeterus. I hope they don't kill me.

When I read my mother's words I didn't feel pain or fear anymore. I felt free. I felt free to be exactly as I am. I felt free from the need to create a reality television show out of my life, like the rest of them. That's something, isn't it? I don't need to be seen, because I've seen myself. And I'm fucking beautiful, a glowing orb. I am the reality. I've put on my warmest, heaviest clothes and I'm going to take the plunge. Caeterus says they'll help me. First I have to help myself.

"Scarlet?" a quiet voice says behind me. I turn and see Sam. She's smiling and moving toward me. It only takes that one moment to send me forward, lunging. I turn from her and it seems like minutes before I hear her speak again. "Do it. Jump," she whispers. I turn back to her, ready to follow her command, but she isn't there. She is figment of my fucked up mind, but that one moment of weakness, of turning to her, is all the slippery roof needs from me. My foot slides sideways. I'm about to fall into a dead drop split and I'm crashing. I'm flying. I'm slipping over the side. *Yes. This.* Someone yells, "Scarlet, no! She's jumping! Grab her."

A hand reaches out and grabs awkwardly at me, under the elbow, squeezing the soft flesh there. *They're early*, I think and come down hard on the roof. My head hits something like concrete. It's wet and the air swells with the smells of algae and fish guts. People are screaming, but I only care that I am not, as the world goes black, and the freezing night swallows me whole. Finally, I'm safe.

CHAPTER 23

My brain is on fire. Nothing seems like the truth any more. I've been in this warehouse for weeks and nothing has changed. They left me here. The world is still spinning on its axle and here I am in this cot. I am a part of it now. Pretty soon my skin will become one with it, like a paraplegic in the apocalypse.

I rub sleep from my eyes as the sun cracks the high window just like it has every day for the past—*how many months has it been?* This time the light plays tricks on the concrete in front of me; a crosshatch pattern like wire mesh slices the floor. I reach for the knob on the camp stove to start up the coffee, but my fingers grab air. The stove is gone. Motherfucker. I gave it back. I quickly take inventory and find that it's all gone. The stove, the duffle bags, the food, my cameras, Brandy's bowl, everything. Gone. I gave it all back.

When I stand, my sleeping bag doesn't hold me in. Instead a flimsy, harsh wool blanket falls to the floor around my grey pants. I'm freezing. I've just realized it. I'm so cold. I sit back down on the cot, but it feels different. Solid. Like metal. I need coffee. I need coffee and a cigarette. I reach into the breast pocket of my scrubs and pull out a crumpled Marlboro and a set of matches. At least I have fire. I light the cigarette, closing my eyes, and inhale instant relief. When I open my eyes I see the date etched into the concrete in front of me, a kind of prehistoric calendar. I remember scraping my knuckles when the screw I was holding to carve the dates slipped. I look at my knuckles. Right there. The knuckle of my middle finger is caked with dry blood and it hurts to bend it, but I do anyway as I inhale again. I only have centimeters left to smoke, but this will do.

Outside, somewhere in the open density of the warehouse, maybe where the dock meets the loading zone, I hear the heavy door scrape and slide. I'm standing when I hear footsteps, two sets, and what sounds like the static of a two-way radio. They're here. I stub the cigarette out and slowly move to the end of the cot. There I drop to my knees as the footsteps grow louder, getting closer. I slink under the cot and pull the wool blanket down to shield me. Beneath the cot rests my carving screw. I remember throwing it now, right after I scraped the skin off my knuckle.

My fingers slowly close on it and I push it through my fore and middle finger just like I was taught to do with my car keys when they made us take that self-defense class my freshman year of high school. I can't count the number of times I've been without keys, but in serious need of them. Now this screw. It's long enough to take someone's eye out. It's long enough to rip open the flesh of cheeks, arms, testicles, whatever. If they come for me I will yell "rape" not "fire" like I was taught. I will call it as it feels.

I hear scraping, like metal on concrete, and it's mind numbing. They must be right outside. My breath quickens and I can feel tasteless white bread caught like a genetically modified lump in my throat. Dinner. It's still there. Two sets of feet stop moving and then a voice, female, but deep and bored says, "Battell, I can see your fucking foot, you idiot. Get out here." I glance at my foot and see that it is in fact sticking out. My eyes dart around the room, looking for an exit, but I don't move. I can't move. I'm pinned.

"Stop playing games, Battell. You want me to call in Oates?" Her voice is mocking, almost singsong. It makes my stomach twist as I rack my brain for an Oates, but find none. Then it hits me like a kaleidoscope: a man, Oates, in a security guard's uniform, holding me against the wall, a concrete wall, his left hand forcing my chin to the ceiling while his right is inside my scrubs and he's kneading my tits like dough. I am not crying. I am gritting my teeth. I am waiting for him to get it the fuck over with. I'm about to do it. I'm about scream rape when my foot is yanked violently and I'm pulled out from under the bed, my scrub top pulled up by the concrete. I feel a burn start near my bellybutton and I kick out to fight them off, but my foot comes out of the wool sock it was nestled in and the woman in front of me falls backward. I have seconds to figure this out, seconds to know where to go.

Before me in light khaki, just likes Oates was wearing, is an imposing boat of a lady. Beyond her is another woman in grey, her partner? The security guard is struggling to get up, but it looks like she whacked her head just hard enough that I have a chance here. I can run. I fumble over her, kneeing her right in the crotch and she yells out in pain but grabs for my other leg as I go. I kick her off of me, landing a heel squarely in her gullet and move fast past the other woman, who only holds her hands to her chest, as if in prayer. She wears dull bracelets and her eyes are squeezed shut.

I'm through a barred door and running, but nothing seems right. It's too clean, too pristine. I am surrounded by doors and like a crack of the sound barrier, suddenly I hear screaming and banging all around me, animals screaming before they attack. I stop. My one naked foot sticks to the shiny poured concrete floor. There is a red light and a siren wailing at me and then I'm flying through the air as a crushing blow from behind catapults me into a metal table. My face smashes on the surface and I taste blood. They've found me. The Marinos. The police. Oates has found me. Sam. Taylor. FX News. The Sigma Alpha Epsilon frat boys. My mother. Hot tears pour down my cheeks.

"What the fuck is wrong with you? We're just bringing in your celly. You were doing so well. Now you're fucked." The lady guard yanks me up by the back of my scrubs and I find that my hands have been bound behind me. Finally, I see the doors circling me. This is not my warehouse. This is not my hiding place. This is nothing like I remembered. And I hear the radio static again, but this time the lady behind me is speaking into it.

"Matthews for Briggs." She waits and then says, "Get Collins on the line. Battell's going to the hole. I need his John Hancock." She is slightly out of breath. Again, I don't hear a response. It must be in her ear. She says, "A month this time." She waits and her big tits are pushing into me from behind, rising and falling between my shoulder blades. I stare into the windows of the doors around me and see faces: white, black, brown, yellow. All of the eyes are white though and they are wide, some smiling, some terrified. I blink, but they are still there. I must be imaging this. I turn my head slightly to try to see her and she continues, "I don't know what the fuck is wrong with you."

When I turn back, Oates is standing in front of me, smirking down at me, his meaty thumb hooked into the waistband of his pants, almost hidden by the underside of his belly. I have a flash and a whiff of Cookie. My legs crumple. I don't see or hear anything after that, but when I wake, I am in a four-walled room with no windows and there is a new calendar on the wall. I've scraped twenty-nine days in what looks like blood. I am wearing the same clothes I went into the hole wearing. There is a burnt brown stain that reaches from my collar down into the material of the neck of my scrubs and ends somewhere near my belly button.

I remember the bloody spit now. I remember everything. I remember REI. I remember the police lights in my warehouse. I remember that video, that fucking video everywhere. I remember Sam and Hollywood and then no Sam. I remember being crushed into the table by Matthews. I remember Oates. I remember the look on my new cellmate's face as I ran past her trying to escape into a circular room full of caged women animals. The look on her face fell somewhere between fear and nervous breakdown. And then I remember that all of our faces look like that in here. IN here. In HERE. #InHere. Inside of here I haven't seen the Internet in months. Inside of here, I only hear rumors about The Marinos and that video. In here they know who I am. Some of them leave me alone because of it.

"Cold, man. Fucking cold."

Most of them want to kill me. Some of them want to be me. All those eyes staring out at me, eating up my guilt, my worthlessness, my fame.

"I wish I'da shot that motherfucker. I'd be a gazillionaire."

"You know the kinda money you coulda got just going on fucking *Ellen* with that shit? Set for life, bitch. But you're just a pussy, aren't you?"

"You taped that shit? What kinda rat are you? Sitting there while that girl gets fucked up. What if we fuck you up? See how you like it." Sometimes they punched me and I'd have to defend myself. Twice there has been a riot over my video. It's all coming back to me now. YouTube commenters in the flesh, every day in here. My new cellmate is probably settled in at this point. We will be strangers going in and going out. I will go back to my cold bunk. No warm sleeping bag to hold me. No camp stove to warm me. I will be disallowed even a pen to put to paper. I can't even get my transgressions out of my head. Inside of here, everything is loud and banging off the walls of my skull. Inside of here I am exactly as they see me, but at least I finally told the truth.

I close my eyes as the electric sun directly above me in the ceiling starts to set, just like it does every night at seven and I hope that my public defender can help me get out of here on time. I need to disappear.

CHAPTER 24

Mary Wolcott is a thin woman. I've only ever seen her eat nut crackers and drink Kombucha. Her makeup is applied in a way that doesn't look like makeup at all and her hair is always tied back in a messy bun. She wears Birkenstocks over thick wool socks and smells like patchouli and the woods of Southern New Hampshire. I can't help but like her. When she smiles at me, she means it.

"Hi, Mary."

"Scarlet. Come on in," she says looking up at me from an open file folder on her desk. Her smile falters at my appearance. I haven't been allowed a shower in three days, so that's where my problems start. Outside of that, I'm sure I'm pasty and too skinny. I can't eat the food when they shove the tray through the slot in the door of the hole because they always scrape the food on the metal and everything tastes like blood and dead, dry, crusty-somethings. I itch my forehead where a pimple has turned into a small volcano of a sore and feel the wetness of blood.

"Jesus. Here." Mary hands me a tissue.

"Sorry," I say and take it, plopping down in the vinyl seat across from her desk.

"You don't have to apologize, Scarlet."

I nod. I know this, but I can't help myself.

"They want to extend my sentence," I say as the vernacular escapes me.

Mary nods and shuffles a few files around on her desk. She licks her finger and opens my file, scanning while saying, "I saw something about that."

"I had a bad dream and acted out," I say a little too quickly. I focus on my breath.

Mary nods again and asks, "They said you attacked Matthews and tried to make a run for it?"

I nod, but interrupt myself by shaking my head. "Yes and no. I was dreaming."

"Hallucinating?"

"No." I shake my head. "I don't think so."

Mary sits back and studies me over clasped hands. Her vinyl chair squeaks as she rocks, "They want to add twenty more days to your sentence."

"No. Please." I breathe the words out like they're all I have left. "I don't deserve—I didn't mean to do it. I swear it will never happen again. Mary, I've been in the hole for almost a whole month this time. I feel like an animal. I've barely seen sunlight or another human other than the guards. They wouldn't let me see you. I didn't do anything bad enough for solitary."

"I know," she says and studies me over intertwined fingers. "They're leaving it up to me to evaluate you."

I lean forward, my cuffed hands clasped in front of me and consider dropping to my knees to beg. "Mary, please. I don't think I'll make it in here. Oates is, he's—" I can't say the words. I put my eyes in my hand and squeeze, making tiny sparks of light shoot into my brain. I can't claim that he's doing to me what's been done before, what Joe did to Quinn, even if it is true. I can't say it. I never could.

"Did Oates do something to you, Scarlet?"

I shake my head. It's not a denial, more of a shaking off of images.

"You wouldn't be the first to make this claim," she says.

I shake my head. She nods and lets me sit in the silence.

"Do you still think that this place is a secret organization of cyber hackers named Caeterus?" she asks me abruptly. She hasn't asked this question in weeks. I shake my head. Five weeks ago the answer was different.

"Do you believe that Caeterus is a real organization?" she asks.

I hesitate, but then shake my head and say, "No."

When I first started seeing Mary I begged her to let me show her my email, to show her the emails that Caeterus had sent me. I wouldn't let it go. Several times I was hysterical. That was before the Paxil. Just after the Paxil, I had a psychotic break and thought bearded men in black suits with no faces were coming to recruit me into their secret organization. During one tirade about Caeterus (I thought they were still waiting for me to meet them on the roof), Mary whipped her laptop around and ordered me to type my Gmail account information in. I felt so relieved. Finally, someone believed me. I pulled up my account and quickly scanned four-months' worth of Sephora and Modell's junk mail, press inquiries, and hate mail.

"Do it quickly, Scarlet. I could get into a lot of trouble for this," Mary said.

I typed Caeterus into the search field, my fingers stumbling over the keys, like an inexperienced lover fumbling to undo a button. I hit enter, looking at Mary with a berserk smile on my face. When I looked back at the screen, my face fell. My search returned zero results. Mary pursed her lips. She felt sorry for me. She slowly turned the computer away.

"I've searched every way I can think for the organization Caeterus, but they just don't exist, Scarlet. You should feel better knowing that it's not real. You have proof now."

I fell back in my seat, tears making my eye sockets swell. After that they switched me to Wellbutrin and I felt practically nothing from that point on besides a dry mouth.

"Do you believe that you acted alone in recording and releasing the footage of the Topsail rape as well as the subsequent videos of yourself on the internet?"

I nod. The answer was different five weeks ago.

"Do you know that you are in the Suffolk County Prison and that you have thirty-seven days remaining of an eight-month sentence for shoplifting, violating the Commonwealth's Wiretapping Law, and negligence in reporting a crime?"

"I do."

Mary nods and thinks on me.

"Did Oates hurt you?"

I look her directly in the eyes and make a choice. "Yes," I say.

She sends me away with a denial of sentence extension, a written note to be released from the hole, and a separate note that grants me permission to have a private shower.

On the way to the showers Matthews lets me stop in the yard where I stand and tilt my head toward the sun. The butches play football. One football blots out the glowing orb above me and as I squint into it, a tall, dark-skinned butch, Jackson, catches it. I can't be sure where it came from. It seems like no one threw it, like it came from the sky itself, over the wall where the barbed-wire keeps us caged like monkeys. I blink again and move back inside where the concrete is cool and dark. I can't trust my eyes. I still can't trust my brain.

CHAPTER 25

Matthews leads me down a long corridor that smells like bleach and it immediately reminds me how unclean I am. They tell me I have a visitor, but I can't imagine who that might be. I have no family. I have no lovers. I only have enemies and fans.

The last time Matthews led me down this too bright hallway and into the visitor's room, I was met by a tiny, ancient black woman, who didn't say a word to me for five minutes. We were seated across from one another and she just stared cold and hard into my eyes. I began to cry and she hissed, "Stop yourself."

This was the first time someone had focused any true emotion in my direction in months, so I held her gaze.

"You took her life," she said and I nodded. "You hateful little girl. You took her soul in that video. You took my grandbaby's soul and held it there and then you kept your dumb trap shut. You are just as responsible as those men. Foul men."

Again, I nodded my agreement. Again, she waited in silence for the right words to come.

"I forgive you," she said and I sucked in relieved, painful breath. Several other inmates turned and she nodded in their direction and said loudly again, "I forgive her." Then she looked back at me, her expression never softening. "You did wrong. You did another human being so wrong. I feel it deep in my bones. But I believe you started out in the right place. I'm not going to pretend I don't know what my—my baby went through. I'm not going to pretend anymore. I suspect you know that pain as well. I can see it in those sad eyes of yours. I suspect this is why you did the foolish things you did when you could have done the right thing."

Tears beat down my cheeks and I nodded again.

"Yes, ma'am," I said and then, "I'm sorry."

"Yes. You are." She stood up slowly, like every bone in her legs might crumble and I stood too, my hands still cuffed, head bowed, like I was hoping for more of a blessing, hoping for a hug maybe. She hooked a gnarled finger under my chin and lifted my head until I was looking her in the eye one more time and then she said, "You do the right thing next time, Scarlet Battell." Then, without hesitating, she smacked me hard, so hard, with an open palm against my cheek. I closed my eyes and listened to her walk away, her shuffling heels clacking, moving slowly, but with purpose against the poured concrete floor. It was the best I could have expected, I suppose. Sometimes I wake and feel her hand connecting with my flesh. It comforts me and I fall back into dreamless sleep.

Today is new. Another visitor. I don't have anyone on my list, so I don't know what to expect. I hope they'll unshackle me in case I'm meeting someone who doesn't look like they'll crumble and blow away in the wind. I enter the intake cell, a glass box really, and Matthews pats me down again, like she did ten minutes ago when we left my cell. Matthews likes to pat me down. She always stops near my hips and her touch gets soft and gooey, like she's got her hands in a fresh batch of Play-Doh. Her fingers are light in the dip of my hip and it makes my brain fuzzy. Matthews is the only touch I get anymore and it's not enough. Her hands slide down either side of my spine. She's quicker when the cameras are on, all business.

I look out into the visitors' room, where roughly ten people sit awaiting their prisoners. There are babies in there. Three of them, to be exact, and the idea that they would let dangerous criminals like me into a room with children unnerves me.

I see a mix of races, black, white, Hispanic, one tiny Asian lady and an even tinier Asian grandmother sitting next to her. They seem the most nervous to be here. Men hold the babies and speak in hushed tones to their prisoners. I recognize Rodriguez, who I buy cigarettes from, sitting across from a big, bulky woman with a lot of tattoos. Butchy is fondling a cigarette in front of her on the McDonald's-style table anchored to the floor. The two women don't make eye contact, but the Butchy looks up when the buzzer goes off to signify the door is opening and a prisoner is entering. Rodriguez glances at me and nods in my direction. I nod back. Matthews unlocks the cuffs, shoves me forward into the room, and says, "Fifteen minutes, Battell."

All the faces in the room are staring at me, except one. His head is bent over his entwined hands, like he's praying. His head is shaved and the dark stubble on his scalp doesn't hide the almost healed scar from stitches holding his flesh together there. His nose looks like it's been broken more times than I'd originally thought, and his lips are hidden under a thick growth of beard, but I know his upper lip, the puffy one, has a deep scar as well. His leg bounces under the table, a nervous jig, but it stops completely when I approach the table, standing over him. I can feel the women behind me craning to get a glimpse of him, but I'm shielding him from their hungry eyes.

"Lucky?"

He looks up when the sandy sound of his name leaves my lips. His eyes are rabid.

"Sit," he says and I do.

"What are you doing here?"

His hands clasp and unclasp, but his eyes are clearing up as he stares into mine.

"I put some cash in your com account."

"Thank you," I say. He looks away from me. "Why did you do that?"

He nods, but not in agreement. He nods like he's psyching himself up to go in the ring, repeating mantras in his head to get past the fear. I know, because I do this. *I am whole, perfect, strong, powerful, loving, harmonious, happy, healthy, and good. I am whole, perfect, strong…*

"Are you okay?"

I nod, but can't make myself say liar's words.

"You get jumped?"

"Not this week." I smile weakly. He doesn't smile back. "I've been in the hole for a month."

He shakes his head, clenching his jaw. "How's your head?"

I immediately touch the healing acne on my forehead, but realize he's not talking about my pimples. "Okay," I say.

"Really?"

"It's okay, Lucky. I'm not like healthy, totally, I guess." The words feel like a confession of sorts, but one that I'm not quite ready to make. He looks at me again and sadness and pity crease the lines of his face.

"You had a lot happen to you," he says.

I nod.

"I did too."

Again, I nod my agreement, waiting. I'm waiting for him to berate me. I'm waiting for him to tear me down, accuse me of ruining his life. I'm waiting for the relief to follow his tirade, but none comes.

"I know. I'm sorry for what I did to you. Truly."

He shakes his head. "Joe did this to me," he says quietly and then adds, "They convicted him today. I just came from the courthouse."

I take a deep breath and let it go into all of the dark corners of the room.

"He got five years…at St. Helen's."

"The mental facility?" I ask. Lucky nods and the nod turns into a soft shake.

"Donnie and Nate got twenty-five a piece. They killed Quinn," he says in a matter-of-fact tone. I think he's made his peace with her name. I stare at my hands, trying not to shake, trying not to show any emotion as he continues, "Jack's still holding office, but he's under a whole new level of scrutiny and a lot of people are saying he might step down as Governor, which means Apolito would succeed him."

Neither one of us knows what to say about this, so we don't say anything. Thirty seconds go by before he speaks again, like he's lining up his thoughts. "Did you know I was in Iraq off and on for three years?" The table moves with the motion of his leg beneath it. I fall into the rhythm and let it soothe me.

I nod. "I saw your soldier headshot on the news."

He looks at his twisted hands, shakes his head, like I've misunderstood something. "I wasn't a soldier. I didn't fight. I was a reporter's assistant and a cameraman."

I pull in a deep breath and imagine him running to catch up with a reporter while munitions cause the dirt all around him to fly. He's covered in tan silt and the dust rests on his eyelashes. I was wrong about him.

"I was in Kabul when that suicide bomb went off near the NATO Compound."

"I had no idea."

"There were babies in the street, bleeding, dismembered, most of them dead. It hit at 4:37 a.m. and the village around the compound was mostly civilian. There was an orphanage. There were babies in the street, bleeding, dismembered, dead." He doesn't catch himself on his repetition. "I had to shoot it. I had to film those kids, those people, dead. It was my job. I had to report the news. Kip, my reporter, had his leg blown off. It happened right in front of John and me. John was the main camera guy. He fucking ran. You believe that?"

I shook my head. I wanted to reach out and grab his lump of hands, wound like angry intestines. They were turning purple under the pressure of his fingers, but I knew as soon as I did, the guard would yell, "No touching!" and my visit might get cut short. So I kept my hands in my lap and listened to his story.

"He ran and left me and Kip with the camera. Kip shoved it into my hands and screamed at me. I don't even remember what he said, but I knew I had to keep shooting. I found an aid worker to take Kip out and I just ran. I ran into a dust cloud and when I came out on the other side, the dirt streets were running with blood and there were babies. I couldn't save them. That's when I turned the camera on. My ears were ringing from the blast. I could only hear myself breathing." A guttural burp of laughter leaves his lips and he smiles at his hands before continuing, "I could hear myself whimpering in the dead space between my ears where my hearing had fucking left me. I was crying in my throat and the children who were alive were screaming silently at me. I thank the universe every day that I couldn't hear them scream. I was able to help a woman get several of the children to safety and the aid workers started their sweep fast. I stepped back and recorded them, recorded the bomb site like a crater in the street, recorded the

men and women taken to safety as the sun came up on their village."
He stops abruptly and looks at me again, his forehead a mess of
wrinkles, thoughts like rivers caught in the lines there.

"My footage was the only footage to air directly following the
attacks. When they analyzed it, they saw three Taliban insurgents
running from the wreckage, carrying the remains of the suicide
bomber."

I think he expects this to mean something to me, but it doesn't.

"The Taliban pledged their commitment to Afghan peace talks
prior to the blast. They obviously weren't really going to go through
with it."

"So your footage showed that the Taliban were responsible?"

He nods. "It also showed a lot of dead bodies and mutilation. A
lot of blood and chaos." He's wringing his hands again and the leg is
going a mile a minute under the table. "I also made the rookie mistake
of uploading the footage to the live server and not to my producers
back at CNN."

I can't stop my mouth from dropping open and inhaling a slow,
strong breath. "You uploaded it to CNN's live server? So…everyone
saw it?"

He nods. "Not everyone, but a lot of people."

"I was fired immediately, sent packing on a plane home with about
four hundred bucks to my name. When I got back, I had
approximately seven thousand emails, most of them death threats and
people telling me what kind of scum I was for airing dead babies. I
had to move home with my dad. I had to get a new job. My girlfriend
left me."

I laugh. I don't mean to, it's just that the story is too familiar.

"So the Topsail?" I ask and he nods, but the nod dissolves into a
shake of the head.

"I thought I was safe. I thought I could meld into the background."

"And I fucked that up for you." I close my eyes, finally realizing why he's here. The last person in the world who is talking to me is about to tell me to fuck off and die. Great.

"No," he says and I stare into his tired eyes. "You reminded me of who I am. You reminded me that there are some things worth fighting for—"

"Battell, five minutes!" Matthews yells from the control booth. My teeth grind down and I stare at my hands, clenched like Lucky's. My leg is starting to move and I realize that the trauma in my body has to find its way out somehow, or I'm going to implode.

"You kept shooting. Most people would have put the camera down. You helped prove my innocence. You showed the world the disgusting truth about what happens to some women. You helped put those shitheads away. You did the right thing, Scarlet."

"Quinn died, I robbed an REI, and I took over a warehouse *illegally* because I'd convinced myself it was a Bat Cave downtown," I remind him. I conveniently leave out the fact that I also conjured up an old lover to keep me company during that time. No one needs to know that but me.

He takes a moment to think about this. "I'm sorry Quinn died. I wish we all could have helped her come forward. I wish they hadn't been such shitty human beings to begin with, but you didn't kill Quinn. You proved that douchebag, Marino, and his two dogs did." He looks at me and I must be begging for more of this with my eyes, because he goes on, "Our brain does fucked up things when it's scared or when it's experienced trauma. Or when trauma becomes a way of life." His knowing glance opens me up and I feel the stinging tears of what would love to become a sob clog up my throat.

"I'm not saying that robbing the REI was right, but it's okay. And you've served your time for that. You didn't hurt anyone. You were only trying to survive."

"What if I'm really fucked up?" I ask, leaning forward as if he has all the answers. But he just shakes his head, lets his lips shrug and for a brief second I fall down the hole of remembering that I wanted to kiss him at one point. I'd wanted to put my body on his and now I understand why and it hurts that I can't.

"You're not. Or you are. We're all a little fucked up." He smiles finally.

"Those videos…the *other* videos. I can't believe you're here talking to me after seeing that shit." I scoff.

He studies me, looks through me, like he's analyzing my blood. "Did you watch your videos?" he asks me.

I don't know what he means. "Only once. I couldn't—they made me sick. I was delusional. I wasn't myself," I explain.

"I watch them a lot," he says and this burns holes right through my cheeks. "I wonder why you edited them so heavily?" he asks.

I shake my head, "I don't know. It's all so hazy for me still. I can barely remember what happened. I can't piece everything together so that it makes sense."

He nods, thinks on it. "Well, you should watch them again. They're interesting. You're interesting," he says and I'm torn between being intrigued by him and a little frightened that he thinks what I did is fascinating.

"Battell! Time's up," Matthews hollers and it shocks my system. Lucky stands. I hear the metal of the barred door scraping behind me and know that Matthews is coming. I stand too.

"I'll keep looking," he says and for a second I think he's trying to tell me something, but know that it's probably just my overactive imagination at play again. I know that when I walk away, that thought, the one of him studying me, studying my body, my habits, my secrets will keep me going.

"I'll be here when you get out. Maybe we can watch them together. I have a new place in Southie. You can see the ocean from my living room window. It's quiet," he says and then, before Matthews has her hands on me, he reaches out and pulls me to him.

"No touching!" Matthews yells and I can hear the misstep in her voice signaling that she's been caught off guard. Lucky goes in for a kiss on my cheek, but he misses and his warm lips hit the corner of my mouth. The affect is instantaneous; my lips quiver and form a smile, something foreign to me, something I thought I'd said goodbye to. His beard tickles me and sends shivers down my legs. There are catcalls and whistles all around us. It makes my smile wider, my teeth bared, like a guilty dog, the high school dream I never knew.

"We'll get that coffee, okay?" he says and his hand grasps mine. My lips touch his nose awkwardly. I can feel a deep scar at the base before they land again, just above his beard. Then Matthews pulls me out of his arms. Her immediate punishment is to whip me around so that I can't see him anymore, but I don't need to. I got what I needed.

When I get back to my cell, my new cellmate, Hernandez, keeps her distance, which is exactly what I want. I drop my blanket and personals bag on the low bunk and crawl in, resting my back against the wall. She stares at me through a wall of thick black hair, only one eye peering out.

"I'm Scarlet."

"Yeah. I know who you are. You're fucking loca. Don't talk to me."

I smile at her like the maniac that she thinks I am. She walks to the bunk and pulls herself up. When I'm completely alone, I open the tiny, sweaty piece of paper I've been clutching in my palm since Lucky put it there ten minutes ago. I open it and read the words: *the shadow over the line.*

I have no idea what it means.

CHAPTER 26

Two weeks later, I understand everything. I'm putting books back on the shelf in the library and my own throaty moans reach my ears. I am embedded in the stacks, so I could hide and listen. At first, I think, *surely it's in my head. Surely I'm hearing the moans of my alter ego as she gets her head bashed in or gets fucked. Stop that. Fucking stop that right now. If you don't stop it, they'll never let you out.* I snap the rubber band Mary gave me to remind myself not to be crazy and it zips the air and stings the flesh on my wrist. But the sounds are still there. Then someone sniggers. My body goes cold with humiliation. I hear myself close to climax and someone nearby grunts low and throaty, "Mmmh. Shit yes," in response to my moan.

I put the battered copy of *East of Eden* back on the shelf between *The Notebook* and a misplaced copy of *The Stand*, straighten the spines, and moved my cart full of books closer to the sound of my sex. I peer over and through the stacks and find three inmates surrounding the old PC that sits at the law library desk. Mahoney is the only one allowed to use it because she's been in for eleven years and has been working at the library for the past seven. But now she has Jackson. I recognize her from the yard. The football. I thought she was a jock, but now that I'm getting a good look at her, I see a bespectacled, burly geek-thug sitting at the keyboard. This warms me to her for some reason. Next to her, Hernandez, my skinny-ass, attitudinal new cellmate.

"Daaay-um," Mahoney says and Jackson shoots her a look of annoyance. Mahoney straightens up. "But I mean seriously, Battell's a freak, Jack. C'mon. Look at this shit," she says and points at the monitor. "She's talking at herself like she's a friggin' super hero."

The monitor looks black to me, dusty even, like it hasn't been used since 1993, but they're all staring at it and from a speaker, my voice emanates. I move toward them slowly until I'm standing right behind them. I'd heard a rumor that Jackson was a hacker, but had no idea she was this skilled. I can't remember video even being able to play on a relic like—then I see it and for a moment, my heart pangs, like I've seen a childhood friend who broke up with me because I fucked her boyfriend—an iPhone, its screen cracked and smudged. One of my videos plays and despite the shattered screen, I can see, and worse, hear everything. Hernandez leans in, getting closer to the screen, a look of disgust on her face. I see myself, naked, writhing on the floor, alone. I flush with embarrassment.

"Dude, she your celly. You hit that?" Mahoney asks Hernandez over her shoulder.

"Shut the fuck up, Mahoney." Jackson says and shoves her glasses into her nose.

"I ain't no dyke," Hernandez says, but I can't hear them anymore. I'm staring at the YouTube video, specifically at the black spray-painted line on the floor under my ass, split by a shard of glass. My heart stops. Literally it stops for three full seconds until I expel the air right onto Hernandez's back and she jumps out of the way before turning on me.

"Let me see that," I mutter. My voice sounds sandy, my words stuck in the back of my throat. The other two jump and Jackson stands quickly, shoving the phone into the waistband of her pants, glancing over her shoulder to the guard seated behind the glass just outside the library door.

"Fuck, Battell. Why you sneaking up on us like that, creepy ass motherfucker," Hernandez says.

"Let me fucking see it," I say again and shove past her.

"Creepy-ass puta fucking yourself on camera." I can feel the spittle from her words hit my ear. She's in my face now, her hot breath on my lips, her forehead inches from my own. Jackson and Mahoney step back to watch, Mahoney with a grisly smile on her face.

"Are you two gonna fuck now?" Mahoney asks through her smirk.

"Nah. Hernandez isn't my type," I say.

"'Cause I don't look like your hand?" she asks.

I smile because none of this shit matters anymore. I've seen the line. Now I need to get rid of Hernandez. I tear my eyes away from hers and stare at Jackson. Her breath is fast as she waits to see what I'll do. I need a new celly. Jackson's the only one on our block up for a new cellmate. I stare back at Hernandez and put my hands on her hips, tight. She kicks my right hand away with the butt of her hand.

"Fuck off me," She hisses.

"You definitely don't smell as sweet as my hand, that's for sure, taco tits," I say and she shoves me hard in the chest. Mahoney doesn't wait around to watch. She splits. But Jackson is rooted to the spot. I smile before I shove Hernandez back harder and she goes down like a lost game of Jenga. When she bounces back up she head butts me as hard as she can in my forehead. I brace myself for it and hope that the split in my forehead will cover the scar of my acne in the future.

It was the last concussion I sustained in prison. After Jackson told the guards what happened— "Hernandez totally jumped Battell and fucked her up."—they traded out Hernandez. "Taco Tits" was just the right amount of fucked up to set her off. They replaced her with Jackson and I finally got laid, with a side of smartphone for my troubles. For the last thirty days of my stay, I study my own videos on the cracked screen and learn so much about myself. For starters, I am not now, nor have I ever been crazy.

CHAPTER 27

I wish I could explain what it feels like to be without your own liberty, to have it stripped from you, to never know when you'll get it back, if ever, but the words don't come easily. I walked out of Suffolk County with nothing, but the items in the personals sack they'd put together when I went in: my wallet with my now expired license, my GoPhone, and four-hundred and seventeen dollars. No one met me at the gate. Well, no one real anyway. There were a handful of reporters who wanted to snap my photo while I stepped into a cab. I'd called Sean O'Toole to pick me up, but his number belonged to someone else now. Lucky didn't come. Being too close to the jail made him uneasy.

The reporters shouted things like, "Your 'web series' has had millions of hits, Scarlet. Have you seen it?" or "How does it feel to know that millions of people have seen your masturbation video?" or "Taylor Blakesley says the last time you saw each other you got physical with her. Can you comment? Did you abuse your ex-girlfriend?" or "What now, Scarlet?"

I didn't answer. I didn't really know. I stepped into the cab and watched out the back window as they followed me TMZ-style to the halfway house I'd been relegated to on Powder House Avenue in Somerville. I had another three-month sentence imposed on me here. I was to live out of this house with several other female strangers for the next 90 days while I became acclimated to my new life as a janitor at Tufts University down the street. For ninety days I would pay the halfway house 25% of my minimum wage income and I would agree to refrain from using cameras at my place of work or in the house. I would also need to search for my own living space upon completion of my probationary period. Though I had no idea how I was going to afford rent anymore on what I was making as a trash picker upper and floor cleaner.

It's not all bad though. I got what little of myself I had back because it was all in my possession when they arrested me on the roof. So I have my laptop. All the raw footage of Battle Scars is there, every video of me. It's hard to see, but I'm glad it's in my hands and not someone else's. I see Lucky almost every day. We've become good friends. We spend hours poring over the footage on my YouTube and hard drive, taking notes and discussing angles. We don't drink anything harder than coffee and I have to say that living and breathing in sober air has changed my perspective on the world. Lucky is kind. He's also an amazing cook and a yogi. He's teaching me yoga. We do it in his apartment in Southie. I take the train over and climb the four flights to his apartment, which is the top floor of an old Captain's house that faces the water. In the eight months that I've been in, Lucky sued the Marinos and won his case and a large settlement from Jack. He deserves it. I call it his hero's pay and he just smiles a sad smile that is broken by a small scar near his flume where Donnie hit him with his class ring. The tooth beneath the lip is brand new though and shines brighter than the rest when he smiles for real. So we do yoga and eat good food and I have to say that life feels like it has potential, especially when Lucky smiles at me. He knows my plan. He wants to help, but I tell him I have to do it on my own.

Before I can know for sure, before I can trust in it, before I know what the future holds, I have some shit to take care of. I don't complain that I'm a graveyard janitor at a University where I clean up after rich kids from foreign lands, hipsters, and locals. I don't complain because there is an end in sight. It's been a really good experience actually. I'm humbled. I'm in a position where I can start over and reinvent myself. I pulled the Topsail attack video off of my YouTube, but it didn't matter. It's been posted so many times on other sites that it will exist forever in the ether. I've left the *Battle Scars* web series up though, as a reminder to keep looking for the truth and also because the videos combined have had eight million hits. It's relevant. I am relevant. I've been releasing more videos too, ones I shot when no one was looking with my old button cam.

Like the one with the cop in Teele who sat right down on the ground next to Janice, one of the local homeless folks. Janice's feet are so swollen and infected that she can barely walk, so sometimes she just sits where she is. This cop on this sunny day before anything bad happened, he bought and shared a lunch with her. A goddamned picnic on the concrete against a chain link fence on Broadway. A few other cops stopped by and joined them. That was a good one. When I went through my button cam footage from my days wandering this city, I found so much, everything I'd been looking for in fact, all the stuff I missed because fear made me angry.

A dad and his daughter on the swings.

A bus driver who stood up and whirled a college girl around his pointer finger as she stepped onto the bus.

Jose and the Pomeranian. That one wasn't the greatest, but I think it spoke to everyone's judgements. And besides the dog was wicked cute and cute dogs get tons of hits.

While Lucky and I upload new ones and scour the old web series videos thousands of hits come through and even more comments. It's an interesting dialogue. Some have called it performance art and I'd have to agree. I was quite the performer.

I watch everything and everyone now. I pull apart every scene in front of me, dissecting it like a roadkill feline in eleventh grade biology. The vernacular, the body stance, the shadows. My body. My movement. That fucking line. Other people have micro-expression-blueprints all over their faces and in the muscles under their skin. They just don't know it, but it all matters.

A kid staring at his phone on the corner, his spine curved like an alien, spinning the wheel of Facebook. He's not really reading humblebrags or vague posts from his friends though. His cautious hidden side eye tells me that he is fantasizing about the group of volleyball players next to him, with their high buns and long legs, their infectious laughter. He wants to be in the middle of a pile of them while they accost him with their tongues and that giggling, nonsensical vocal fry. The lady sitting next to him with the bad perm and Princess Leia t-shirt? She wants the same, but with kittens. Lots of kittens.

The old man in a cabby hat and cable knit sitting at a table on the patio of the local café, reading the paper? He's read the same line four times because the young barista who is sweeping the patio around him reminds him of his son, who died in Iraq seven years ago. He keeps asking the kid about his plans for the future and then going back to his paper to read the line about the fifth shooting in East Boston this month. He smiles and tears up as he reads it before turning back to the barista and asking, "You like the Sox?" and the kid, uncomfortable with conversation with a stranger, just shakes his head. The old man turns back to his paper, reads the line again, tears pooling. A lot of what we say doesn't come from the mouth, but the eyes. My eyes, for instance, used to scream fear, but they reflect a lot more now. I don't hide anything. It's a waste of a life. Honesty is the air I breathe.

I have eleven days left. In eleven days I will be free of this house and though I don't have a new place yet, I have a plan. Lucky says I can stay with him if I need to, but I don't think I will, well maybe not more than a few days. First I'm going to New York.

"You fucking take my soap, Batt—"

"No," I say before Nico, who sticks her head in my room angry, squinty eyes first, can finish, "Try Cooper."

"She says you did it."

"Well she's a fucking liar. Close the door."

Eleven more days of this. No more communal shower where I have to tromp through Cooper's thick pubic hair that I swear she shaves every other day. No more missing food from the refrigerator or underwear stolen from the wash. Maybe I could live at Lucky's for a minute. Maybe New Hampshire, Vermont. Who knows. I only know that I'm not running anymore and I'm not desperate. Isn't that funny? I should be. I should feel that I have nothing, but I have everything.

I swipe my phone open and click on the voicemail. I listen to a message from so long ago, the only one preserved in my phone since before I went in. It's 29 seconds long and that kid's voice saying, "It's her." It gives me nervous chills, so I listen to him again. *I know this voice.* I listen another five times just to be sure and then I drop my phone in my bag. I make a note on my to-do list.

Get the call sheet.

CHAPTER 28

I take the bus into the city. It's a five-hour trip that gives me time to think. There's no one next to me, so I stretch out and stare up through the window at the slow moving stars above me. I'll arrive at Penn Station at 7:30 tonight, grab a bite at Starlight and make my way uptown. They'll be in Midtown I assume, close enough to walk. I'll need to be there between 9:00 and 10:00 just after day wrap. I have a lot of questions for him, but *why* is the biggest one. It weighs on me because there could be a lot of reasons, none of which are big enough to garner this kind of sabotage, but we'll get to that, I'm sure.

I've been studying the schedule online and know that they're shooting for another month. I check my bag to make sure I have my equipment with me one more time. It's all there just like the last five times I've checked. I close my eyes. When I open them I will be in New York City.

I have to catch myself. I am having a mini panic attack. It comes in waves, my heart cathunking in my chest, making my whole body pulse, and my skin feel like it's on fire. My cheeks flush and it's not just because it's hot in the city tonight. It's not just because the sticky subway steam is coating me and the stench of composting trash is making me dizzy. I am in full panic mode. I step away from the doorman and the revolving door behind him. I walk away, sucking at the air. Then I jog. It's the only thing, besides yoga, that calms me down anymore. I should have changed at the diner. *Stupid.* It was part of the plan, but I jumped the gun.

I walk past Madison, past 5th and head for the park. I use a bench to stop my legs from wobbling and from my bag I pull my Yankees cap, a grey hoodie, an old walkie-talkie and an old Midland ear bud I stole from production many years ago when I was a PA. The walkie's batteries are dead, but I don't need them. I put the ear bud in and strap the walkie on the hip of my worn jeans. I stuff the laminated side of the lanyard into my jeans pocket. The Doc Martens, circa 1998, add a nice touch. My breathing is back. I'm normal. I check the buttons of my chambray work shirt and feel confident that I'm ready. I just need to stick to the plan. Get him to talk to me. Keep him talking. I head back to the hotel.

When I stand before the doorman in front of the Four Seasons, he doesn't seem to notice me. I head toward the door and pull out my lanyard, flashing it at him too quickly to read and say, "Production."

He nods, but doesn't give me a second glance. I'm below his radar. When I get inside, I find who I'm looking for immediately. It's almost too easy. She's dressed in a t-shirt and jeans and she's picking up a stack of papers from the front desk. She too wears a walkie and earbud. I check my phone. It's 9:00 on the dot.

"Hey! Excuse me," I say and when she doesn't turn around, I yell, "Hey!" again, a little more frantic this time. She turns to me, glaring. "Hey, sorry. I'm Michelle. Are you on TRRL?" I ask as she gives me a thorough once over and says, "Yeah."

"Oh god. Good," I say through an exhalation of relieved breath. "I'm the new overnight PA and they sent me over to help you distribute call sheets so I can get used to where everyone is. I'm wicked late aren't I?"

"They got rid of Roddy?"

I shrug and shake my head, playing dumb. "Who's Roddy?"

She rolls her eyes and sighs heavily. "For fuck's sake," she says and splits her call sheet stack in half, handing me the second pile, "Check the door numbers. Do not fuck up and give a call sheet to someone who's not crew." She points at the call sheet to where the door numbers are, "Seriously don't fuck it up. They'll shitcan us both and I need this job."

"Got it. I will not fuck it up," I say and attempt to lighten her up with a smile. I glance at the call sheet and see the name I need immediately. "So I'll take floors five and up," I say.

"Well what the fuck are you waiting for? Go," she says and I walk away from her quickly, grab the elevator, and hit the 7th floor. I dump the rest of the call sheets in a bin and stop to study the one I have in my hand. *Room 711.* I have just under an hour. I hope it's enough time.

I get inside room 711 relatively easy. I learned to open locked hotel doors with a credit card a long time ago on my first season of TRRL when the gaffer had left his personal kit in the Line Producer's room after a night of very vanilla (I'm sure) sex. He needed to get it out before her husband, the EP, found it there. He brought me along as a lookout. Everything is exactly as I expect it to be. Clean. Housekeeping swept this place of any evidence of loneliness or desperation hours ago.

The MacBook is open and resting atop a stainless steel riser on the desk in front of the giant picture window. The curtains are gently moving in swirls from the narrow open windows on either side of the large pane. A rubber outfitted rugged G Raid terabyte hard drive is attached to the computer. It's there. I'm sure of it.

I move quickly, dropping my ass into the seat and pulling my own terabyte drive out of my bag. I type in the password TRRLS7CR and hold my breath. If the show has changed their password schematic, I'm fucked. This is the only hiccup I foresee, but it doesn't demolish my plan. I'd just have to adjust. The password box shakes. *No.* My password isn't accepted. I try again, hoping I just missed a cap or letter and it goes. The screen takes a few seconds to warm up. When the screen comes to, the desktop comes to life in in a full color snapshot of the most recent production crew of TRRLS7. They're all down on the docks in front of a tall ship. There he is. Right in the front. Right next to Sam.

My blood heats up, my pulse quickens. I preemptively start deep breathing so I don't lose control. Ever since I kicked the Wellbutrin habit, it comes at me hard and fast sometimes. I can't afford it right now. I pull up the finder, click on the GRaid drive, typing in the first thing that comes to mind: my name. Nothing. I type: SCAR. Nothing. Next I type: BATTELL, but before I hit enter, I know that it's too easy. I erase it and hit two keys: BS and enter. A long list of files pops up. I click on a file called BS000001 and hit the space bar. It opens up a preview window and a video starts playing inside the warehouse.

A slow pan around the empty space shows the warehouse before it was spruced up for my stay. It's cold and broken, but the light is beautiful. The camera moves slowly toward the back of the room and I can see the large barn door where I lived for eight days.

"Perfect." A male voice off camera says and I know it's him. It's the same voice on my voicemail. I want to watch all of them, but I don't have time. I plug my drive in and start dumping. As the completion bars moves at the slowest pace known to Macintosh, the hour ticks down. Not a lot of time. 37 minutes to dump everything, but it's 9:30 already. I may not make it before he comes in for the night. In about 30 minutes he's going to walk in and I will not be finished. I close out the tab that is simultaneously uploading all of the videos and minimize the browser.

I pull out my phone and type in a message to Lucky: *I'm in. It's all here. I'm in room 711. Uploading to server. If you don't hear from me in two hours, please publish all.*

I hit send and less than 10 seconds later, he responds: *Protect yourself. Don't let them hurt you.*

Me: *I'll be okay. I'll call soon. Thanks, Lucky.*

Lucky: *Just be careful. I'll be here waiting for you.*

I shove aside the lilt that flips through my gut and focus on the task at hand. I check the computer's clock. It reads 9:45 and the dump has twenty-five minutes. I hide my G Raid behind the silver riser and keep my ears perked up for the door. At 10:13 I hear the scrape of a key card. My download has two minutes remaining. I choose not to hide.

Clark Robertson doesn't look any different than I remember, except he has a better haircut, an undercut with a deep part and gentle highlights. He still wears chucks, just like he did when he was my PA, but now it looks like he's wearing them to declare his status as CrossFitter, not lowly production assistant fresh from film school. He's bulkier in the arms and thighs since I knew him. He's yammering on the phone when he walks in and glances at me, but pays me no mind.

"Can you leave extra towels when you go?" he covers the mouthpiece and asks me without eye contact, assuming I'm housekeeping. Then he stops with his back to me. He stares in the mirror over the minibar. Then he drops his bag and his eyes.

"Katie, I have to call you back," he says and turns slowly to meet my eyes.

"I thought you were in prison."

The very edge of my lip curls into a smile. I imagine I look like a psychopath. I pull the hoodie off of my head, revealing my scars and he swallows hard.

"Call her," I say.

"Who?" he squeaks.

"Your partner."

"I—I don't—You shouldn't be here. Isn't this like a violation of your parole or something?"

I shake my head. "Call her right now, Clark, and tell her to come to your room. It's an emergency."

He sighs hard and looks at his phone, but doesn't make the call. I use the moment that his eyes aren't on me to check my status. 99% complete.

"I only want an explanation," I say, "and then I'll leave you both alone. I just want to know why."

"You know why, Scar." He smirks at me, getting some of his power back. "But maybe you've forgotten about the people's lives you've ruined," he says.

"You've been listening to too much TMZ, I think."

He shakes his head and turns from me to the bar. While he's focused on a bottle, I snatch the G Raid and drop it into my bag, but he sees the computer screen open and lit. He throws back a shot.

"You found the footage?"

"Stellar editing on your part," I say.

He nods, pours another nip, and downs it. "I always wanted to be an editor."

"But now you're a what?"

"Production Coordinator," he says, squeezing his eyes shut to bite back the liquor or because of the pain he experiences every time he says his crappy job title out loud. "How'd you figure it out?" he asks.

"You left a voicemail. You thought you'd hung up. You said, 'It's her.' Where were you waiting for her that night?"

"In the cab, the one we followed you in from the hotel," he says and I can hear the relief in his voice as he is finally able to tell the truth. I know that feeling of release well. It is my religion now. "She called and told me to meet her downtown at REI."

"On the day that the story broke, I called what I thought was Sam's phone and you answered. I didn't realize it at the time. It took many months in solitary confinement, while I was being molested by guards and force fed antidepressants, to figure it out. Then Lucky came to visit me. He said I should look at the line on the floor. The shadows told me a lot," I say.

Clark turns to me. He's gripping the bottle like he might hurl it at my head.

"But I found more than shadows. So I let this stone butch who was in for internet fraud fuck me in my bunk every night. In exchange, she would let me hold the iPhone she smuggled in so I could watch myself phantom fuck someone on camera in my very popular web series. And then I saw it. A finger. Her finger. Just the tip of it. The one with the tattoo. Just the edge of a tattoo. It comes into frame for about 1.2 seconds at 3:57."

"Shit," he says breathing the word into the air between us. "I told her she crossed it. She said no one would notice. She said it looked like a part of your hand." He looks like he's about to laugh hysterically.

"Where were you hiding while it was happening? Where were you watching from?" I ask, taking slow steps toward him, making sure I get everything he's saying. "Where was command central?"

"Upstairs. There was a lofted area over your room. It was boarded up. I could see everything."

"How many cameras?" I ask.

"I don't know. At least ten in the warehouse."

"And REI?"

"I broke into their security system and deleted angles and substituted empty frames, so it looked like you were alone," he says.

A breath filled with laughter leaves me. They thought of everything.

"What'd she promise you?"

"A bump up," he says, but not very loudly.

I laugh out loud. "To Production Coordinator? Boy, you must feel like a piece of shit?"

His eyes narrow and he shakes his head. Incredulous.

"You are, you know?" I say.

"I don't feel bad about what I did," he says. "Not after she told me what you made Jenny do."

I swallow hard. "Jenny?"

"Don't play dumb. Jenny Lang," he says.

"What did I do to her except let her tell her story?" I'm wracking my brain, buzzing. This just took a turn I wasn't expecting. *Jenny Lang?*

"You're completely delusional," he says.

"Get her here," I say. "I want to hear what she has to say. I want to know why you two tore down the minute existence I had left."

"What are you going to do?" he asks and takes a step forward.

"Nothing yet. I just want to know the truth, Clark."

"Scarlet, I'm sure we can work something out."

"Call her," I repeat. I'm done waiting. "Get the bitch here so she can answer for herself. You're obviously not the one in charge."

240

He hesitates, pleading with me with just his hazy, buzzed eyes and then takes a huge meditative inhalation of breath before he swipes his phone open, taps the screen twice, and holds it to his ear. My pulse quickens. I had expected fear and nervousness, dread, even, but I am none of those things. Instead power is surging my veins as Clark says into the phone, "You need to come to my room. It's an emergency," with very little sense of urgency in his voice. Rather, he sounds completely and utterly defeated. "No. This isn't a joke. Come now," he says and hangs up, downs what's left in his glass, and offers me the bottle. The gesture isn't lost on me. In fact, I appreciate his willingness to *go quietly* as it were. I smile at him and say, "Thanks, but I quit." As I stare at the bottle, I realize my mistake too late. Something's don't change.

Clark smashes the bottle against the side of my face and it breaks near my temple. My vision is static and then it's black.

CHAPTER 29

I had been watching him all night. Every move he made worked my skin into a frenzy of static and stress. He was going to take another one home and I was going to have to watch from Control. I was going to watch it happen and if I didn't, if I did anything to stop it, I'd be out on the street, tied with a gag order and the 1-800 number for unemployment.

Sam handed me a bottle of water and stood next to me scanning the pulsing, neon crowd in front of us. I moved my headset away from my mouth and leaned into her, raising my voice above the incessant drilling of the DJ's bass. "If you see Jaron getting friendly, let me know. We need to keep all eyes on him. Copy?"

She nodded and pointed to the dance floor. "He's been all over that girl for about ten minutes."

"Yeah. I'm aware. We just need to keep eyes on him."

"What happens if he gets too friendly?" she asked.

"We'll make it work," I said and popped my headset back in. "Charlie, grab an angle on the bar. Our boy's definitely going in for a drink soon. He's been away from the watering hole too long. Does anyone have eyes on Vanessa?"

Over my walkie Clark's voice came back, "She's still in the bathroom. Lotsa sniffing and snorting going on in there, of the 8-ball variety. You want me to get her out?"

"We can't. She's in a stall," I said. "Ask her to come back to the party. Be persuasive. Copy?"

"Copy that, boss."

Jaron drops the ass of the girl he's been dancing with and swaggers to the bar. My camera guy is on him, the boom right behind hugging tight to camera and Sam and I fall in behind them. He's heading for Jenny. I roll my eyes, reach around camera, and snag Jaron by the arm.

"Cut camera, guys. Give us a sec," I said and pull Jaron away from the bar by the sleeve.

"Scarlet," he said and smirked down at me, his white teeth florescent in the black lights. He stared at my hand on his arm. "Why you wanna impede my flow?"

"Your flow is all over the fucking place tonight. What's the goal, Jare?"

"The goal is to find a fine ass lady to converse with," he said and his attention turned from me to Jenny behind the bar.

"Yeah? Conversation's your thing now? Thought you were more about hooking up than meaningful convo."

He smirked at me, grabbed me by the hips and forced my hips to move to the rhythm of the music, then he spun me and in my ear said, "Lighten up, Scar. Have a drink. Dance a little."

I pulled my hand out of his and said, "Okay. Okay. Seriously though, not Jenny." It's not what I wanted to say. It's not the angle I expected to take. It just came out because I was dizzy. He started to nod, like he knew I had been wanting to spit that out for some time and then his smirk dropped into something like fishface, and his eyes got dark.

"So it's like that, Ms. Producer?"

"Oh come on, Jaron. I'm not trying to produce you."

"The fuck you're not," he said and turned from me, headed straight for the bar. He flagged Jenny, the pretty bartender with three kids and a diabetic mother at home. She beamed at him. He'd been flirting with her a lot of late and I could tell Jenny liked the attention and the cameras. I signaled to roll camera, but I was defeated and feeling sick inside. I was going to have to do something. I waited. I watched them get heavier and heavier all night, until Jaron was leaning over the bar, about to flip ass over head, and was trying to talk her into a kiss. The crowd egged her on. She did it and they made out to the swollen room full of cheers. It was heading downhill fast.

I waited for her to take a bathroom break and I followed, grabbed her by the arm and pulled her into the bathroom.

"Everyone out," I said and the room cleared. "Charlie, I'm going off air for a minute."

"Copy that."

"Sam, don't let anyone in here," I said.

"Copy, Scarlet." She came back quickly on the walkie and I imagined her standing sentinel at the swinging bathroom door.

"What the fuck's going on?" Jenny said and ripped her arm out of my grip.

"You can't have sex with him," I said.

She just looked at me, but didn't fight it.

"You understand?" I asked.

She nodded.

"I'm serious, Jenny."

"Why?"

I thought long and hard about this. I thought about her kids and her mom and the deadbeat who left her and hadn't paid a dime of the child support he owed her. I thought about her looks and her brains. She was going to make something of herself.

"He's positive," I said. She faltered, stepped back from me like I had it myself.

"Ya'll know that he is? Like for sure?" she asked.

I nodded, but couldn't meet her eyes.

"Pieces of shit," she said. I nodded my agreement. I'd been calling myself that for a while. "Ya'll motherfuckers. He's been hooking up with everyone, all those girls on campus."

"I'm only telling you this because I like you a lot and I don't want you to get fucked. If my producers knew I was telling you, I'd get fired. Not to mention I'm outing someone who hasn't given me their permission," I said, trying to keep us on track. I didn't have a lot of time.

"Well I'm already fucked," she said and fell back against the sink, her hands holding her up. My heart sunk.

"No. You didn't?"

"Not with Jaron."

"Then—what?" I said, confused.

"I already got it too," she said, holding up her chin.

"Got what?"

"It. I've been positive for three years."

"Get the fuck outta here," I said.

She raised her eyebrows and looked like she wanted to laugh at me. I bent over, touched the nasty, sticky tiled floor, took a deep breath, and came up with a red face; the only yoga I knew back then.

"I'm sorry. I'm so sorry that happened to you," I said.

"Will the audience know about Jaron?" she asked and I found it an odd question. I couldn't figure out the angle.

I shook my head and said, "Nope. Not unless he has a change of heart and decides to come clean. I know Cass is looking for a way to bring it out without outing him, but in the meantime the half dozen girls he's fucked could all be infected and we have to keep our mouths shut. NDA bullshit. He told us too late."

"That's royally fucked up. My NDA keeps me from talking?" she asked.

"You could get into a lot of trouble—money trouble—if you say anything," I said.

"Then I'll fuck him."

"I'd love to fuck him, Jen, but I don't see how we—"

"No. I. Will. Fuck. Him," she clarified. "I'll have sex with him."

It took me a minute. I had to let my head fall to the side and then allow my brain to right itself before I understood the scope of what she was talking about and then it hit me, sadly.

"Scarlet, Cass is on her way over here. She wants to know why we're not rolling," Sam says popping her head in through the swinging door, unannounced. The interruption caused me to jump back against the wall. I glared at her and pointed to the outside.

"Shut the fucking door, Sam!" I yelled. I waited for the door to shut and turned back to Jenny, the door swinging behind us as Sam exited. "You'll have sex him?"

She nodded, looked a little scared. I stepped toward her and took her arms in my hands. "You don't have to, but it would be—"

"I know," she said and tears started to well up in her eyes.

"I can get you some money," I said and she nodded. "All you have to do is have sex with him somewhere where the cameras have access, Jen. It doesn't have to be on camera, but sound needs to pick it up."

"We can do it tonight. I can't go home with him with the kids and my mom there, but some place—"

"His car. It's his favorite spot," I offered a little too fast.

The look on her face punctured my soul. *I can't do this shit anymore,* I thought. I heard a scuffle outside of the door and Cass smashed into the room, nearly dragging Sam in behind her. Sam stared at me, a strange mix of fear and repulsion on her face, over Cass's shoulder. I didn't fully register it at the time.

"What the fuck are you doing, Scarlet? Why aren't my cameras rolling?" She took one quick glance at Jenny, but didn't seem impressed or moved at all by her tears. She glared at me, arms crossed over her chest.

"We just needed a moment, Cass. We'll be out shortly. We're just discussing Jenny's date with Jaron," I said and gave her a knowing look. She nodded at me, never cracking an expression.

"Well hurry the fuck up. Every minute we're down is costing me," she said and though I expected her to walk out, leaving a cloud of angry entitled dust behind, she turned from me to Jenny and yanked the shoulder of Jenny's blouse down a bit so that it showed more of her neck and clavicle and then she pinched Jenny's cheeks roughly turning them pink as she let go. "There. All camera ready," she said and winked at Jenny before turning on her very expensive heels to leave us. The pulsing sound of the club ate up the room for a few seconds and in the depths of it, I heard her say, "Cam! You! Whatever your name is—Sam. PA! Follow me." Then all was quiet again. When I turned back to Jenny she was staring at herself in the mirror and trying to do away with her own tears. She had a strength about her, like Cass pinching her cheeks had turned on her power.

"I'll wait two months and get tested. I'll call you and tell you that I'm positive," Jenny said, all tone gone from her voice, the plan taking shape in her very capable brain.

"I'll set up a 'confession' and we'll tell Jaron that you're naming him because he's the only one you've slept with in—"

"I haven't had sex in four years," she said. I take a deep moment of silence for the sadness in her voice.

"We'll get Jaron tested and we'll do it all on camera, so all those girls will know. We'll make a special out of it. He'll have to agree."

"Maybe it'll help some people," she said.

I grabbed her by the arms again and it forced her to look at me. "It will help so many people, Jen. I promise you. This is the right thing to do."

She nodded her agreement and then hugged me ferociously, shaking in my arms, but by then we were both shaking.

CHAPTER 30

My skin is pulsing. The room is fuzzy and moving all around me. I taste blood, but know it's coming from my head and not my mouth. *How long have I been out?* I Can see out of the slit in one eye; two sets of feet standing in front of the computer, their backs to me. The taller of the two takes the rugged drive and tucks it into a back pocket and then a woman's voice said, "Just delete everything. Don't leave any traces."

As quietly as I can I get to my feet. The room starts to slow to a soft spin and when I finally am able to stand, I can make out their backs clear as day. I touch my chest, just under my clavicle. I hit the side of the bed going down and it feels bruised, but more importantly, my button has come undone. I do it up, stand up straight, and say, "Thanks for joining us, Sam."

They turn to me. Sam backs away into the wall like she's just been touched from behind by an actor in a haunted house. I can see that her fear embarrasses her, but it makes me practically giddy inside. I hold my hands up to show that I have no weapons. She glances at Clark and the computer processing the deleted files and I say, "It's okay. I don't need them. I just want the truth, Sam."

"You're a scumbag," she says and again I want to laugh.

"I'm the scumbag?"

Sam nods and Clark just rests his head in his hands on his knees from his spot in the desk chair. I almost don't need him anymore, but if I let him go, he'll call security, and I won't get to hear the truth. No one will ever hear the truth.

"Okay, Scarlet, what do you want?" she asks me, like there's a price she can pay to be rid of this little problem.

"Oh, I don't know…the past two years of my life back maybe? My sanity? My dignity?"

She sneers at me and says, "You haven't had a shred of dignity since you—well, I'm not sure you've ever had any dignity actually. You were a shallow hole of nothingness when I met you and you're even more empty now," she says and her words fill her legs with adrenaline. She steps away from the wall. I imagine the little monkey in her brain is awake again and remembering its purpose and the reasons why it hates me so much, but I still can't fathom how this started.

"Clark said this is about Jenny."

She laughs, a clipped bark of a laugh, and glances at Clark. "Yeah. Jenny and then Quinn. You never fucking changed. I thought you'd think about who you are, about what you'd done after Cass fired you, after Taylor dumped you, after you were homeless, certainly after the industry turned its back on you and you were reduced to schlepping burgers in a dive, but I misjudged your ego, I guess. I underestimated your ability for extreme denial and your need to be significant, because there you were fucking up someone else's life for 10 minutes of glory. You're a piece of shit," she says and looks like she wants to spit.

"I never did anything to Jenny," I say and while the words are leaving me, I dissect my actions again. "I agreed to the plan because it was the right thing to do, no matter how fucked up it might have seemed. I went along with what *she wanted* because I knew in the long run that it would stop Jaron from infecting anyone else. I knew also that it would give Jenny another start. She'd have a different—a better life, so yeah, I agreed to go along with it. Honestly, I don't even understand how you know. No one, but me, Jenny and Cass know."

Sam laughs again. I'm not sure she's hearing me, but Clark definitely is. He stands up, massages his temples. "Wait. It was Jenny's idea? Why would she *allow* herself to be infected?" he asks while Sam starts to pace, shaking her head.

"Allow herself? What are you talking about?"

"She," he points to Sam and says, "said she overheard you coercing Jenny into fucking Jaron so she would get infected and that you'd pay her to—" He stops himself and thinks hard about what he's saying. His face drains of color. He takes a deep breath and closes his eyes.

"You obviously only heard part of the conversation, Sam," I say this quietly like I'm trying to soothe a kid who has innocently fucked up. "Jenny was already positive. The guy who got her pregnant gave it to her. It was *her* idea. It was a convenient fix to get Jaron to stop running around like an asshole, infecting innocent coeds. Jenny wanted him to be accountable. She, *and I*—even Cass—wanted to put a stop to it. You know that I tried everything I could think of to get him to stop. He wouldn't. So we forced him to."

"That's not what I heard," she says, turning on me, defeat seeping from her pores, mixing with the stench of embarrassment. She starts to come at me, but this time, Clark stops her, his hands on her chest. He shoves her back and she hits the wall almost getting tangled in the billowing curtains from the open window. She sits down on thin sill to the left of the big window pane in front of the desk.

"Just stop, Sam," he says and starts to pace in front of her. "Just shut the fuck up."

"I'm sorry," I say to Clark, to both of them really. I'm not sure why an apology comes to my lips. They should be apologizing to me, but it feels like the right thing to say. Clark's hands are shaking as he looks from my eyes to Sam's reddening ones. I can see the veins bulging in the sides of her eyeballs, running tracks through her temples. I can't tell if it's all becoming clear to her, or if she's still in denial. I take a step toward her and she flinches like a wounded animal. I don't stop slowly moving toward her, until I'm standing in front of her.

"You made a mistake. I know you thought you were doing the right thing," I say and take her face in my hands. Hot tears stream her cheeks and squish between my palm and her cheeks before she yanks her head away.

"I. Know. What. I. Heard," she says, but won't look in my eyes.

"We're both going to jail," Clark says behind me and when I turn to look at him, he's glaring at her, ready to charge. I hold my hand out to keep him from her, but he shoves my hand away and very quietly says, "You know what I did for you?"

Sam's face twists, condescension filling the lines near her mouth. "She's a murderer!" she screams and shoves me hard in the chest and then turns to him, "I saw Quinn's body!"

"I didn't kill Quinn," I say quietly. "Joe had her ki—"

Sam cuts across me, never breaking eye contact with Clark. "You were her donkey. She treated you like shit too, but you were too far up her ass to see it. You did what you did to get ahead, Clark. Don't fucking put this on me. I saved you."

He's laughing now and they're both pushing against me, like I'm the cream filling in their anger sandwich. "I'm a slave for you!" he yells and I hold my hand out again. "I trusted you. You said she was evil, you said she was a monster. I believed you."

Sam glares at me and spittle hits my face as she says, "You said, 'All you have to do is have sex with him somewhere where the cameras have access.' You said, 'I'll get you money.' You told Jen to fuck him in his car."

I nod in agreement and say, "It was part of the plan. I only said that after she told me she was already positive and that *she wanted* to do this so we could put a stop to it, Sam. I swear."

She hiccups out a sob, "But then I saw you in the hotel and followed you and there was a dead body—" She switches to Quinn so fast, like it's all running together in her brain. "—I saw you standing over her and I followed you back to that shithole apartment and you showed me the video and I knew you were doing it all over again, only this time someone got raped and you murdered her! I know you did," she says and the tears are streaming for real. Clark is pushing against my hand, which is becoming weak at the memories of Quinn's body.

"No," I say because it's all I can muster and she continues, "I couldn't believe what you were doing. I couldn't believe you were still—still trying to be validated, no matter who got hurt."

"Bobby and Nate killed Quinn. I saw Joe pay them off. They've been convicted, Sam," I say, trying desperately to reason with her.

"She called me and told me to bring the equipment to the warehouse in East Boston and then to meet her out back at the REI on Newbury. When I got there, you were passed out." Clark's voice is near a whisper and so calm as he says this to me, while staring without blinking at Sam. "You were slumped against the wall and she told me you were fucked up and that you'd be out for a while. She let me into the store and told me to wipe any and all images of her off the security system. I did it. I already knew about Jenny. I wanted to fuck you over too. So bad. You were so shitty to me, Scarlet," he says and his voice sounds too wet.

"You're right. I was horrible to you. I'm sorry, Clark."

He stops glaring at Sam long enough to finally make eye contact with me. I nod for him to go on. I'm so ready to hear about what happened when I was unconscious for three whole days. "Then we went to the warehouse and rigged a skeleton house setup with a tiny command upstairs. And we wrote the WIKI for Caeterus and threw together the website. It was completely juvenile, but she said you'd buy it."

"I did. I was too scared not to," I say.

"We called the show *Battle Scars* and then when the news picked it up. They called it that too and we laughed so hard. Remember how we laughed, Sam?"

Sam stares at me, her eyes about to burst from her skull and then she says, "And I erased all of the data from your phone and the websites we made for Caeterus and the emails and I stayed on my side of the line." She smirks at me through insane tears. Clark shakes his head, his eye twitching slightly.

"I liked fucking you, Scar. It's the one part I struggled with, the one part I loved."

"You're a sociopath," Clark says quietly and the words scrape against his throat. I think he'll have no voice tomorrow, if any of us make it that far.

My breath catches and I want to shove her out the window, but I don't get the chance as Clark swipes my hand out of the way and lunges at her, she falls back, out the window, her legs anchored against me.

"No!" I scream and the sudden sound breaks the chords in my throat. I taste blood again. My arm is twisted around the windowsill and Sam's boots are digging into my thighs. The skin on my fingers is tearing, caught in the clump of material from Sam's shirt. I'm holding onto her just below the collar and her head is back like she's laughing bigger and louder than is humanely possible. Clark slithers down the wall at my feet and grabs my leg. At first, I think he's going to push me too, but he's holding on so I don't go over, anchoring me and I'm grateful.

It's a slow motion kind of thing, watching her hang suspended over the park, lush and black underneath us, a soft landing, if not for the street directly below. She is a swinging trapeze artist in a fit of passion. She tilts her chin to look down at me from outside and she smiles and shakes her head and then she kicks off with her feet and I feel my fingers stretch and rip through the material of her blouse. The force of her kick-off is so great that three of my fingers bend all the way back to the top of my wrist and snap in unison. The sound echoes somewhere behind my eyes. I fall back into the room, the carpet burning my elbows. I know she's doing me a favor. I know she's making it so I can't watch her fall. It's a last will, an apology. Clark's hand twists in the folds of my jeans and his scream of "No!" coats the walls of my brain. I hit the ground hard and a burst of life is expelled from my lips. I close my eyes and immediately hear honking horns and screams. I keep my eyes shut until the cops get here.

AFTER

I don't have to take the bus back to Boston. For that, I'm eternally grateful. Lucky rents a Zipcar and comes for me. While hugging, we accidentally kiss and I'm immediately comforted and embarrassed. He lets my head sink into the space between his shoulder and his neck and I let my tears soak both of our collars.

I don't have to release the footage or the confessions. Clark, after the police were done questioning him, agreed to release all of the footage from the other side of the camera from *Battle Scars* and I'm holding onto the footage I took on my button cam in that room. It's a time capsule now. I gave a copy to the police as evidence that neither Clark nor I pushed Sam, but I don't have the heart to release it like an *I told you so*. Vengeance doesn't make sense to me anymore.

I've watched the video five times. I can't stomach more than five, but it's very clear that she pushed herself, so to speak. The idea of it, the feeling of her boots digging into me, kicking me away doesn't ever leave me. I still have the yellow of the bruises on my thighs to remind me. And her eyes. I've felt the regret and the sadness in her eyes. I only wish I had conversations with her in real life instead of the video of her suicide to commiserate with.

My life has changed. It seems to do that every few months or so. Today, I'm going down to Copley with Lucky and we're going to capture a peaceful protest about black lives and violence. Quinn's grandmother, Evelyn, asked me to shoot the rally and walk with her. She has hit me hard in the face and hugged me later and we have made some sort of amends. Now we walk together.

I have advertisers on the Battle Scars site. They pay the bills. They don't ask me to change anything on my YouTube and website and I don't accept any company I can't personally get behind. It's enough to live on. Every day I upload new footage of people being people. It's not always pretty. I always think about Jose from the train and how horrible the cops were to him.

Fear makes us do stupid things. But the thing I didn't capture after his face was pressed to the dirty floor of the train, after he had been racially profiled, the thing that happened moments later that not many of us saw because we've grown accustomed to thinking the worst of people, was the old lady, bent by years, who took him by the arm and dusted him off and then stood arm and arm with him while they traveled up the escalator together. She tilted his chin up, did the same with her own and they walked into the sun together. Those moments represent us. Those moments, the ones we've already looked away from, seem to make us human and bind us to one another. Those moments are our life blood. It flows in you. It courses through my veins. We are alive with it.

I am alive with you.

ABOUT THE AUTHOR

M.A. Barrett is a writer, photographer, screenwriter, and poet. Her works have appeared in the New York International Film Festival, The Academy Awards, and in publications such as the Huffington Post, The April Perennial, Visibilities Magazine and IN OUR OWN WORDS: A Generation Defining Itself. She lives in Boston with her wife and French Bulldog, Grace Kelly.